HIGH SPIRITS

HIGH SPIRITS

ROBERTSON DAVIES

RosettaBooks®

Rosetta Books New York, 2019

Cover jacket design by Lon Kirschner
ISBN e-Pub edition: 978-0-7953-5234-8
ISBN POD edition: 978-0-7953-5250-8

Contents

HOW THE HIGH SPIRITS
CAME ABOUT

A chapter of Autobiography

Ghost stories came into my life before I could read. How well I remember the first one; it was at a party given by my parents, and it was not yet time for me to go to bed, because I remember that the sun was sinking outside the windows, and as the guests ate tulip jellies—they were streaked red and yellow and topped with whipped cream of a deliciousness that seems to have departed from the earth—Mrs. Currie told the strange tale of the Disappearance of Oliver Lurch. He was a farm youth in Kentucky who had gone out one night from a gathering just like ours, to fetch some wood for the fire, had not returned and when the others went to seek him he could be heard calling from the sky, 'Here I am! Here I am! Help me! I am Oliver Lurch!' The cries became fainter and fainter, and Oliver was heard and seen no more. There were those who said he had been carried off by a great eagle but—a grown man? What sort of eagle was that? It must have been Something Else.

I fell asleep that night fearing the Mighty Clutch. And since then I have always felt that any party would be the better for a ghost story.

The first uncanny tale I read, when I was ten, was *Frankenstein*, which terrified me unforgettably and gloriously. None of the film versions, in my opinion, comes near the effect Mary Shelley produces by her special quality of prose. A story in this collection, *The Cat That Went To Trinity*, obviously owes much to this favourite of mine, and although it is far from serious, it is not meant to be derisive of the great original. No disrespect toward serious spectres is intended herein.

Although I have read tales of ghosts and the supernatural eagerly all my life I never thought of writing one until I went to Massey College in the University of Toronto, in 1963. The college had a Christmas party for its members and their friends, and some sort of entertainment was needed. There were lots of gifted people to call on—poets and musicians—but I was expected to make a contribution, and I decided on a ghost story, the one which appears first in this book. For the eighteen years I was at the college a story was called for every Christmas, and here they are, gathered together, in the hope that other enthusiasts for this sort of tale will enjoy them.

It was never my intention to frighten anyone. Indeed I do not think that would have been possible; the audience was too big and to me, at least, terror is best when the group of listeners is small. No, these stories were to amuse, and perhaps to add a dimension to a building and a community that was brand-new. University College has a ghost, of which it is justifiably proud, and doubtless there are others around the University which have not yet found their chroniclers. Massey College is a building of great architectural beauty, and few things become architecture so well as a whiff of the past, and a hint of the uncanny. Canada needs ghosts, as a dietary supplement, a vitamin taken to stave off that most dreadful of modern ailments, the Rational Rickets.

Let no one suppose that I was the first to think that a few hauntings might be acceptable in the new college. Very early in its first autumn I was told that a figure had taken to appearing on the stairs, and in dark corners, who frightened some people, and disappeared when bolder people pursued it. I have never thought of myself as a ghost-catcher, but my work at the college demanded some unusual tasks, and I accepted this one as part of the job. I captured the ghost at last—sneaked up on him from behind— and he proved to be one of the students who, with a sheet and an ugly rubber mask, was trying to cheer the place up. That was his explanation, but there was a gleam in his eye that suggested to me that the ghost game fulfilled some need in his own character. That was not hard to understand, for he was engaged in a particularly rational and hard-headed form of study, and too much rationality, as I have suggested, calls for a balancing element.

Writing ghost stories, and in particular, cheerful ghost stories, set me to the task of examining the literature of the ghost story, and its technique. There are some very famous ghost stories, and perhaps the acknowledged masterpiece is Henry James' *The Turn of the Screw*. James casts it in the form of a tale read at Christmas time to a party of friends in an English country house; what could be better? It is without doubt the best of James' substantial and distinguished contribution to this branch of literature. There are also the fine stories written by Montague Rhodes James, which he composed and at first read aloud to groups of friends at King's, Cambridge, and later at Eton, where he was Provost. My father-in-law heard him on a few of these occasions and many years later described to me the special pleasure they gave. Parties of friends, college occasions: yes, we could provide these elements at the Massey College Gaudy Nights; the word comes from the Latin *gaude,* and has long been applied to college parties. But what about style?

Ghost stories tend to be very serious affairs. Who has ever heard of a ghost cracking a joke? I wanted my ghosts to be light-hearted, if not in themselves, at least as they appeared to my hearers. No new style would suit a ghost story, so it would be necessary to parody the usual style. And the parody would have to be affectionate, for cruel parody is distasteful in itself, and utterly outside the spirit of a party.

Joseph Le Fanu

I think I know the traditional ghost story style pretty thoroughly. It is solemn, and it frequently makes use of unusual words, designed to strike awe into the minds of the reader or the hearer. It is a style that can very easily become ridiculous, and even such a great master of the ghost story as Joseph Sheridan LeFanu does not always escape this peril. Poor LeFanu not only wrote uncanny tales, he lived one. The story has been told many times that he suffered from a recurrent nightmare, in which he stood at the foot of a macabre and menacing house which towered high in the air, and which he knew was about to collapse on him. When he died in 1873, of a heart seizure, his physician remarked dryly that the house had fallen at last.

It is one of the regrets of my life that I missed seeing, and perhaps even having some conversation with, a man who was a great scholar in the realm of magic, uncanny happenings, and of course ghost stories. He was, to give him his full resounding title and name, the Reverend Father Alphonsus Joseph-Mary Augustus Montague Summers, chiefly known for his work in the realm of Restoration drama, but also the author of *The History of Witchcraft* and many other books about werewolves, Satanism and the supernatural. He was a rum customer. He had left his home in Oxford shortly before I went there in 1936 and was remembered with affection, some mirth, and now and then with unexpected venom. He appeared in the streets dressed like a European priest, in cassock and shovel-hat, with a cloak and a

5

bulky umbrella; some stories insisted that he always walked in the gutter, for no determinable reason. But—and it was this that raised eyebrows—he was invariably accompanied on his afternoon walk *either* by a pallid youth dressed in black, who was supposed to be his secretary, *or* by a large black dog, but never by both! Tongues wagged.

Although I never met Father Summers, I have all my life collected his books, among which are several collections of ghost stories, some of which he wrote himself, and to all of which he appends learned discussions of the kind of literature he knew and loved so well. His prose style, which sets the teeth of more austere readers on edge, fills me with delight. He had read so many tales of the supernatural, pored over so many old manuscripts and *grimoires,* that his writing had been infected by them, and displays a fruit cakyness and portwinyness that makes for very rich literary feeding. He delights in words like 'sepulture' and 'charnel' which it would be a pity to allow to fall out of the language. So when I set to work to write some ghost stories, with a glint of parody in my eye, I determined also to lay a few laurels on the tomb of that not always wholly admired scholar, Montague Summers. I shall be pleased if those who know his work feel that I have not altogether failed.

My ghosts are sufficiently traditional, in that they all appear in search of something. This is the usual reason for ghostly appearances; something has been lost, or some revenge or justice is sought, and the spirit cannot rest until this unfinished business

Sepulture
Charnel

is concluded. If that is established, it is obvious that the proper greeting to a ghost is not a shriek of terror but a courteous 'What can I do for you?' It was Shelley who wrote—and I echo him—

While yet a boy I sought for ghosts, and sped
    Through many a listening chamber, cave and ruin,
    And starlit wood, with fearful steps pursuing
    Hopes of high talk with the departed dead.

In my ghost stories I have tried to explore where such high talk might lead.

Anybody who writes ghost stories is sure to be asked: Do you believe in ghosts? And the answer to that must be, I believe in them precisely as Shakespeare believed in them. People who want further discussion may be referred to that model of good sense, Dr. Samuel Johnson, who said:

It is wonderful that five thousand years have now elapsed since the creation of the world, and still it is undecided whether or not there has ever been an instance of the spirit of any person appearing after death. All argument is against it, but all belief is for it.

All belief? The Doctor speaks with his accustomed certainty. Much belief, undoubtedly, for in 1954–55 the popular Swiss fortnightly, *Schweizerischer Beobachter* published a series of articles on prophetic dreams, coincidences, premonitions and ghosts, and then asked readers who had any experience of such things to write to the Editor. The response was overwhelming; more than 1200 readers wrote in, giving more than 1500 cases of personal experience; and these writers were people of education and discretion. It is interesting that most of the letter-writers confided their names to the Editor but asked that they be not made public; few people will admit to all the world that they believe in the supernatural. These letters were confided by the paper to the late Dr. C. G. Jung, whose secretary, Mrs. Aniela Jaffe, published them with psychological comment, and extremely interesting reading they make. So it may be said that if not everybody believes in ghosts, there are a great many people who certainly do not disbelieve in them.

One word remains to be said: I have not edited these stories specifically for the reader; they remain in the form in which they were first spoken aloud, and I beg you—you readers—to grant them the attention of the ear, as well as of the eye. Perhaps, as in my case, your first ghost story was *heard*.

The names of several living people, associated in one way or another with Massey College, appear in these stories. Never, let me say, are they mentioned in anything except an affectionate and genial spirit, as befits a Gaudy Night, and I hope that the bearers of these names will not feel that I have been impudently free with them, or suggested an acceptance of the supernatural which they may disclaim. These are, after all, party-ghosts, emanating from high spirits.

REVELATION FROM
A SMOKY FIRE

At the outset of a personal ghost story, it is accepted practice to say that one is the least fanciful person in the world, that one has not a nerve in one's body, doesn't believe in ghosts, and can't understand how it happened. I am therefore at a disadvantage, for I am a more than ordinarily fanciful person, I am extremely nervous, I don't find anything intrinsically improbable in the notion of a ghost, and I have a pretty shrewd idea how it happened. Therefore I am more likely to distress myself than to alarm you by what I am going to recount; I know that in the ghost controversy you are all overwhelmingly of the anti-ghost party. But I can assure you that I found it a disquieting experience.

The fire in my study smokes. It is not merely that the Bursar buys green wood; something is amiss with the chimney. Sometimes it smokes so much that I feel like those Jesuit missionaries who used to fling themselves on the floor in the longhouses of the Canadian Indians, because only within six inches of the floor could one breathe the air without tearing the lungs.

My fire was smoking yesterday afternoon at dusk, as I sat reading the précis of an M.A. thesis. My nerves would have been quieter had I been reading a ghost story; thesis abstracts are, with a very few exceptions, the least credible and most horrifying productions of imaginative literature. Nevertheless you will understand that I was not in the least disposed to see a ghost, though I was rather far advanced in asphyxiation.

At last, reluctantly, like a man approaching a task he knows to be outside human power, I went to the fire and knelt to poke it, thinking perhaps I might alter the quality of the smoke, and thus secure change, if not relief. Of course I simply made it worse. I grew impatient, and, holding my breath, put my head into the worst of the smother, to see if anything—a bird's nest, or a dead squirrel, or anything of that sort, might have stuck in the chimney.

Nothing. Defeated, and with the disgruntled resignation of one used to such defeats, I crawled backward into the room, and stood up.

There was a man sitting at my desk.

Nothing in the least alarming about that. People quite often come into my study without being heard; when I am busy I often do not notice what is happening around me. I assumed he was a visitor. He looked like a senior faculty member—a tall, rather lean, bald man, with professorial eyebrows. He was wearing his gown, but so was I, for that matter for, though smoky, my study was cold.

'Good afternoon,' I said; 'can I help you?'

'You can help me by doing something about that smoking chimney,' he replied.

He smiled as he spoke, and I assumed that this was some form of donnish humour. Nevertheless, I thought it rather cool of him to complain about what was, after all, *my* chimney. I decided to take the line of extreme and disarming courtesy, which sometimes works well with impudent people.

'I assure you I am doing the best I can,' said I.

'Not a very good best,' said he; 'take another look up the flue.'

I obeyed. Not, you understand, because I was awed by him, but because I wanted time to think. Slowly I knelt, and poked my head into the fireplace again, and thought.

Who the devil is he? There is something familiar about his face, but what is his name? I wish I could either forget both faces and names, or remember both. It is this perpetual dealing with nameless faces that makes my life a muddle of uncertainty. Is he one of those architectural critics who still push their way into the college, and take on airs? How dare he give me orders? I *must* have met him somewhere. Is he one of those dons who suffers from the delusion that he is Dr. Johnson, and is rude on principle?

By this time I had thought all I could, without drawing in huge breaths of smoke, so I crawled back into the room and stood up again.

'If I were you I'd go up on the roof and put a rod down that chimney,' said the stranger. 'Or why don't you come down it again?'

'Down the chimney?' said I. Aha, this was the clue. Here was a madman.

'Yes,' said he; 'you didn't knock at the door, so I assume you must have come down the chimney. You weren't here a minute ago.'

One of my cardinal rules in life is always to humour madmen. It is second nature to me. I do it several times every day.

'Quite so,' said I. 'I came down the chimney.'

He looked at me closely, and I thought somewhat insultingly.

'Tight squeeze, wasn't it?' said he.

'Not in the least,' I replied. 'A chimney with a good clear draught might be a little swift for a man of my age and quiet habit of life, but this is a superbly smoky chimney—and the smoke, as you readily understand, gives just that density to the atmosphere in the flue which permits me to float down as gently as a feather. Science, you observe.' I said this airily, for I was beginning to enjoy myself.

'Look here,' said he; 'I don't believe you're a chimney sweep at all.'

'Your perception is in perfect order,' said I. 'I am not a chimney sweep; I am the Master of this College. Now may I ask who you are?'

'Aha,' he cried, 'just as I thought. You're a madman. I don't believe in humouring madmen. Out you go!'

The Ninth Master

'As you please,' said I. He looked as though he might become violent, and I wanted time to edge myself toward the bell which calls the Porter. 'But before I go, would you have the goodness to tell me who you are?'

'I?' he shouted, working the tremendous eyebrows in a way which I could tell had been effective in quelling undergraduates. 'Certainly I'll tell you. *I* am Master of this College.'

'Of course,' said I, in my silkiest tones, 'but which Master are you?'

'Damn your impudence,' he roared, 'I'm the ninth Master.'

I confess this made me feel very unwell. I can't tell why, but it did, and although I cannot fully describe the sensation, I thought I was going to faint; for a time my consciousness seemed to come and go in rhythmic waves; it was like vertigo, only more intense; I was horribly distressed. But my visitor seemed even more so.

'Stop! Stop!' he cried; 'for God's sake don't fade and reappear like that. You make me giddy.' And to my astonishment he fell back into my chair and closed his eyes, as white as—well, as white as a ghost. I forgot all about the Porter, and hurried to his side. I put out my hand to feel his brow, just as he opened his eyes. I was amazed to see unmistakable fear in his face, and he shrank from my touch.

'Don't be afraid,' I said, 'I only want to help you.' His voice was faint, and came from a dry mouth. 'Who did you say you were?' he asked.

13

'I am the first Master,' said I. Presumably I was distressed more than I realized, for though I was trying to reassure him my voice sounded sad and eerie, even to myself.

'Then you are—Finch?' he said.

Again the inexplicable malaise overcame me, and I could tell by the fear in his eyes that, to his vision, I must be fading and reappearing again. My sensations were mingled; to be mistaken for Robert Finch—painter, poet, musician, scholar, wit and distinguished diner-out—presented me with an extreme of temptation. Should I risk all, and bask for a moment in another's glory? But decency prevailed. I denied, reluctantly, that I was Finch.

'Good God! then—you must be the other fellow who was here, briefly, even before Finch,' said he.

Condemn me, if you will, as an egotist, but in such a situation which of you could have contained his curiosity? 'What became of him—that other fellow who was here, briefly, before Finch?' I asked. And again I heard in my own voice that hollow, eerie note.

He shook his head. 'I don't really know,' he said; 'it was whispered that something happened that occasionally happened to professors in those days; something called "making a composition with his creditors", or some quaint phrase of the kind, and he went.'

'Where did he go?' I persisted. The man looked as if he needed fresh air, but the subject was of such importance to me that I put my own interest first.

'I don't think anybody knew,' he said. 'The story that has come down to us is that there was a full-dress enquiry in the Round Room, and it is presumed that the Visitor broke the Master, for when it was over he stumbled out into the quad, and it was seen that the russet rosette had been torn from his gown. After that—well, some said it was the pool, and some said he leapt from the tower, and some said'—here his voice thickened with repugnance—'that he went off and got a job at York. The College behaved very well toward the wife and girls; they kept going by taking in washing for some of the Junior Fellows who couldn't afford the Coin Wash. Finch was a man of very delicate feeling, by all accounts, and he saw to it. But it was all so long ago ... '

My concern for his suffering had considerably abated. Madman he might be, but... 'How long ago?' I asked.

'A century, at least,' said he. 'Let's see—this is Christmas, 2063—oh, yes; a full century.'

'A century, and nine Masters?' said I. And again that dreadful sensation, like going down too rapidly in an elevator.

'A distingusihed group,' said he, with complacency, 'Let's see—before me—I'm in my fourth year now—there was Kasabowszki for twenty-one years, poor Sawyers who died after three, Taschereau who made it for ten, Gamble for twelve, Meyer for seven, Duruset for fifteen, poor Polanyi—worn out with waiting, really,—for three, and of course Finch's glorious first mastership of twenty-five long, sunny years. Yes, nine Masters from the beginning.'

I knew I was dealing with a madman. I knew that I was behaving foolishly, but I couldn't help myself. 'Nine, you idiot!' I shouted. 'Ten, ten, ten! I was first Master—' I stopped, shocked at what I had said, and hurried to change the dreadful word. 'I *am* first Master,' I screamed.

I suppose I must have looked dreadful, waving my arms and shouting, for he shrank back into my chair, and covered his face with his hands. But I could hear him muttering.

'It isn't true,' he was whispering to himself. 'Reason and science—everything I have lived by— are against it. I'm not seeing a ghost. I utterly deny that I am seeing a ghost.'

These words affected me dreadfully. I felt as though every fibre and bone of my body were melting into something insubstantial, and my control of myself deserted me utterly. 'Ghost!' I screamed; 'ghost yourself! Ghost yourself!' But even as I protested a fearful sickness of doubt was mounting to my heart. I needed help, not for the madman in my chair but for myself. I pushed the bell for the Porter; that way lay sanity; an old army man would know what to do.

The Porter came faster than I could have hoped—but what a Porter! Six feet four of ex-naval man, a bo'sun if ever I saw one. He went at once to the figure in my chair.

'I heard you shouting, sir,' said he; 'anything I can do?'

'Get rid of that—thing there by the fireplace,' said the impostor, pointing toward me, but keeping his eyes closed.

'Nothing there, sir,' said the Porter. 'Better let me help you out into the air, sir. Terrible smoky fire you have today.'

Nothing there! The words struck me like a heavy blow, and I swooned.

How long it was I do not know, but some time later I was aroused to find Mr. McCracken helping me to my feet.

'Better let me help you out into the air, sir,' he said. 'Terrible smoky fire you have today.'

'Yes,' I said; 'we must ask the Bursar for some seasoned wood.'

THE GHOST WHO
VANISHED BY DEGREES

Some of you may have wondered what became of our College Ghost. Because we had a ghost, and there are people in this room who saw him. He appeared briefly last year at the College Dance on the stairs up to this Hall, and at the Gaudy he was seen to come and go through that door, while I was reading an account of another strange experience of mine. I did not see him then, but several people did so. What became of him?

I know. I am responsible for his disappearance. I think I may say without unwarrantable spiritual pride that I laid him. And, as is always the case in these psychic experiences, it was not without great cost to myself.

When first the ghost was reported to me, I assumed that we had a practical joker within the College. Yet—the nature of the joke was against any such conclusion. We had had plenty of jokes—socks in the pool, fish in the pool, funny notices beside the pool, pumpkins on the roofs, ringing the bell at strange hours—all the wild exuberance, the bubbling, ungovernable high spirits and gossamer fantasy one associates with the Graduate School of the University of Toronto. The wit of a graduate student is like champagne—Canadian champagne—but this joke had a different flavour, a dash of wormwood, in its nature.

You see, the ghost was so unlike a joker. He did not appear in a white sheet and shout 'Boo!' He spoke to no one, though a Junior Fellow—the one who met him on the stairs—told me that the Ghost passed him, softly laying a finger on its lips to caution him to silence. On its lips, did I say? Now this is of first importance: it laid its finger where its lips doubtless were, but its lips could not be seen, nor any of its features. Everybody who saw it said that the Ghost had a head, and a place where its face ought to be—but no face that anybody could see or recognize or remember. Of course there are scores of people like that around the university, but they are not silent; they are clamouring to establish some sort of identity; the Ghost cherished his anonymity, his facelessness. So, perversely I determined to find out who he was.

The first time I spotted him was in the Common Room. I went in from my Study after midnight to turn out the lights, and he was just to be seen going along the short passage to the Upper Library. I gave chase, but when I reached the Upper Library he had gone, and when I ran into the entry, he was not to be seen. But at last I was on his trail, and I kept my eyes open from that time.

All of this took place, you should know, last Christmas, between the Gaudy and New Year. Our Gaudy last year was on December the seventeenth; I first saw the Ghost, and lost him, on the twenty-first. He came again on the twenty-third. I woke in the night with an odd sensation that someone was watching me, and as this was in my own bedroom I was very angry; if indeed it were a joker he lacked all discretion. I heard a stirring and—I know this sounds like the shabbiest kind of nineteenth century romance, but I swear it is true—I heard a sigh, and then on the landing outside my door, a soft explosion, and a thud, as though something had fallen. I ran out of my room, but there was nothing to be seen. Over Christmas Day and Boxing Day I had no news of the Ghost, but on the twenty-eighth of December matters came to a head.

December the twenty-eighth, as some of you may know, is the Feast of the Holy Innocents, traditionally the day on which King Herod slaughtered the children of Bethlehem. In the Italian shops in this city you can buy very pretty little babies, made of sugar, and eat them, in grisly commemoration of Herod's whimsical act.

I was sitting in my study at about eleven o'clock that night, reflectively nibbling at the head of a sugarbaby and thinking about money, when I noticed that the lights were on in the Round Room. It troubles me to see electric current wasted, so I set out for the Round Room in a bad humour. As I walked across the quad, it seemed that the glow from the skylight in the Round Room was more blue and cold than it should be, and seemed to waver. I thought it must be a trick of the snow, which was falling softly, and the moonlight which played so prettily upon it.

I unlocked the doors, walked into the Round Room, and there he was, standing under the middle of the skylight.

He bowed courteously. 'So you have come at last,' said he.

'I have come to turn out the lights,' said I, and realized at once that the lights were not on. The room glowed with a fitful bluish light, not disagreeable but inexpressibly sad. And the stranger spoke in a voice which was sad, yet beautiful.

It was his voice which first told me who he was. It had a compelling, 'cello-like note which was unlike anything I was accustomed to hear inside the College, though our range is from the dispirited quack of Ontario to the reverberant splendours of Nigeria. The magnificent voice came from the part of his head where a face should be—but there was no face there, only a shadow, which seemed to change a little in density as I looked at it. It was unquestionably the Ghost!

This was no joker, no disguised Junior Fellow. He was our Ghost, and like every proper ghost he was transporting and other-worldly, rather than merely alarming. I felt no fear as I looked at him, but I was deeply uneasy.

'You have come at last,' said the Ghost. 'I have waited for you long—but of course you are busy. Every professor in this university is busy. He is talking, or he is pursuing, or he is in a journey, or peradventure he sleepeth. But none has time for an act of mercy.'

It pleased me to hear the Ghost quote Scripture; if we must have apparitions, by all means let them be literate.

'You have come here for mercy?' said I.

'I have come for the ordeal, which is also the ultimate mercy,' he replied.

'But we don't go in for ordeals,' said I. 'Perhaps you can tell me a little more plainly what it is you want?'

'Is this not the Graduate School?' said he.

'No indeed,' said I; 'this is a graduate college, but the offices of the Graduate School are elsewhere.'

'Don't trifle with me,' said the Ghost sternly. 'Many things are growing very dim to me, but I have not wholly lost my sense of place; this is the Graduate School; this is the Examination Room. And yet'—the voice faltered—'it seemed to me that it used to be much higher in the air, much less handsome than this. I remember stairs—very many stairs...'

'You had been climbing stairs when you came to me in my bedroom' said I.

'Yes,' he said eagerly. 'I climbed the stairs—right to the top—and went into the Examination Room—and there you lay in bed, and I knew I had missed it again. And so there was nothing for it but to kill myself again.'

That settled it. Now I knew who he was, and I had a pretty shrewd idea where, so far as he was concerned, we both were.

Every university has its secrets—things which are nobody's fault, but which are open to serious misunderstanding. Thirty or more years ago a graduate student was ploughed on his Ph.D. oral; he must have expected something of the kind because when he had been called before his examiners and given the bad news he stepped out on the landing and shot himself through the head. It is said, whether truly or not I cannot tell, that since that time nobody is allowed to proceed to the presentation and defence of his thesis unless there is a probability amounting to a certainty that he will get his degree.

Here, obviously, was that unfortunate young man, standing with me in the Round Room. Why here? Because, before Massey College was built, the Graduate School was housed in an old dwelling on this land, and the Examination Room was at the top of the house, as nearly as possible where my bedroom is now. Before that time the place had been the home of one of the Greek-letter fraternities—the Mu Kau Mu, I believe it was called.

'The Examination Room you knew has gone,' said I. 'If you are looking for it, I fear you must go to Teperman's wrecking yard, for whatever remains of it is there.'

'But is this not an Examination Room?' said the Ghost. I nodded. 'Then I beg you, by all that is merciful, to examine me,' he cried, and to my embarrassed astonishment, threw himself at my feet.

'Examine you for what?' I said.

'For my Ph.D.', wailed the Ghost, and the eerie, agonized tone in which it uttered those common-place letters made me, for the first time, afraid. 'I must have it. I knew no rest when I was in the world of men, because I was seeking it; I know no rest now, as I linger on the threshold of another life, because I lack it. I shall never be at peace without it.'

I have often heard it said that the Ph.D. is a vastly overvalued degree, but I had not previously thought that it might stand between a man and his eternal rest. I was becoming as agitated as the Ghost.

'My good creature,' said I, rather emotionally, 'if I can be of any assistance—'

'You can,' cried the Ghost, clawing at the knees of my trousers with its transparent hands; 'examine me, I beg of you. Examine me now and set me free. I'm quite ready.'

'But, just a moment,' said I; 'the papers—the copies of your thesis—'

'All ready,' said the Ghost, in triumph. And, though I swear that they were not there before, I now saw that all the circle of tables in the Round Room was piled high with those dismal, unappetizing volumes—great wads of typewritten octavo paper—which are Ph.D. theses.

'Be reasonable,' said I. 'I don't suppose for a minute I can examine you. What is your field?'

'What's yours?' said the Ghost, and if a Ghost can speak cunningly, that is exactly what this one did now.

'English literature,' I said; 'more precisely, the drama of the nineteenth century, with special emphasis on the popular drama of the transpontine London theatres between 1800 and 1850.'

Most people find that discouraging, and change the subject. But the Ghost positively frisked to one of the heaps, drew out an especially thick thesis, and handed it to me.

'Shall I sit here?' he asked, pointing to the red chair, which, as you know, has a place of special prominence in that room.

'By no means,' said I, shocked by such an idea.

'Oh, I had so hoped I might,' said the Ghost.

'My dear fellow, you have been listening to University gossip,' said I. 'There are people who pretend that we put the examinee in that chair and sit around the room in a ring, baiting him till he bursts into tears. It is the sort of legend in which scientists and other mythomaniacs take delight. No, no; if you will go away for a few hours—say until tomorrow at ten o'clock—I shall have the room set up for an examination. You shall have a soft chair, cheek by jowl with your examiners, with lots of cigarettes, unlimited water to drink, a fan, and a trained nurse in attendance to take you to the Examinees' W.C. and bring you back again, should the need occur. We are very well aware here that Ph.D. candidates are delicate creatures, subject to unaccountable metaphysical ills—'

The Ghost broke in, impatiently. 'Rubbish,' he said; 'I'm quite ready. Let's get to work. You sit in the red chair. I'm perfectly happy to stand. I think I'm pretty well prepared'—and as he said this I swear that something like a leer passed over the shadow that should have been a face—'and I'm ready as soon as you are.'

There was nothing for it. The Ghost had taken command. I sat down in the red chair—my chair—and opened the thesis. *Prologomena to the Study of the Christ Symbol in the Plays of Thomas Egerton Wilks,* I read, and my heart, which had been sinking for the last few moments now plunged so suddenly that I almost lost consciousness. I have heard of Wilks—it is my job to have heard of him—but of his fifty-odd melodramas, farces and burlesque extravaganzas I have not read a line. However, I have my modest store of professor-craft. I opened the thesis, riffled through the pages, hummed and hawed a little, made a small mark in the margin of one page, and said—'Well, suppose for a beginning, you give me a general outline of your argument.'

He did.

Forty-five minutes later, when I could get a word in, I asked him just where he thought the Christ symbol made its first appearance in *My Wife's Dentist, or The Balcony Beau* which is one of Wilks' dreary farces.

He told me.

Before he had finished he had also given me more knowledge than I really wanted about the Christ symbol in *Woman's Love or Kate Wynsley the Cottage Girl, Raffaelle the Reprobate, or the Secret Mission and the Signet Ring, The Ruby Ring, or The Murder at Sadlers Wells,* and another farce named, more simply, *Bamboozling.*

By this time I felt that I had been sufficiently bamboozled myself, so I asked him to retire, while the examination board—me, me, and only me, as the old song puts it—considered his case. When I was alone I sought to calm myself with a drink of water, and after a decent interval I called him back.

'There are a few minor errors in this thesis which you will undoubtedly notice during a calm re-reading, and a certain opaqueness of style which might profitably be amended. I am surprised that you have made so little use of the great Variorum Edition of Wilks published by Professors Fawcett and Pale, of the University of Bitter End, Idaho. Nevertheless I find it to be a piece of research of real, if limited value, which, if published, might be—yes, I shall go so far as to say, will be—seminal in the field of nineteenth century drama studies,' said I. 'I congratulate you, and it will be a pleasure to recommend that you receive your degree.'

I don't know what I expected then. Perhaps I hoped that he would disappear, with a seraphic smile. True enough, there was an atmosphere as of a smile, but it was the smile of a giant refreshed. 'Good,' he said; 'now we can get on to my other subjects.'

'Do you mean to say that nineteenth century drama isn't your real subject?' I cried, and when I say 'I cried,' I really mean it; my voice came out in a loud, horrified croak.

'Sir,' said he; 'it is so long ago since my unfortunate experience at my first examination that I have utterly forgotten what my subject was. But I have had time since then to prepare myself for any eventuality. I have written theses on everything. Shall we go on now to History?'

I was too astonished, and horrified, and by this time afraid, to say anything. We went on to History.

My knowledge of History is that of a layman. Academically, there is nothing worse, of course, that can be said. But professor-craft did not wholly desert me. The first principle, when you don't know anything about the subject of a thesis, is to let the candidate talk, nodding now and then with an ambiguous smile. He thinks you know, and are counting his mistakes, and it unnerves him. The Ghost was an excellent examinee; that is to say, he fell for it, and I think I shook his confidence once with a little laugh, when he was talking about Canada's encouragement of the arts under the premiership of W. L. Mackenzie King. But finally the two hours was up, and I graciously gave him his Ph.D. in History.

Next came classics. His thesis was on *The Concept of Pure Existence in Plotinus*. You don't want to hear about it, but I must pause long enough to say that I scored rather heavily by my application of the second principle of conducting an oral, which is to pretend ignorance, and ask for explanations of very simple points. Of course your ignorance is real, but the examinee thinks you are being subtle, and that he is making an ass of himself, and this rattles him.

And so, laboriously, we toiled through the Liberal Arts, and some of the Arts which are not so liberal. I examined him in Computer Science, and Astronomy, and Mediaeval Studies, and I rather enjoyed examining him in Fine Art. One of my best examinations was in Mathematics, though personally my knowledge stops short at the twelve-times table.

Every examination took two hours, but my watch did not record them. The night seemed endless. As it wore on I remembered that at cockcrow all ghosts must disappear, and I cudgelled my brain trying to remember whether the kosher butchers on Spadina keep live cocks, and if so what chance we had of hearing one in the Round Room. I was wilting under my ordeal, but the Ghost was as fresh as a daisy.

'Science, now!' he positively shouted, as a whole new mountain of theses appeared from—I suppose from Hell. Now I know nothing whatever of Science, in any of its forms. If Sir Charles Snow wants a prime example of the ignorant Arts man, who has not even heard of that wretched law of thermodynamics, which is supposed to be as fine as Shakespeare, he is at liberty to make free with my name. I don't know and I don't care. When the Ghost moved into Science I thought my reason would desert me.

I needn't have worried. The Ghost was as full of himself as a Ghost can possibly be, and he hectored and bullied and badgered me about things I had never heard of, while my head swam. But little by little—it was when the Ghost was chattering animatedly about his work on the rate of decay of cosmic rays when they are brought in contact with mesons—that I realized the truth. The Ghost did not care whether I knew what he was talking about or not. The Ghost was a typical examinee, and he wanted two things and two things only—an ear into which he could pour what he believed to be unique and valuable knowledge, and a licence to go elsewhere and pour it into the ears of students. Once I grasped this principle, my spirits rose. I began to nod, to smile, to murmur appreciatively. When the Ghost said something especially spirited about the meiosis-function in the formation of germ-cells, I even allowed myself to say 'Bravo'—as if he had come upon something splendid that I had always suspected myself but had never had time to prove in my laboratory. It was a great success; I knew that dawn could not be far away, for as each examination was passed, the Ghost seemed to become a little less substantial. I could see through him, now, and I was happily confident that he could not, and never would, see through me. As he completed his last defense of a doctoral dissertation, I was moved to be generous.

'A distinguished showing,' I said. 'With a candidate of such unusual versatility I am tempted to go a little beyond the usual congratulations. Is there anything else you fancy—a Diploma in Public Health, for instance, or perhaps something advanced in Household Science?'

But the Ghost shook his head. 'I want a Ph.D. and that only,' said he. 'I want a Ph.D. in everything.'

'Consider it yours,' said I.

'You mean that I may present myself at the next Convocation?'

'Yes; when the Registrar kneels to take upon him the degrees granted to those who are forced by circumstances to be absent, I suggest that you momentarily invest him with your ectoplasm—or whatever it is that people in your situation do,' said I.

'I shall; Oh, I shall,' he cried, ecstatically, and as he faded before my eyes I heard his voice from above the skylight in the Round Room, saying, 'I go to a better place than this, confident that as a Ph.D. I shall have it in my power to make it better still.'

So at last, as dawn stole over the College, I was alone in the Round Room. The night of the Holy Innocents had passed. Musing, my hand stole to my pocket and, pulling out the sugar baby, I crunched off its head. Was it those blessed children, I wondered, who had hovered over me, protecting me from being found out? Or had it perhaps been the spirit of King Herod, notoriously the patron of examiners?

All things considered, I think it was both great spiritual forces, watching over me during the long night. Happy in the thought that I was so variously protected, I stepped out into the first light, the last crumbs of the sugar-baby still sweet upon my lips.

THE GREAT QUEEN
IS AMUSED

The first christmas we celebrated in College I told a Ghost Story on this occasion because I had had an odd experience just before the Gaudy, and thought it might amuse you. The second Christmas I told another, only because it was true and a footnote to the first. It was never my intention that these stories should multiply. The last thing I desire for Massey College is the shabby notoriety of being haunted. I am not a man who particularly likes, or seeks, ghosts: I never saw a ghost till I came here— came to a brand-new building, every brick of which I had seen set in place, and all the furnishings of which have been known to me since they came from the makers. I had always thought that ghosts were superstitions. I wish I thought so still.

It happened a week ago last Sunday. I perceive that you have gone at once to the heart of the matter; it is a pleasure to address a truly perceptive audience. You have recognized immediately that the date was December the fifth—the Vigil of Saint Nicholas, patron of scholars, and therefore an unseen but real presence in this College. It was near to midnight, and I lay in my bed, reading myself to sleep, when I felt stealing over me that special uneasiness which I have learned—but only since I came here—to associate with a particular kind of trouble. In university life one quickly becomes expert in identifying several sorts of disquiet; I have one which I believe is all my own, and I call it the Ghost Chill. My temperature drops suddenly; my breathing is laboured; my vision is disturbed so that stable objects seem to advance and retreat before my eyes, and I feel a stirring in my scalp, as though my hair were rising. I see some medical men in the audience smirking; simple fright, they think. Oh no, nothing so easy as that; I am not frightened, but disagreeably *aware*. I know that something quite out of the ordinary—something untoward—something both inescapable and exhausting—is about to happen to me. I know that I have slipped out of the groove of one sort of life and am trapped for a time in an alien realm.

The Ghost Chill also makes one sensitive to sounds which other people do not hear. As I lay in my bed I became conscious of sobbing and sighing and wailing—as of a great number of people shaken with grief and despair and (this was the worst of it) expecting something of me. How did I know this? I cannot tell you. But I knew it, quite clearly. I was not frightened, but I was deeply disturbed and depressed. I knew that things would be worse before they were better, and I knew also that I could not escape whatever lay before me. So I rolled up my book, put it back in its locked case, put on my dressing-gown and slippers, and set out for the scene of the disturbance.

How did I know where to look? That is another of the characteristics of the Ghost Chill. One knows where to go. I do not make any pretentious claim that one is guided to a particular spot; one just knows where to go. So I trudged downstairs, and through the passage on the lowest floor that leads to the Lower Library.

The lights are always burning there, with a hard, charmless blaze that should be enough to discourage the most insensitive ghost. I could see at once that there was nobody in the Reference Room, but from the room which is marked 'Press Room and Stacks' the sound that was drawing me was audible—to my sensitive ear, you understand—in dreadful volume. As I unlocked the door I felt fear for the first time.

How does fear manifest itself in you? With me it is like being stabbed with a cruelly cold knife; for an instant it is a paralysis, then a pain, then a shock. Why was I afraid now? Because I had remembered something that was in the stacks.

Our library has, from time to time, been given generous gifts of books. Even before the College opened one gift came to us of a hundred or more volumes, of which all but five were works of Canadian literature. We are already modestly famous for our collection of Canadian literature, you know. But those five were books to which the

Librarian paid scant attention, because they did not fit into any of the categories of our collection. They were the works of a man of whom some of you will have heard, and whose name may raise a smile. It was Aleister Crowley; he died not long ago, putting an end to a life that had been spent in trying to impose himself on the world as a magician. Most people laughed at him, but there is no doubt that his career was an unsavoury one, and he was involved in scandals that were disastrous, and sometimes fatal, to people who had come under his influence. There were five of Aleister Crowley's books in the stacks, piled together on a shelf of unclassified volumes, and once or twice I had suggested to the Librarian that we should get rid of them, or put them in the vault. But I had forgotten them, and so had he. I remembered them now with the terrible onset of fear that I have already described.

But as I have told you, when the Ghost Chill is upon me, I have to do what lies before me, afraid or not. So I turned the key in the lock, pushed back the heavy door, and walked inside.

There I saw a scene of such complex disorder that I do not know where to begin to describe it. The light was extraordinary, to begin with; it was not the electric glare of the Reference Room, but a wavering blue light, as though I stood in the middle of a gas flame. There was one other living creature in the stacks, and I recognized her with dismay. I cannot reveal her name, for she is well-known to many of you, and I do not wish to involve her in unseemly gossip. I must say, however, that she knows our library well, for she has spent many hours in the stacks, doing some research in Canadian literature for her husband. She stood, tall, straight and unafraid, looking about her in wonder, and as the door slammed into place she turned to look at me.

'You had better step inside this circle if you don't want to get into trouble,' she said, in the soft, yet deliberate and pleasing accents which tell of a childhood spent in the Hebrides. I saw that she stood in a chalk circle that had been carefully drawn on the floor, and I hastened to her side. She was calm in the midst of the frantic disturbance that surrounded us. I suppose President's wives are always calm before scenes of despair and tumult; they learn that art at faculty receptions.

'What on earth are you doing?' I demanded.

'I'm afraid I've been careless with the books,' she replied, and in her hand I recognized one of Crowley's volumes, opened at a drawing that looked like a mathematical diagram. 'I just wanted to see if this recipe worked as well as the author said it did, and it seems to have caused a little trouble.'

A little trouble! I detest understatement; it always seems to me to be dangerous frivolity. A little trouble! My eyes were now accustomed to the strange light, and I could see that the whole area of the stacks was filled with agitated, insubstantial figures; each one was clear to the eye, but it was also transparent. The floor stood thick with them, leaping, writhing, shoving and jostling as they attempted to stand on their hands and fell to the floor every time with shrieks of despair. Some others danced about on their hands, laughing in derisive triumph, and still others crowded all the space immediately below the ceiling. These were even stranger than the dervishes on the floor, for they were curled into balls, their heads tucked into their stomachs, their legs drawn up toward their bodies, and their hands clasped loosely before them, as they bobbed, somersaulted and turned gently in the air, like hideous balloons. And, most extraordinary circumstance of all, every one of these figures was stark naked.

What does one say under such circumstances? Almost any remark one can think of is unequal to the occasion. Undoubtedly mine was so. 'What in the world have you done?' I said.

'Well, I've been reading a lot of these Canadian books, getting together material for Claude's anthology,' she replied. 'I got a bit curious about some of the authors—thought what fun it would be to talk to them, and all that—foolishness, I suppose. Then to-day I came across this book by this man Crowley, and he says it isn't hard to bring back the dead if you go about it in a respectful and proper manner. For the past two weeks I've been wishing I could have a word or two with Sara Jeanette Duncan; there's a bit in *The Imperialist* that always sounds to me as if something had been cut out of it and the gap never properly patched, and I thought—'

'You thought you'd get hold of Miss Duncan and ask her,' I interrupted. The leisureliness of the beautiful anthologist's explanation nettled me.

'Well, Crowley didn't seem to think there was much to it,' she said.

'I think that before monkeying with Crowley you might have had the courtesy to speak to me,' said I.

'Oh don't be so pompous,' said she.

Women always think that if they tell a man not to be pompous they will shut him up, but I am an old hand at that game. I know that if a man bides his time his moment will come. 'Well,' I said, 'if you and Crowley are such a great pair, suppose you explain what has happened.'

'That's just the difficulty,' she said, with terrible Scottish patience; 'I don't understand what has happened. I did all the right things, and called the name of Sara Jeanette Duncan, and these articles began to appear. Look at them, would you! Did you ever see such a sight in your life? What do you suppose they are?'

This was my moment of triumph. You see, I knew what they were.

It has been a lifelong habit of mine to read myself to sleep. Some people read light books—mystery stories and the like—in bed, but my custom has always been to read works of greater substance before sleeping. And not just to read them once, carelessly, but to read and re-read a group of selected classics ove and over again, year in and year out, for in this way they become a part of oneself. For many years a bedtime favourite of mine has been that very famous commentary on the Pentateuch, the *Midrash of Rabbi Tanhuma bar Abba,* most learned of the fourth century Talmudic mystics and sages. My copy of the Midrash is rather a nice one—a fine tenth century scroll, beautifully illuminated though not particularly suited to reading in bed, because it is fourteen feet long, and as it must be read from right to left this means a lot of winding and rewinding. It is encased at both ends in copper and gold; the rubies on the casing scratch my hands now and then, but I don't greatly mind. It is a small price to pay for keeping my Hebrew alive. As luck would have it, I had been reading the scroll of Rabbi Tanhuma when the Ghost Chill came upon me.

Of course you have guessed what the explanation was. Not all of you will have read the great Midrash, but certainly you have read Louis Ginzberg's seven volume compilation of Jewish legends, and will have formed your own conclusions. But Hebrew studies are neglected in the Hebrides and so, for the sake of completeness, I must continue exactly as if you were as much in the dark as was my companion.

She had asked me what I supposed these apparitions were. 'Why,' I said, 'this is hell, and these are spirits of the dead.'

'Don't be silly,' she replied, 'it isn't a bit like hell, except perhaps for the noise.'

'What do you suppose hell to be?' said I. 'The word merely means a dark and enclosed place, inhabited by spirits. A perfect description of the stacks in

Massey College Library. Rabbi Tanhuma says it is indistinguishable from Paradise; both damned and saved pass a few millenia there. I suppose you called up a single spirit, and have received a wholesale delivery; Crowley is a most untrustworthy guide.'

'But who are they?' said she.

'It is only too clear that they are the ghosts of the Canadian authors whose books are here,' said I.

'Then why are they so noisy?' she asked. Every time I think of it, I realize what a wealth of national feeling was compressed into that one enquiry.

'They are clamouring to be reborn,' I explained, for my long acquaintance with Rabbi Tanhuma was at last showing its practical applicability. 'Look, you see those who are floating in that strange, curled-up posture; they have placed themselves in the foetal position, so that, when a child is conceived, they are ready at once to take possession of it in the womb, and come to earth again.'

'Whatever for?' said she.

'Perhaps they hope that this time they might be born American authors,' said I.

Our conversation had not been unnoticed by the spirits, who now began to float uncomfortably near us. Ernest Thompson Seton, though foetal in posture, was still clearly recognizable by the obstreperous outdoorsiness of his appearance; one spirit, naked like the rest, was walking on her hands, and it was only by the invincible dignity of her person, back and front, that I recognized Mrs. Susanna Moodie. Robert Barr looked particularly smug, and I knew why; a Junior Fellow of Massey College is making a fullscale study of him, and he was flattered. A floating foetus bumped me—though spectrally—and I turned just in time to see that it was Nellie McClung, avid for re-birth. It was an eerie experience, I can tell you. I had just time to reflect that Canadian authors appeared, on the whole, to have been neglectful of their physiques.

'You don't suppose they mean us any harm, do you?' said my companion, with the first show of nervousness that I had observed in her.

I do not think that I am a cruel man, but I confess that there is a streak of austerity in my character, and it showed itself now. 'They certainly do not mean *me* any harm,' I replied; 'I have not disturbed their rest; I have not frivolously routed them out of Paradise. What their intentions may be toward *you* I have no way of telling.'

'What are you going to do to get us out of here?' she asked, as if I had not spoken. It is thus that women rule the world.

'There is a practical difficulty,' I said. 'These ghosts can be put to rest only by the command of a king—a Hebrew king. They are uncommon nowadays, even in Massey College. We have one or two men of aristocratic birth, but they are unfortunately Aryan. We have a man whom I strongly suspect of being a chieftain in his homeland, but I am quite sure that an African chief would not fill the bill. Even a royal ghost might help us, but you know Canadian literature—no use looking there.'

'I'm not so sure,' said she. From the triumph in her voice I knew that she had an idea. The circle in which we stood was not too far from the stacks for her to reach over into what the Librarian calls the Matthews Collection, and this is what she did now, handing me two weighty volumes bound in half-calf. I looked at the title. It was *Leaves from the Journal of Our Life in The Highlands;* the date, 1868.

'But this is by Queen Victoria,' said I.

'Of course,' said she; 'and a queen worth a dozen ordinary kings, and I'm pretty certain that she even qualifies as a Hebrew ruler. Disraeli used to tell her that she was descended from King David, and I doubt if a rabble of middle-class Canadian ghosts can say she wasn't. What's more, she also qualifies as a Canadian author. Wasn't she Queen of Canada?'

Women are very, very remarkable people.

'Come on,' she said; 'get to work. See what you can do.'

I was glad of my long acquaintance with the works of the great Rabbi Tanhuma; it meant that I knew how to raise a spirit without resorting to the slipshod conjurations of Aleister Crowley. I did what was necessary with, I think I may say, a certain style, and gently and slowly there appeared, between me and the beautiful anthologist that small, immensely dignified figure, familiar from a hundred portraits and statues. She wore the well-known tiny crown, from the back of which depended a beautiful veil; across her bosom was a sash of a splendid blue, and on her left shoulder was pinned the Order of the Garter.

I am a democrat. All of my family have been persons of peasant origin, who have wrung a meagre sufficiency from a harsh world by the labour of their hands. I acknowledge no one my superior merely on grounds of a more fortunate destiny, a favoured birth. I did what any such man would do when confronted with Queen Victoria; I fell immediately to my knees.

'Rise at once,' said the silvery voice with the beautiful, ac-tress-like clarity of articulation, which has been so often described that it sounded almost familiar in my ears. 'We have work to do that cannot wait. We presume that you wish to set at rest this disorderly group of my colonial subjects.'

'If you would be so good, Your Majesty,' said I. 'These are Canadian writers, and here in Massey College our library is, it appears, a Paradise for the repose of all such as are represented on our shelves. The blessed in Paradise invariably appear to mortals either walking on their hands, or in a posture convenient for re-birth—'

'Master,' said Queen Victoria; 'do not presume to teach the great-great-grandmother of your Sovereign how to suck eggs—or to lay ghosts either. We shall have these spirits right-side up and safely at rest in the squeezing of a lemon—to use an expression dear to our faithful ghillie, John Brown. But look what has happened. We wish an explanation.'

I had been so occupied with Queen Victoria (who, even though I could see right through her, was, I assure you, much the most imposing and awesome person I have ever seen through in this world or any other) that I had not noticed what was going on among the ghosts. I saw that there had been a great reversal; those who had formerly been standing on their hands were now on their feet; those who had formerly been foetal in posture were now normally postnatal: but the others—those who had been trying to stand on their hands before—were now standing on their heads, and bitter tears were pouring from their eyes.

'Who can they be?' I murmured to myself.

'Those, Master,' said Queen Victoria, 'are impostors in Paradise—persons loosely attached to literature who are not themselves authors but who fatten upon authors. What place have they in Paradise? Surely you recognize them? Those, when they lived, were literary critics!'

I looked more closely, and indeed it was so. I saw—never mind who, and with him was—but the less said, the better. They were critics, all right.

'Away with them,' cried the Queen, and the effect of her words was horrible. There was a roaring, as of a mighty rushing wind, and a tumult filled the room. I was thrown to the ground, but even as I fell I saw a figure, black and glistening, as of a naked man of extraordinary but frightening beauty, carrying a cruel scourge, who swooped upon the unfortunate critics. I thought I heard Queen Victoria say

'Good evening, Rhadamanthus,' in a tone of genial politeness, as one monarch to another, but I cannot be sure, for the howls of the critics mounted to a scream. 'No!' they shrieked, 'it's unfair. We really *were* authors. We too were creative! Living critics say so!' But it was unavailing. In an instant the critics were gone, and stillness filled the room. But, in our shelves, there were smoking, blackened gaps where their books had stood.

Then the great Queen made a splendid gesture of dismissal, and all the Canadian authors made their farewell. It took a long time, for they did so one by one, basking in the royal presence. The ladies curtsied—some like Sarah Jeanette Duncan and Frances Brooke with quite a fashionable air, and others—as though they were improvising. Nakedness is unfriendly to a clumsy curtsy. The men bowed—all sorts of bows, from Kerby's splendid gesture with hand on heart and his right foot advanced, to Ralph Connor's strange giving at the knees. But at last all of them had gone back into the shelves, and there we stood—Queen Victoria, the beautiful anthologist and myself, in a room cleansed and calmed.

'You may leave us,' said the Queen.

I bowed. 'I cannot sufficiently express my gratitude—' I began, but as I spoke a smile of extraordinary sweetness broke over the royal features, which had already begun to fade, and before she vanished altogether there came to my ears, unmistakably—'The Queen was very much amused.'

THE NIGHT OF
THE THREE KINGS

A fortnight ago I prepared a Ghost Story to read to you on this occasion. It was a lame affair, because I had to manufacture the whole thing. For three years at this time I have told you of things that really happened—of supernatural visitations to the College which I deeply regretted (because being haunted is considered unseemly in an institution dedicated to truth and scholarship) but which nevertheless provided me with a story to tell. This year I waited, half hopeful that another ghost would turn up, half fearful that our corporate image might receive yet another brutal blow from the unseen world. As nothing happened, I wrote a story, as I said, to pass a few minutes this evening; perhaps I had better be quite frank and admit that I stole a story out of an old volume of *Chums*, and adapted it clumsily to a College setting. I was sorry for the plagiarism, but there seemed no other way out. And then—

But it would not do to raise your expectation too high. It is not of a haunting that I shall tell you tonight. Rather, I must inform you of a haunting that is yet to come. I was there when it was planned. Indeed I—but let me not anticipate.

It happened last night, which as those of you who live in the College know, was one of our High Table nights. There had been guests at dinner, and a great deal of general conversation, and finally an adjournment to the rooms of one of our Senior Fellows for one of those convivial gatherings which are such an enlarging aspect of College life. When the guests had gone, I walked about the College, as I often do on such occasions, expecting to finish with a stroll in the quadrangle. A little fresh air helps one to organize one's recollection of the brilliant and pithy observations on life with which High Table conversation invariably teems. I began with a tour of the lower floor—the *sous sol* as Professor Finch so elegantly calls it; we deplore the word 'basement'. And as I was walking through the corridor on the north side of the building, I smelled, unmistakably, the aroma of a cigar.

Nothing in that, you will say. That is what I said. Indeed, I had been smoking a cigar myself not long before, and traces of it may yet have hung about me. So I went on, humming the Antiphon for the Day, which as you will recall, is the one that begins *O Sapientia*. But as I was peeping into the Chapel, an uneasiness began to assert itself. A cigar—but not any cigar that I had smoked. A cigar, rather, that raised a question in the mind's nose. What *was* that scent? I sat down in the Chapel and mused. Then it came to me; it was the fragrance of a Hoyo de Monterey, and it was quite fresh. Well!

I see that you share my astonishment. Still, in case there are a few of the ladies present who have led very sheltered lives, or who perhaps have never known any really first-rate men, I shall explain. The Hoyo de Monterey was certainly one of the finest cigars ever manufactured, but it was exported only to England and none has been made since 1939!

I retraced my steps. I paced up and down the north corridor sniffing like a great hound. Who had a Hoyo de Monterey? Who, having such a treasure, was smoking it after midnight in our *sous sol?* I sniffed ... and sniffed ... and my sniffs brought me to a locked door.

You know the door; it is to what will be called the Muniment Room when it is completed. It is the room which will contain the personal papers of our Visitor. Great quantities of those papers are in there now, in roped and sealed filing cabinets, waiting to be catalogued. Who was smoking a Hoyo de Monterey in there, among those inflammable papers? The Visitor himself? Doesn't smoke cigars. The Librarian? Smokes a pipe, of what had better be called a characteristic odour. It was my duty to unravel this mystery. I have a master-key. I unlocked the door.

There he was, the scoundrel, crouched behind a row of filing cabinets. These cabinets are sealed, but he appeared to have broken a seal and was rootling in a drawer. The Hoyo de Monterey, in all its tawny magnificence, was nestling between the silki-est moustache and the most elegantly spiked Navy beard you ever saw; he was wearing the full dress uniform of an Admiral of the Fleet, and on top of the filing cabinet rested a gold-laced admiral's fore-and-aft hat. He spotted me. I insist upon the term; he did not see, or observe, or take notice; he spotted me.

'You, there,' he called, much more loudly than was necessary in a small room; 'do you work here?'

Of course I do work here. I work like a dog—nay, like a Trojan. But one of the necessary fictions of Massey College—what Ibsen would have called the Life-Giving Lie—is that I am a person of limitless scholarly leisure. I replied sternly.

'I am the Master of this College,' said I. 'What do you think you are doing?'

'I don't think anything about it, my good man,' said he. 'I'm looking for a valuable stamp.'

I do not like being called 'my good man'; in the particular minority of which I am a member, it is a discriminatory and offensive term.

'Who are you?' said I. But I knew. Already I knew.

My question made him hesitate for a moment. 'Oh—I'm Baron Killarney,' he replied, trying to make it sound like John Smith.

'So you are,' said I, courteously, I hope, 'and you are also the late George the Fifth, King of Great Britain, Ireland and the British Dominions beyond the seas, and Emperor of India. Now sir, what are you doing snooping in Mr. Massey's papers?'

He looked at me closely for the first time. Never have I looked into eyes of so bright a blue.

'You're not as big a fool as you look,' said he. I acknowledged the compliment with a half-bow; I didn't think it called for a whole bow. 'Well, I wrote a letter to Vincent Massey in 1934 and my ass of a secretary put a very valuable stamp on it. I was keeping the stamp, which had a unique reversed border— only one of its kind—and I suppose the fella hooked it to save himself trouble. I couldn't sack him—he was a Balliol man—but I made his life a perfect hell till he quit. And I swore I'd get that stamp back in this world or the next. Well, as you see, I didn't get it in this world. And only now have I found out where the letter is. Give me my stamp.'

'I haven't got your beastly stamp,' said I, 'and I think you are an impostor. Royalty never stamps letters. Everybody knows that.'

'Do they, b'God!' said he. 'I always stamped mine. I liked stamps. Why, I even designed a few stamps. Now, where's my stamp?'

'I suppose it has been thrown away,' said I; 'nobody files letters in envelopes.'

'That shows how much you know,' said the King, with what I thought quite unnecessary rudeness. But then I remembered that he had been a Navy man all his life, and forgave him. He went on: 'You must have heard about filing: what you do is this—you cut open your letter with an ivory paperknife and when you have read it you replace it in its envelope, and make a concise *précis* of what the letter says on the envelope. Then you chuck it into your locker. That way you preserve the stamp. That's what I always did. That's what every sane man does. So my stamp must be in here.'

'But as you see,' said I, 'these letters are not filed in envelopes.'

A look of suspicion came into the King's blazing eyes, and he became as frantic as a man in the uniform of a full Admiral can possibly be. 'Then he's filed the envelopes separately,' he roared; 'obviously because he was a collector! Where are the envelopes?'

'I don't know,' said I.

'Then help me find them,' he shouted.

'I cannot prevent you, as a monarch and a ghost, from doing as you please,' said I, 'but you must not ask me to join in rummaging through our Visitor's papers; it is contrary to my duty to Mr. Massey, to the College, to the Librarian—'

The King made a very unsuitable proposal regarding the Librarian, which I do not think it proper to repeat. It was increasingly obvious that his character and vocabulary had been formed in the Navy.

'Here's a rum start!' he continued. 'My time is short, and I need expert help. Who were Mr. Massey's correspondents?'

I was flummoxed by that one. 'Oh, just about everybody,' I replied.

'Any collectors?' he asked. 'You know our rules, I suppose; I can't call up anybody who isn't represented somehow in this room. *Supernatural Regulations* 64 A. What about my son? He was a very fair collector; not in my class, of course, but good enough. Any letters from him in these boxes?'

It seemed likely, and I nodded. The King began to shout in a quarter-deck voice. 'Bertie!' he roared. 'Bertie, come here at once; I need you. Bertie!'

A voice spoke behind me—a voice I remembered well—the quiet, careful voice of a man who has overcome a distressing stammer.

'Father,' it said; 'I've been looking all over the Commonwealth for you. We are due to haunt the chartroom of the Royal Naval College at Greenwich. Do hurry.'

'Bertie, my boy,' shouted King George the Fifth. 'We've got a good ten minutes. My three-penny with the reversed border is in here someplace, and we've got to find it. Hurry up, boy, hurry up!'

Nothing in my experience is stranger than the scene that followed. There was George the Fifth, and with him George the Sixth, in full Naval kit, tearing open those carefully sealed filing-cabinets. They severed the rope bindings with their swords (I had never before believed that those swords would cut anything) and tore out double handfuls of papers, which they threw about the room until it was like a snowstorm. The monarchs were in the grip of collectors' mania—than which there are few more terrible passions in the world. The short King and the tall King whisked about the room with extraordinary speed, searching, sifting, seeking, while I dodged hither and thither, expostulating and now and then hopping out of reach of their terrible swords.

What time passed, I cannot tell; a few minutes, I suppose, though it seemed hours. Then George the Sixth, far too excited to speak, discovered in some obscure corner an envelope, upon which a few words had been written, and thrust it at his father. The senior monarch was overjoyed; as he seized it, the blue eyes filled with tears.

'Bertie, my boy,' he sobbed; 'you've found it! Good fella! Oh, good fella!'

But my distress was greater than before. 'You can't take it away!' I cried. 'You mustn't!'

'Who's going to stop me?' said King George the Fifth.

Who, indeed? Consider: this was a ghost; the ghost of a king, armed with a sword that seemed to have the very unghostly property of being able to cut real objects. Such a threat was more than enough to daunt me. In my anguish I cried aloud: 'Oh help!' I sighed, and then, remembering my national obligation to be fully bilingual I added 'Au secours! Au secours!'

I like to think it was the bilingualism that did it. A soft, self-possessed voice behind me said, 'Perhaps I might be of assistance?'

All three of us turned to see who had spoken. It was George the Sixth, oddly enough, who spoke first.

'Mr. Prime Minister,' said he.

Yes, that was who it was. Not any Prime Minister, but preeminently and solely *the* Prime Minister. That lock of hair that always dangled over the forehead;

the lips parted in childlike wonderment; those exquisitely beautiful brown eyes, of which an Edwardian
beauty might have been vain; the expensive clothes
so negligently worn; above all that air of imperturb-
able, toad-like dignity: it could be but one person. It
was William Lyon Mackenzie King.

'There are a great many letters from me here,'
said Mr. King, 'and when I sensed that I might be
of assistance to my dear old friend and colleague,
Vincent Massey, I made haste to come.'

For a moment my senses swam. But as rapidly as
I could I explained the situation.

'It is clear that the ahnvelope must remain where
it is,' said Mackenzie King.

'What!' roared George the Fifth, in such a Navy
bellow as I had not yet heard. 'Look here, Mr. Prime
Minister: I know just as much about constitutional
monarchy, and Dominion status, and the Statute of
Westminster and all that frightful bilge as you do,
but fair's fair. It's my stamp, and I want it.'

'Your Majesty has failed to remember that in the
case of a letter, only the literary content continues to
be the property of the writer; the physical letter—
paper, ink, and of course the stamp—become the
indisputable property of the receiver. Your Majesty
would not wish to rob one of his subjects of a personal possession. You would not think, for instance,
of taking Mr. Massey's cufflinks, or his cigarette case.'

'But it's a stamp,' murmured the King; it was not
the voice of a monarch, or of an Admiral, but of a
collector, and it was so wistful that my heart ached

toward him. For I too am a collector, though not of stamps.

'He's got you up a tree, Father,' said George the Sixth, hardly less dejected.

'He always had us all up trees,' murmured his father.

But Mackenzie King was magnanimous in victory. 'Canada would not wish to be ungenerous. Perhaps you might come back from time to time and look at it, finger it, play with it—even perhaps lick it,' said he.

This last was an unhappy inspiration. The senior monarch fixed him with a look of fathomless scorn.

'Anybody who would lick a unique specimen would fabricate a constitutional issue,' said he, and Mackenzie King veiled his beautiful eyes and moved his lips, as though in silent explanation of some old, unhappy, far-off thing. 'Still—could I come here once a year?'

'I think that is for the Master to say,' said Mackenzie King.

It was at this moment that I was visited with an inspiration. 'Will your Majesty grant me a favour?' said I.

'Anything in reason,' said George the Fifth. 'What would you like? What do you college-wallahs fancy? Star of India? Posthumous, naturally. You'd get it when you became one of us.'

I knew why he was so generous; he wanted to get at that stamp. But before I could speak, Mackenzie King intervened.

'Your Majesty has forgotten that Canadians are not permitted to accept titles, even posthumously.'

King George the Fifth spoke at length on that subject, in terms I shall not repeat. His simple, sailor's eloquence burned like a refiner's fire. I was lost in wonder at some of the uses he made of the simplest Anglo-Saxon words, but Mackenzie King's eyes were once more closed. I sensed that he was thinking of his mother. When the King had finished, I spoke again.

'It was not a personal favour I sought, but something for the College. We have had some ghosts here—shabby, detrimental spooks who ran the place down. Now, if your Majesty—and of course you also, sir,' said I, looking at George the Sixth, 'wish to come here to look at this remarkable stamp, you are welcome at any time. All I ask is that for some part of your yearly visit you will permit yourselves to be seen. It would do so much to establish a good College tone.'

Before the King could answer, Mackenzie King had spoken again. 'If any monarch, or monarchs, are to set foot—even posthumous foot—upon Canadian soil, it is desirable that a Canadian Minister of the Crown should be with them at all times,' said he. And because ghosts are not always careful to conceal their thoughts, I could hear, passing through his mind, the objectionable phrase, 'to keep an eye on them'.

It was at this moment that my inspiration completed itself in a dazzling flash. I spoke in a courtier-like tone which I had not found necessary with the two Georges. 'Mr. Prime Minister,' said I; 'you were certainly included in the invitation.'

He seemed dubious, even then, and closed his eyes. In that instant I winked at the two kings; like the sailors they were at heart, they winked back.

'When shall we manifest ourselves?' said George the Fifth.

'I question if it is at all desirable to manifest ourselves,' said Mackenzie King. 'There are a great many young scientists living in this college, and it would be discourteous—nay, wantonly cruel—to do anything that would tamper with their simple faith in materialism.'

'Oh, come on,' said the senior monarch. 'Let's do the thing properly. I hate all this invisible hooting and rattling windows and so forth. That is for the lower order of ghosts. Be a sport, man; everybody knows you were a keen spiritualist. We'll manifest ourselves.'

'Yes,' I assented, eagerly; 'if you would consent to walk around the quadrangle at midnight, for instance—.'

'Capital!' said the old King. 'We'll walk ahead, Bertie, arm-in-arm, and the P.M. can follow us, three paces in the rear. How's that?'

Mr. King looked sour. 'We shall see,' said he. 'Let us leave it at this: manifestation if necessary, but not necessarily manifestation.'

'Oh, it will be necessary,' said George the Fifth. 'When shall we come?' he asked, eagerly. I could see that his mind was on the stamp.

'Would January the sixth be agreeable to your Majesties?' said I. It was clear by now that Mr. King did not count. The collectors were only too ready to co-operate.

'You may depend upon us,' said the old King. 'Now Bertie, we must go, or we shall be late for the haunted chart-room at Greenwich.' And as he began to fade before my eyes, he drew from some inner recess of his uniform a handome and completely real cigar and pressed it upon me.

A few minutes later I was strolling about the quad, smoking that admirable Hoyo de Monterey, as contented as any man in Canada, I suppose. For I had managed something for the College which I do not think had been apparent to my distinguished guests. Why should they know what I knew—two men educated as Naval officers, and a statesman of Presbyterian background and spiritualist leanings? But I knew that by far the most appropriate day for their manifestation was January the sixth, which is, of course, the last of the Twelve Days of Christmas, and the Feast of the Three Kings.

The Charlottetown
Banquet

The range of guests who come to our fortnightly High Table dinners is wide, and provides us with extraordinarily good company. Sometimes we get a surprise—an economist who turns out to be a poet, for instance. (I mean a poet in the formal sense: all economists are rapt, fanciful creatures; it is necessary to their profession.) Only last Friday we had a visitor whom I found a most delightful and illuminating companion. I shall not tell you what his profession is, or you will immediately identify him, and I shall have betrayed his secret, which is that he is a medium.

He does not like being a medium. He finds it embarrassing. But the gift, like being double-jointed or having the power to wiggle one's ears, can neither be acquired by study nor abdicated by an act of will. His particular power lies in the realm of psychometry; that is to say that sometimes—not always—he finds that when he is near to an object that has strong and remarkable associations, he becomes aware of those associations with an intensity that is troublesome to him. And occasionally psychic manifestations follow.

He confided this to me just as we were leaving the small upstairs dining-room, where we assemble after dinner for conversation and a reasonable consumption of port and Madeira. We were standing at the end of the room by the sideboard, for he had been looking at our College grant-of-arms; he put his hand on the wall to the left of the frame, to enable him to lean forward for a closer look, and then he turned to me, rather white around the mouth, I thought, and said—

'Let's go downstairs. It's terribly close in here.'

I thought it was the cigar smoke that was troubling him. Excellent as the Bursar's cigars undoubtedly are, the combustion of a couple of dozen of them within an hour does make the air rather heavy. So I went downstairs with him, and thought no more about the matter.

It must have been a couple of hours later that I was taking a turn around the quad for a breath of air before bed, when I saw something I did not like. The window of the small dining room was lighted up, but not by electricity. It was a low, flickering light that seemed to rise and fall in its intensity, and I thought at once of fire. I dashed up the stairs with a burst of speed that any of the Junior Fellows might envy, and opened the door. Sure enough, there was light in the room.

But—! Now you must understand that we had left the room in the usual sort of disorder; the table had been covered with the debris of our frugal academic pleasures—nutshells, the parings of fruit, soiled wine-glasses, filled ashtrays, crumpled napkins, and all that sort of thing. But now—!

I have never seen the room looking as it looked at that moment. How shall I describe it?

To begin, the table was covered with a cloth of that refulgent bluey-whiteness that speaks of the finest linen. And, what is more, there was not a crease in it; obviously it had been ironed on the table. The pattern that was woven into it was of maple leaves, entwined with lilies and roses. At every place—and it was set for twenty-four—was a napkin folded into the intricate shape known to Victorian butlers as Crown Imperial. At either end of the table was a soup tureen, and my heightened senses immediately discerned that the eastern tureen contained Mock Turtle, while that at the western end was filled with a Consommé enriched with a *julienne* of truffles— that is to say, Consommé Britannia. A noble boiled salmon of the Restigouche variety was displayed on one platter, with a vessel of Lobster Sauce in waiting, and on another was a selection of Fillets of the most splendid Nova Scotia mackerel, each gleaming with the pearls of a Sauce Maitre d'Hotel.

And the Entrees! Petites Bouches a la Reine, and Grenadine de Veau with a Pique Sauce Tomate— and none of your nasty bottled tomato sauce, either, but the genuine fresh article. There was a Lapin Sauté which had been made to stand upright, its paws raised as though in delight at its own beauty, and a charming fluff of cauliflower sprigs where its tail had been a few hours before; you could see that it was served au Champignons, for two button mushrooms gleamed where its eyes had once been. There was a Cotellete d'Agneau with, naturally, Petits Pois. There was a Coquette de volaille, and a Timbale de Macaroni which had been moulded into the form of—of all things—a Beaver.

In addition there were roasted turkeys, chickens, a saddle of mutton and a sirloin of beef, and there were boiled turkeys, hams, corned beef and mutton cutlets. And it was all piping hot.

The flickering soft light I had seen through the window came from a gasolier that hung over the table, and through its alabaster globes gleamed the gaslight—surely one of the loveliest forms of illumination ever devised by man.

You have recognized the meal, of course. Every gourmet has that menu by heart. It was the Grand Banquet in Honour of the Colonial Delegates which was held at the Halifax Hotel in Charlottetown on September 12, 1864. This was the authentic food of Confederation. A specimen of the menu, elegantly printed on silk, and the gift of Professor Maurice Careless, one of our Senior Fellows, hangs on the wall of our small dining-room, just at the point where our guest, the medium, had laid his hand.

Nor was this all. What I have described to you at some length leapt to my eye in an instant, and my gaze had turned to the sideboard, which was laden with bottles of wine.

And what bottles! Tears came into my eyes, just to look at them. For these were not our ugly modern bottles, with their disagreeable Government stickers adhering to them, and their high shoulders, and their uniformity of shape, and their self-righteous airs, as though in the half-literate, nasal drone of politicians, they were declaiming: 'We are the support of paved roads, general education and public health; we are the pillars of society.' No, no; these were smaller bottles, in a multiplicity of shapes and colours. There were the slim pale-green maidens of hock; the darkly opalescent romantic ports; the sturdily gay clarets and the high-nosed aristocrats of Burgundy; there were champagnes that almost danced, yet were not gassy impostors; and they were all bottles of the old shapes and the old colours—dark, merry and wicked.

My knees gave a little, and I sat down in the nearest chair.

It was then that I noticed the figure by the sideboard. His back was toward me, and whether he was somewhat clouded in outline, or whether my eyes were dazzled by the table, I cannot say, but I could not quite make him out. He was hovering—I might almost say gloating—over a dozen of sherry. That should have given me a clue, but you will understand that I was not fully myself. And, furthermore, I had at that instant recalled that the menu given to us by Professor Careless was said by him to have been the property of the Honourable Geroge Brown. On such a matter one does not doubt the word of Maurice Careless.

'Mr. Brown! I believe?' I said, in what I hoped was a hospitable tone.

'God forbid that I should cast doubt on any man's belief,' said the figure, still with its back to me, 'but I cannot claim the distinction you attribute to me.' He picked up a bottle of sherry and drew the cork expertly. Then he drew the cork of another, and turned toward me with a wicked chuckle, a bottle in either hand;

'These are Clan Alpine's warriors true,
And, Saxon, I am Roderick Dhu—'

said he, and I was so astonished that I quite overlooked the disagreeable experience of being addressed as a Saxon. For it was none other than Old Tomorrow himself!

Yes, it was Sir John A. Macdonald in his habit as he lived. Or rather, not precisely as we are accustomed to seeing him, but in Victorian evening dress, with a red silk handkerchief thrust into the bosom of his waistcoat. But that head of somewhat stringy ringlets, that crumpled face which seemed to culminate and justify itself in the bulbous, coppery nose, that watery, rolling, merry eye, the accordion pleating of the throat, those moist, mobile lips, were unmistakable.

'If you were expecting Brown, I am truly sorry,' he continued. 'But, you see, I was the owner of this menu.' (He pronounced it, in the Victorian manner, meenoo.) 'Brown pocketed it as we left the table. It was a queer little way he had, of picking up odds and ends; we charitably assumed he took them home to his children. But it's mine, right enough. Look, you can see my thumb-mark on it still.'

But I was not interested in thumb-prints. I was deep in awe of the shade before me. I started to my feet. In a voice choking with emotion I cried: 'The Father of my country!'

'Hookey Walker!' said Sir John, with a wink. 'Tuck in your napkin, Doctor, and let us enjoy this admirable repast.'

I had no will of my own. I make no excuses. Who, under such circumstances, would have done other than he was bidden? I sat. Sir John, with remarkable grace, uncovered the Mock Turtle, and gave me a full plate. I ate it. Then he gave me a plate of the Consommé Britannia. I ate it. Then I had quite a lot of the salmon. Then a substantial helping of mackerel. I ate busily, humbly, patriotically.

I have always heard of the extraordinary gustatory zest of the Victorians. They ate hugely. But it began to be borne in upon me, as Sir John plied me with one good thing after another, that I was expected to eat all, or at least some, of everything on the table. My gorge rose. But, I said to myself, when will you, ever again, eat such a meal in such company? And my gorge subsided. I began to be aware that my appetite was unimpaired. The food I placed in my mouth, and chewed, and swallowed, seemed to lose substance somewhere just behind my necktie. I had no sense of repletion. And little by little it came upon me that I was eating a ghostly meal, in ghostly company, and that under such circumstances I could go on indefinitely. Not even my jaws ached. But the taste—ah, the taste was as palpable as though the viands were of this earth.

Meanwhile Sir John was keeping pace with me, bite for bite. But rather more than glass for glass. He had asked me to name my poison, which I took to be a Victorian jocularity for choosing my wine, and I had taken a Moselle—a fine Berncasteler—with the soup and fish, and had then changed to a St. Emilion with the entrees. (It was particularly good with the rabbit, a dish of which I am especially fond; Sir John did not want any, and I ate that rabbit right down to the ground, and sucked its ghostly bones.) But Sir John stuck to sherry. Never have I seen a man put away so much sherry. And none of your whimpering dry sherries, either, but a brown sherry that looked like liquefied plum pudding. He threw it off a glass at a time, and he got through bottle after bottle.

You must not suppose that we ate in silence. I do not report our conversation because it is of slight interest. Just—'Another slice of turkey, my dear Doctor; allow me to give you the liver-wing.'

And—'Sir John, let me press you to a little more of this excellent Timbale de Macaroni; and may I refill your glass. Oh, you've done it yourself.' You know the sort of thing; the polite exchanges of men who are busy with their food.

But at last the table was empty, except for bones and wreckage. I sat back, satisfied yet in no way uncomfortable, and reached for a toothpick. It was a Victorian table, and so there were toothpicks of the finest sort—real quill toothpicks such as one rarely sees in these weakly fastidious days. I was ready to put into effect the plan I had been hatching.

In the bad old days, before the academic life claimed me, I was, you must know, a journalist. And here I found myself in a situation of which no journalist would dare even to dream. Across the table from me sat one whose unique knowledge of our country's past was incalculably enhanced by his extraordinary privilege of possessing access to our country's future! Here was one who could tell me what would be the outcome of the present disquiet in Quebec. And then how I should be courted in Ottawa! Would I demand the Order of Canada— the Companionship, not the mere medal—before I deigned to reveal what I knew? And how I should lord it over Maurice Careless! But I at once put this unworthy thought from me. Whom the gods would destroy, they first make mad. I wound myself up to put my leading question.

But, poor creature of the twentieth century that I am, I was mistaken about the nature of our meal.

'Ready for the second course, I think, eh Doctor?' said Sir John, and waved his hand. In a moment, in the twinkling of an eye—the Biblical phrase popped into my mind—the table was completely re-set, and before us was spread a profusion of partridges, wild duck, lobster salad, galantines, plum pudding, jelly, pink blancmange, Charlotte Russe, Italian Cream, a Bavarian Cream, a Genoa Cream, plates of pastries of every variety—apple puffs, bouchées, cornucopias, croquenbouche, flans, strawberry tartlets, maids-of-honour, stuffed monkeys, prune flory, tortelli—it was bewildering. And there were ice creams in the Victorian manner—vast temples of frozen, coloured, flavoured cornstarch—and there were plum cakes and that now forgotten delicacy called Pyramids.

And fruit! Great towers of fruit, mounting from foundations of apples, through oranges and nectarines to capitals of berries and currants, upon each of which was perched the elegantly explosive figure of a pineapple.

You see, I had forgotten that a proper Victorian dinner had a second course of this nature, so that one might have some relaxation after the serious eating was over.

But Sir John seemed disappointed. 'What!' he cried; 'no gooseberry fool? And I had been so much looking forward to it!' He proceeded to drown his sorrow in sherry.

I had no fault to find. I began again, eating methodically of every dish, and accepting second helpings of Charlotte Russe and plum cake. During this course I drank champagne only. It was that wonderful Victorian champagne, somewhat sweeter than is now fashionable, and with a caressing, rather than an aggressive, carbonization. I hope I did not drink greedily, but in Sir John's company it was not easy to tell.

I do not mean to give you the impression that Sir John was the worse for his wine. He was completely self-possessed, but I could not help being aware that he had consumed nine bottles of sherry without any assistance from me, and that he showed no sign of stopping. I knew—once again I was in the debt of Professor Careless for this information—that it was sherry he had favoured for those Herculean bouts of solitary drinking that are part of his legend. I was concerned, and I suppose my concern showed. Before I could begin my interrogation, might not my companion lose the power of coherent speech? I sipped my champagne and nibbled abstractedly at a stuffed monkey wondering what to do. Suddenly Sir John turned to me.

'Have a weed?' he said. I accepted an excellent cigar from the box he pushed toward me.

'And a b. and s. to top off with?' he continued. Once again I murmured my acquiescence, and he prepared a brandy and soda for me at the sideboard. But for himself he kept right on with the sherry.

'Now, Doctor,' said Sir John, 'I can see that you have something on your mind. Out with it.'

'It isn't very easy to put into words,' said I. 'Here am I, just as Canada's centennial year is drawing to a close, sitting alone with the great architect of our Confederation. Naturally my mind is full of questions; the problem is, which should come first?'

'Ah, the centennial year,' said Sir John. 'Well, in my time, you know, we didn't have this habit of chopping history up into century-lengths. It's always the centennial of something.'

'But not the centennial of Canada,' said I. 'You cannot pretend to be indifferent to the growth of the country you yourself brought into being.'

'Not indifferent at all,' said he. 'I've put myself to no end of inconvenience during the past year, dodging all over the continent—*a mari usque ad mare*—to look at this, that and the other thing.'

I could not control myself; the inevitable question burst from my lips. 'Did you see Expo?' I cried.

'I certainly did,' said he, laughing heartily, 'and I took special trouble to be there at the end when they were adding up the bill. The deficit was roughly eight times the total budget of this Dominion for the year 1867. You call that a great exposition? Why, my dear Doctor, the only Great Exposition that made any sense at all was the Great Exposition of 1851. It was the only world's fair in history that produced a profit. And why was that? Because it was dominated by that great financier and shrewd man of business Albert the Prince Consort. If you had had any sense you would have put your confounded Expo under the guidance of the Duke of Edinburgh; no prince would have dared to bilk and rook the country as your politicians did, for he would have known that it might cost him his head. Expo!—' And then Sir John used some genial indecencies which I shall not repeat.

'But Sir John,' I protested, 'this is a democratic age.'

'Democracy, sir, has its limitations, like all political theories,' said he, and I remembered that I was talking, after all, to a great Conservative and a titled Canadian. But now, if ever, was the time to come to the point.

'We have hopes that our mighty effort may reflect itself in the future development of our country,' said I. 'Because you have been so kind as to make yourself palpable to me I am going to ask a very serious question. Sir John, may I enquire what you see in store for Canada, the land which you brought into being, the land which reveres your memory, the land in which your ashes lie and your mighty example is still an inspiration? May I ask what the second century of our Confederation will bring?'

'You may ask, sir,' said Sir John; 'but it won't signify, you know. I see, Doctor, that I must give you a peep into the nature of the realm of which I am now a part. It is a world of peace, and every man's idea of peace is his own. Consider the life I led: it was one long vexation. It was an obstacle race in which my rivals were people like that tendentious, obstructive ass Brown, that rancorous, dissident ruffian Cartier, even such muttonheaded fellows as Tupper and Mowat. It was a world in which I would be interrupted in the task of writing a flattering letter to an uncomprehending Queen in order to choke off some Member of Parliament who wanted one of his constituents appointed to the post of a lighthouse-keeper. It was a life in which my every generous motive was construed as political artfulness, and my frailties were inflated into examples to scare the children of the Grits. It was, doctor, the life of a yellow dog. Now—what would peace be to such a man as I was? Freedom, Doctor; freedom from such cares as those; freedom to observe the comedy and tragedy of life without having to take a hand in it. Freedom to do as I please without regard for consequences.'

During this long speech Sir John had finished the final bottle of his dozen of sherry. Those which he had drunk before had all floated, each as it was emptied, to the sideboard, where they now stood in a cluster. He picked up the twelfth bottle, and whirled it round his head like an Indian club, closing one eye to take more careful aim.

'You ask about the future of Canada, my dear sir?' he shouted. 'Understandably you want to tell the world what I know it to be. But you can't, my dear Doctor, because I haven't taken the trouble to look. And the reason for that, my dear sir, is that I DO NOT GIVE A DAMN!'

And as he uttered these fearful words the Father of My Country hurled that last sherry bottle at the eleven on the sideboard. There was a tremendous smash, the gaslight went out, and I lost consciousness.

How much later it was I cannot tell, but when I was myself again I was walking around the quad, somewhat dazed but strangely elated. For, although I had been baulked in my wish to learn something of the future in this world, had I not been admitted to a precious, soothing, heartlifting secret about the next? To be a Canadian, yet not to have to give a damn—was it not glorious?

And to have eaten the Charlottetown banquet in such company! A smile rose to my lips, and with it the ghost of a hiccup.

Needs of new Story not just any Ghost Story

WHEN SATAN GOES HOME

FOR CHRISTMAS

Ectoplasmic Elitism of the most disgusting Kind

One of the Fellows of this College—a distinguished scholar whose name is familiar to all of you—said to me a few weeks ago: 'Well, I suppose we are going to have *another* of your ghost stories at the Gaudy.'

My ear is sensitive, and it seemed to me that his remark contained less of eager enquiry than of resigned acceptance. I asked him at once what it was he disliked about my ghost stories.

'The ghosts,' he said, bluntly. 'We've heard about your meetings with the shades of Queen Victoria, and George V and George VI, and Sir John A. Macdonald; it is as if nobody was fit to haunt you who had not first gained a distinguished place in history. It's ectoplasmic elitism of the most disgusting kind.'

I could have told him that these ghosts were not inventions; I did not seek them—they sought me. But it is useless to argue with jealous people who, if they are haunted at all, are clearly haunted by ghosts

Useless to argue with jealous people

drawn from the lower ranks of the Civil Service. But I determined that I would show him. I did not expect a real ghost this year; after all, five in a row is surely enough even for the most-haunted College in the University. I knew I should have to invent a ghost; it would be a simple matter to invent a ghost who would be acceptable to listeners with strong egalitarian views.

I did so. It is an excellent story—what used to be called in an earlier day 'a ripping yarn'—and quite original. It is about a Junior Fellow of this College called Frank Einstein, a brilliant young biologist who discovers the secret of life in an old alchemical manuscript, and manufactures a living creature out of scraps he steals from the dissection lab. in the new Medical Building. He fits it together secretly in his bedroom. But because he cannot give his creation a soul, it is a Monster, and kills the Bursar and the Librarian and finally deflowers and then eats Frank's girl-friend, a graduate student called Mary Shelley. It is a lively narrative, and I had looked forward to reading it—especially the soliloquies of the Monster—but last night—

Last night we held our College Christmas Dance, and there was no sleep till morn, as is entirely proper when Youth and Pleasure meet to chase the glowing Hours with flying feet. It was about one o'clock, and I had been to look at the dancing in the Round Room, where the flying Hours were being chased in a circle, which is after all what you would expect in a Round Room. I then went downstairs to the Chapel;

Wearing a cut of suit that made him look like an America Beautiful Man

it seemed unlikely that any couples would be sitting out there, and I would gain ten minutes of blessed quietness. But the Chapel was not empty.

The man who was standing at the altar, gazing so intently at the reredos, was not odd in any way, and yet I felt at once that he was extraordinary in every way. He seemed to be middle-aged, and yet he was not an academic; you can always date an academic by the cut of his dress suit, which he buys before he is thirty and uses very sparingly for the next forty-five years. But this man's tail-coat might have been made yesterday, though its cut was conservative. His hair was rather long, and curly, but it was most elegantly arranged. His bearing was distinguished. I am somewhat too old to describe a man's face as beautiful without self-consciousness, yet he was undeniably beautiful—beautiful but of an icy *hauteur*. I recognized the type at once; obviously a visiting lecturer from some Mid-Western American University.

'It is a handsome piece of work, isn't it?' said I, referring to our reredos.

He did not look at me. 'Quite interesting, as these family portraits go,' he murmured. I concluded that he must be deaf.

'It is Russian, seventeenth century, what is called a travelling iconostasis,' I said, raising my voice.

'A pity there is no picture of Father here. Still, not bad of its kind,' said he, still ignoring me.

'I take it you are a visitor to our Department of Fine Art,' I shouted.

The look of Pity and Contempt

He turned then and looked at me. It was a look in which pity and contempt vied for supremacy. I was taken aback, for I have not been looked at in that way since my final oral examination, now some thirty years ago.

'You do not know me?' said he.

This nettled me. I am not very good at names, but I am first-rate at faces. I knew that I had never seen him before. And yet—there was something familiar about him.

'Does this give you a clue?' said the stranger, and in an instant he was transformed. A scarlet, tight-fitting costume, and a voluminous red cloak appeared where the fashionable dress-suit had been, and the murmur of the discotheque upstairs seemed suddenly to be changed to some familiar bars of—who was it—yes, Gounod. *Faust Opera*

'Of course I know you now,' I cried; 'you are the new director of the Opera School. How good of you to come in fancy dress.'

'No!' he shouted, impatiently, and once again he was transformed. This time he wore a rough, hairy costume, the feet of which were like hooves; great ram's horns sprang from his brow, and at the back, where the seat of his trousers had been, there was now an ugly face from the mouth of which a long red tongue lolled obscenely.

'Of course,' I shouted, and laughed foolishly, for I was becoming somewhat unnerved; 'you must be one of the actors from the medieval play group, the Poculi Ludique Societas. What a good disguise!'

'Disguise!' he roared, and his voice was like a lion's. At the same moment the pendulous tongue of that nether face blew a loud raspberry—the very trumpet-call of derision. 'Wretched child of an age of unbelief, what is to be done with you?' And suddenly, to my intense dismay, there was—right before me in the Chapel—a red dragon, having seven heads and ten horns, and seven crowns upon his heads. The noises made by those seven heads were very hard on the nerves, and the delicate scent of the beautiful man's cologne had given place to a stench of brimstone that made me gasp. I leapt backward, tumbled over a chair and crashed to the ground.

'O the Devil!' I exclaimed, and suddenly the dragon was gone and the beautiful man stood before me. 'Well, you've got it at last,' said he, and helped me to rise.

I did not stay on my feet for an instant. I know when I am outclassed; I dropped immediately to my knees. 'Great Lord,' I said, and as my voice did not seem to be trembling enough naturally I added a shade more tremolo to it by art, 'Great Lord, what is your will?'

'My will is that you stand up and forget all that medieval mummery,' said the Devil—for now it was as plain as could be who the visitor was. 'You wretched mortals insist on treating me as if I had not moved forward since the sixteenth century; but living outside time as I do, I am always thoroughly up-to-date.'

'All right,' said I, getting to my feet, 'what can I do for you? An excellent supper is being served in the Upper Library, or if you would fancy a damned soul or two, I can easily give you a College list, with helpful markings in the margin.'

'Oh dear, dear, dear,' said he; 'what a cheap Devil you must think me. I don't want any of your Junior Fellows, or any of your colleagues, either; I leave such journeyman's work as they are to my staff.'

A thought of really horrible dimension—of blasting vanity—swept through me. Trying to keep pride out of my voice, I whispered, 'Then you have come for me?'

The Devil laughed—it was a silvery snicker, if you can imagine such a thing—and poked me playfully in the ribs. 'Get along with you, and stop fishing for compliments,' said he.

It was that poke in the ribs that reassured me. I had always been told the Devil has a common streak in him, and now he had shown it I was not so afraid. 'Well,' said I, 'I am sure that you have not come here for nothing; if you don't want souls—even so desirable a spiritual property as my own soul—what can I offer you?'

'Nothing but a really good look at this handsome reredos,' he replied. 'Doubtless you will find this strange, but at this time of year, when so much Christmas celebration is going on, I feel a little wistful. I hear so many people saying that they are going home for Christmas. Do you know, Master, I should very much like to go home for Christmas.'

I was too tactful to offer any comment.

'But of course I shan't be asked,' he said, and a look of exquisite melancholy transformed the beautiful, proud face into the saddest sight that I have ever beheld.

When I was a boy there was still a large public for a novel by Marie Corelli called *The Sorrows of Satan,* but even she never guessed that not being asked home for Christmas was one of them.

I was in a quandary. Against overpowering and insensate Evil I could have thrown myself, and been consumed in defence of the College. But against sentimentalism I did not know what to do. This was a time for the uttermost in tact.

'Do they have a pretty lively time at your old home, when Christmas rolls round?' I asked, thinking that this colloquial tone might disarm him.

'I can't say,' he replied; 'as I told you, I've never been asked back since my difference of opinion with my Father, such a long time ago. Christmas didn't begin until aeons after that.'

'Ah, I think I understand your situation,' I said. 'No wonder you are so wicked. It's not your fault at all. You are what we now call the product of a broken home.'

The Devil gave me a look which made me profoundly uneasy. 'Just because I am enjoying your sympathy, don't imagine that I cannot read you like a book,' he said. 'You think you are cleverer than I; it is a very common academic delusion.'

'I certainly do not think I am cleverer than you,' said I; 'I know only too well what happens to professors who get that idea; the unfortunate Dr. Faustus, for instance. But I do think you might play fair with me; you ask for my sympathy, and when I do the best I can you threaten me and accuse me of hypocrisy. Please let us talk on terms of intellectual honesty.'

Once again the Chapel resounded with that startling and lewd raspberry, and I became aware that though the Devil chose to appear in the guise of a gentleman of impeccable contemporary taste, all those other aspects of his personality, including the one with the seven dragons' heads and the one with the unconventionally placed tongue, were present, though invisible.

'Intellectual honesty just means playing by your rules,' said he, 'and I like to play by my own, which I make up as we go along. Do you think I am so stupid I can only hold one point of view at a time? Why, even you foolish creatures of earth can do better than that. I enjoy being sentimental about Christmas; after all, it is my Younger Brother's birthday. But don't imagine that because of that I don't take every opportunity to make it distasteful.'

He paused, and I could see that he was in a mood both reminiscent and boastful, so I held my peace, and very soon he continued.

'I think the Christmas card was one of my best inventions,' he said. 'Yes, I think the Christmas card has done as much to put Christmas to the bad as any other single thing. And I began it so cleverly; just a few pretty Victorian printed greetings, and then—well, you know what it is today.'

I nodded, and rubbed my arm, which was still aching with writer's cramp.

'Gifts, too,' he mused. 'Of course they originated with the Gifts of the Magi. I knew the Magi well, you know. Gaspar, Balthazar and Melchior—very good chaps and their offerings of gold, frankincense and myrrh were characteristic of their noble hearts. But when I got to work on their idea and spread the notion that everybody ought to give a Christmas gift to virtually everybody else I was really at the top of my form. The cream of it is, you see, that most people want to give presents to people they like, but I have made it obligatory for them to give presents to people they don't like, as well. Look at it any way you will, that was subtle—downright subtle.'

It sickened me to see that the breakdown in his style of conversation was accompanied by a coarsening in his appearance. He was now red-faced, heavy-jowled and wet-lipped. And somewhere in the background I could hear the seven heads of the red dragon hissing like great serpents.

'Santa Claus,—yes, Santa Claus is all mine,' he continued. 'Look at his picture here on your reredos—St. Nicholas the Wonder Worker. A fine old chap. I knew him very well when he was bishop of Myra. Loved giving gifts. Lavish and open-handed as only a saint knows how to be. But when I went to work, and advertising got into high gear, the job was done. Now you see his picture everywhere—a boozy old bum in a red suit peddling everything you can think of; magazine subscriptions, soft drinks, junk jewellery, dairy products, electric hair driers, television sets, Wettums Dolls—you name it, Santa's got it. I meet Saint Nicholas now and then; he's still in existence, trying to rescue Christmas, and I don't mind telling you that when we meet I'm almost ashamed to look him in the face. Almost, but not quite.'

By this time the degeneration of the Devil had gone very far indeed. His beautiful dress suit was a crumpled mess, his hair had become thin and greasy, his stomach and also his posterior had swollen so that he was positively pear-shaped, and the handkerchief he pulled out to wipe tears of cruel mirth from his eyes was disgustingly dirty.

I had no idea what to do. I felt that the situation was desperate. And then I had an idea.

There is a form of activity very popular now in education, called 'counselling'. Several times each year I receive letters which say, "What counselling staff do you provide in your College?" and I always reply with a monosyllable—"Me". Obviously this was the moment for some counselling, and all that held me back was a strong conviction that counselling, too, had been invented by the Devil. Would he fall for his own nonsense? I could but try.

'You came here to look at our reredos,' said I, putting my arm around his shoulders in what I hoped was a fatherly, yet respectful manner. 'Look at it now, and think of your old home, of your family. Unfortunately we have no likeness of your Father—'

'The Michelangelo portrait is by far the best,' he interrupted; 'catches Him to a T.'

'—but look here, at your brothers—the Archangel Michael, the Archangel Gabriel. How handsome they are! Observe what fine physical condition they are in, despite an age almost equal to your own. Remember that you too were once like that—'

I quickly removed my embracing arm; all the disgusting symptoms of spiritual and physical degeneration had fled in that instant, and he stood beside me, naked as the dawn, and equipped with splendid black wings. 'I am like that now,' he said proudly. But to my astonishment, I saw that the Devil was a richly endowed hermaphrodite. Still, five years of Massey College has prepared me for any unusual development.

'Good—ah—archangel!' I cried. And then I brought out the tried-and-true counsellor's phrase of encouragement. 'You see, you can do anything if only you will try. Now, this dreadful assault on Christmas is unworthy of you. Don't you think you've done enough? People still celebrate Christmas, you know, in a spirit quite outside the reach of the Christmas card, the perfunctory gift, the degraded figure of Santa Claus—' I was set to go on, for I was thinking of tonight, and of all of us here, but the Devil looked balefully at me.

'Yes, but it is all for Him—my Younger Brother, you know. One would imagine nobody else had ever had a birthday. Nobody celebrates *my* birthday.' I looked, and I assure you he was pouting.

I am not a professor of drama for nothing: I know a cue when I hear one.

'Grieve no more,' I said; 'I will celebrate your birthday.'

'Pooh,' he said; 'who are you?'

'Aha,' said I; 'you are trying to trap me into the sin of Pride. Nevertheless, without my telling you, you know very well who I am.'

He had the grace to look somewhat abashed. 'Well, be that as it may, who's going to know?'

'The whole College will know,' said I.

'Pooh! The College!' said he, rudely, but he was wavering.

'It's a graduate College,' said I; 'more than that, it's a think-tank.' I knew the Devil could not resist a really up-to-the-minute bit of jargon.

'It's a bargain,' he said. 'What will you do?'

'I'll fly the College banner and the St. Catharine bell will ring twenty-one times.'

'Just as if I were one of the Fellows?' he asked, and there was a gleam in his eyes which looked very much like pleasure.

'Precisely the same,' I replied. 'Now, what is the date?'

He hesitated, but only for a moment. 'Do you know, I've never told a soul. It's—' and he whispered the date into my ear. His breath made my ear disagreeably hot, but today I notice I hear better with it than the other.

Everybody says the Devil has a vulgar streak, but they are the very same people who will say, on other occasions, that he is a gentleman. This was the side of his character he chose to show now.

'You are really most considerate,' he continued, 'and I should like to make some suitable return. What would you like—don't restrict your ambitions, please.'

Not a word would I say, and almost at once the Devil laughed again—that silvery laugh I had heard before. 'Of course, I quite understand, you are thinking of Faust. But he only gave me a rather shopworn soul; you have given me something nobody ever offered me before—the most cherished privilege of a Fellow of Massey College. But come—if you won't have anything for yourself, will you accept something for the College? What about a handsome endowment? Academics always want money. Name your figure!'

But the Devil had underestimated me. I know what makes colleges, and it isn't money—delightful though money is. This time it was my eyes that were fixed on the reredos. At the extreme of the third row of pictures is one that very few people recognize. It is a symbol so extraordinary, so deep in significance and broad in application that even Professor Marshall McLuhan has not been able to explode it. It is the Santa Sophia, the Ultimate Wisdom.

The Devil knew what I was looking at.

'I'll say this for you,' said he, 'you certainly know how to ask.'

'It is for the College, after all,' I replied.

He sighed. 'Very well,' said he; 'but you must understand that I have only half that commodity you ask for—Ultimate Wisdom—in my possession. You shall have it for the College, and it is a considerable gift. When you'll get the other half I can't say.'

'I can,' I replied; 'I shall expect it promptly the very first time you go home for Christmas.'

He laughed for the last time, folded his splendid wings, and disappeared.

I made my way reflectively toward my study, to make a note of yet one more day when—perhaps until the end of time—we shall display our banner, and ring twenty-one strokes of the Catharine bell. Once again, under circumstances I could not have foreseen or prevented, the College had been visited by—not precisely a ghost, for he was plainly of an order of being vastly more energetic and powerful than our own—but by a spirit of the highest distinction. I sighed for the egalitarians who would confine us to ghosts drawn from the *petit bourgeoisie*. The dance, I observed, was over, and our Christmas celebrations were well begun.

REFUGE OF INSULTED
SAINTS

'I see you have guests,' said the youngest of the Fellows, when we met last week at High Table. As he said it I thought he winked.

I made no answer, but I was conscious of turning pale.

'I noticed them in your guest-room a couple of times last week when I was at breakfast,' he persisted.

Of course he would have noticed them. He is an almost professionally observant young man. When he goes back to New Zealand I hope he puts his gift at the disposal of the Secret Service.

The design of this College is such that when the Fellows are taking their leisurely breakfast in the private dining-room they can look directly into the windows of my guest-chamber. Guests have often complained about it. Two or three ladies have used a disagreeable term: ogling. But the guests who are there now I had hoped—trusting, unworldly creature that I am—to keep from the eyes of the College, and if they have been seen it must be taken as evidence that whatever influence I once had over them is now dispelled. I long ago accepted the fact that this College is haunted, but until recently it has been my determination to keep apparitions out of my own Lodging. But I know now that I have been cruelly betrayed by what, in justice to myself, I must call the nobility and overflowing compassion of my own nature.

It all began this autumn, on the thirty-first of October. To be more accurate, it was a few minutes after midnight, and was therefore the first of November. The date and time are important, for of course the Eve of All Hallows, when evil spirits roam the earth, extends only until midnight, after which it is succeeded by All Hallows itself—All Saints' Day, in fact. I was lying in bed reading an appropriate book—the *Bardo Thödol.* For those of you whose Tibetan may have grown rusty I should explain that it is the great *Tibetan Book of the Dead,* a kind of guide book to the adventures of the spirit after it leaves this world. I had just reached the description of the Chonyid State, which is full of blood-drinking, brain-pulping and bone-gnawing by the Lord of Death, and as I read, I munched an apple. Then I became aware of a rattling at the College gate.

This happens often when the Porter has gone off duty and I have retired for the night. I frequently vow that never again will I get up and put on a dressing-gown and slippers and traipse out into the cold to see who it is. But I always do so. It is the compassion I have already spoken of as amounting almost to a weakness in my character that makes me do it. The rattler is often some girl who assures me that she simply must get back a paper that is being marked by one of the Teaching Fellows in the College. Or it may be that some young man has ordered a pizza and is too utterly fatigued by his studies to go down to the gate and get it for himself. It would be heartless to disregard such pathetic evidences of what it is now fashionable to call the Human Condition. So up I got and down I traipsed.

The night was cold and wet and dark, and as I peered through the gate—for of course I was on the inside—I could just make out the form of a girl, who seemed to have a bicycle with her.

'Make haste to open gate,' she said in a peremptory voice and with a marked foreign accent. 'I vant to see priest at vonce.'

'If you want a priest, young woman, you had better try Trinity,' said I.

'Pfui for Trinity,' she snapped, insofar as an expression like 'Pfui' may be snapped. 'Is here the Massey College, no? I vant Massey College priest. Be very quick, please.'

I was a prey to conflicting emotions. Who was this undeniably handsome, rudely demanding girl? And whom could she mean by the Massey College priest? Our Chaplain lives out. Could it be our Hall Don? A priest undoubtedly but—was he leading a double life? Or was this girl a bait to lure him forth on an errand of mercy, so that he might be destroyed? I would defend him.

'We have no priest here,' said I, and turned away. But I was frozen to the spot by the girl's compelling cry.

'Babs!' she shouted; 'show this rude porter what you have!'

Who could Babs be? Suddenly, there she was, right behind the other, with what I thought was another bicycle. But oh! (I hate using these old-fashioned and high-flown expressions, but there are no others that properly express my emotions at this instant) as I looked I became transfixed, nay, rooted to the spot. For what Babs had—and it seemed to make it worse that Babs was no less a beauty than the other, with splendid red hair instead of black—was a cannon, and it was pointed straight at the College gates! Babs looked as if she meant business, for she had a flaming linstock in her hand, dangerously close to the touch-hole of the cannon.

'Now,' said the dark girl, drawing a huge sword—a horrible two-handed weapon—from the folds of her cloak, 'will you open the gate, or will Babs blow it off its hinges, as she very well knows how to do?'

Here was student power as even our President has never encountered it! But my mind worked with lightning swiftness. All that I had ever read of von Clausewitz came back to me in a flash: 'If the enemy's attack cannot be resisted, lure him forward, and then attack his rear.' I would admit these girls, then, and with a sudden rearward sally I would shove them and their cannon into the pool. I flung open the gate.

'Enter, ladies,' said I, with false geniality, 'and welcome to Massey College, home of chivalry and courtesy.'

But they did not rush forward as I had hoped. Babs, who really looked a rather jolly girl, turned and waved her linstock in what seemed to be a signal, and the other one—the dark one who spoke English so clumsily—cried aloud in unimpeachable Latin, 'Adeste, fideles!'

Suddenly the whole of Devonshire Place was filled with a turbulent rabble that I, still under the delusion that these were students, took to be the New Left Caucus in more than their usual extravagance of dress. Half-naked, hairy men, dirty girls whose hair blew wildly in the wind, girls carrying roses, lilies and flowers I could not identify, men carrying objects which I took to be the abortive creations of ill-mastered handicrafts, people with every sort of flag and banner—you never saw such a gang. They rushed the gate, and I was forced to retreat before them, shouting 'Stop! Wait!' as loudly as I could.

You may imagine how relieved I was to hear another voice, unmistakably English, crying 'Stop! Wait!' as well. Suddenly, right through the middle of the crowd rode a man in full armour, on a splendid horse; it is true he had a naked girl, not very effectively wrapped in his cloak, clasped in one arm, but in these permissive days such things are not unknown in our university, and whoever he was, he brought with him an atmosphere of trustworthiness that contrasted very favourably with the hostile spirit of Babs and her friend. He looked down at me, and I knew at once I was in the presence of an officer of Staff rank.

'You are the seneschal, I suppose,' he said.

'No,' I replied, 'the seneschal is at home in Leaside, and at this moment I would to God that I were with him. But I am the Master of this College, and I will defend it with all my strength, though it be but that of a poor old man, sore stricken in years; and I shall defend it also with all my art and craft, which is virtually unlimited. Now, sir, who in Hell are you?'

'It is to avoid Hell that I, and all this rabble (for I know no other way to describe most of them) seek your hospitality,' said he. 'I am Saint George of Cappadocia, formerly patron saint of England. This lady, with the wheel and the great Sword of Truth, is Saint Catherine of Alexandria. This other lady— the red-head with the cannon—is Saint Barbara, patroness of artillery. And we are all, every one of us here, deposed, degraded, denuded, despoiled, defeased, debauched, and defamed by that arch tyrant Giovanni Batista Montini, pseudonymously describing himself as Supreme Pontiff, Servant of the Servants of God, Bishop of Rome and Pope Paul the Sixth!'

There is something about other people's rhetoric that reduces my own language to the lowest common denominator. I regret my reply. It was unworthy of an academic. But history is history and truth must out.

'What's your beef?' I said.

It was the girl who shared the horse who replied. 'He means that Pope Paul announced last ninth of May that all this lot weren't really saints any more. Demoted them to legends, you see. A stinking trick, when you consider what they've been worth to the Papacy, over the centuries. But he wanted to make places for some Africans, and Americans, and other trendy riffraff. So since then we've been racketing all over Christendom trying to find someplace to stay. My name is Cleodolinda, by the way, and I'm not a saint. I just have to travel around with Georgie here because I'm a reminder of his greatest triumph. You remember, when he slew the dragon? I was the girl the dragon was—well, nowadays they call it molesting. Will you take us in? It's All Saints, today; if we don't get a home, and a place where we are respected, before midday, it's Limbo for us, I'm afraid. And Limbo is the absolute end, you know.'

I liked Cleodolinda. As I listened, her history came back to me. Daughter of the King of Lydia. I've always got on well with princesses. But as I looked at that streetful of sanctified hippies and flower-children, my heart misgave me.

'Why Massey College?' I asked her. 'With all the earth to choose from, why have you come here?'

It was Saint George who answered. He never let Cleodolinda get a word in edgewise. The way he insisted on having all the good lines for himself, you might almost have thought they were married.

'You need us,' he said, 'to balance the extreme, stringent modernity of your thinking; nothing grows old-fashioned so fast as modernity, you know; we'll keep you in touch with the real world—the world outside time. And we need you, because we want handsome quarters and you have them. It is our intention to set up a Communion of Saints in Exile, and this is the very place to do it. We wouldn't dream of going to the States, of course, But here in the colonies is just, the spot.'

Cleodolinda saw that I didn't like Saint George's tone; she leaned forward and whispered, 'He's begging, you know, really; please let them in.'

Compassion overcame common sense, and I nodded. Immediately the crowd began to surge forward, and that tiresome girl Saint Catherine shouted 'Adeste fideles!' again. I began to dislike her; she reminded me of a girl whose thesis I once supervised; she had the same quality of overwhelming feminine gall.

'One moment,' I shouted. 'It must be understood that if you enter here, I'm running the show. There'll be no taking over, do you understand? The first rule is, you must keep out. of sight. I presume you are all able to remain invisible?'

'Oh, absolutely,' said Saint George; 'but we really must resume physical form for a little while each day. You've no idea how cold invisibility is, and most of us are from the East; we have to warm up, every now and then.'

'Five minutes a day,' I said, 'and I don't want you scampering all over the College. I'll tell you where to go, and there you must stay. Oh, yes, you may run along to the Chapel daily, but don't loiter. And no ostentatious miracles without written consent from the House Committee. We have participatory democracy here I'd like you to know, and that means you mayn't do anything without getting permission from the students. Now, one at a time please, and no shoving.'

Saint George helped me to check them in, and it was no trifling job. There were about two hundred of them, but the trouble was that they all insisted on bringing what they called their 'attributes'—the symbols by which they have been recognized through the ages. Saint Ursula, for instance, brought her eleven thousand virgins with her, and insisted that they were simply personal staff, and only counted as one; they were a dowdy lot of girls, and I sent them to the kitchen, thinking the Chef would probably be able to put them to work. Saint Barbara I packed off to the Printing Room; I thought that brass cannon of hers wouldn't be noticed among all the old presses down there. Because of his association with travel I sent Saint Christopher to the parking-lot; many College people have remarked that they have never had any trouble finding a space since that moment. Saint Valentine was tiresome; he insisted that he must be free to roam at large through the living quarters, or I would regret it. I mistrusted the look in his eye. Indeed, I quickly realized that all of these saints had a strong negative side to their characters, and could turn ugly at a moment's notice. So I told Valentine to go where he liked, but that I would hold him responsible for any scandal.

Saint Lucy seemed a nice little thing, but conversation was made difficult by her trick of carrying her eyes before her on a salver. Still, she was simplicity itself compared with Saint Agatha, who walked up to me, confidently carrying her two severed breasts on a platter; I was so disconcerted that, before I grasped the full implication of my deed, I sent her to the kitchen. I made the same mistake—so full of potentialities for College cannibalism—with Saint Prudentiana, who was carrying a sponge, soaked in some jam-like substance that she insisted was martyr's blood. I can tell you that after these it was a relief to admit Saint Susanna, who carried nothing more disconcerting than a crown. As for Saint Martin, I recalled that he had once rent his cloak in two, in order to share it with a beggar, so I knew that he had experience in tearing up rags, and sent him down to our Paper-Making Room. Nor was Saint Thomasius a problem: I knew that his knack was for turning water into wine, and I thought he could make himself useful in the bar.

In fairness I must say that I foresaw certain problems that did not arise. Saint Nicholas, for instance. I was sure he would miss children, but he assured me he did not care if he never saw a child again this side of the Last Judgement; he said he wanted to re-establish himself as what he originally was—a treasurer, an administrator, a dealer in money. I shipped him straight off to the Bursary, and I understand he has since made himself very comfortable in that grandfather's clock.

Many of the saints had animals, and these gave me a lot of trouble. Saint Hubert, for instance, had brought a large white stag, which was interesting enough because it bore a blazing cross between its horns; I told him to put it to work cropping the croquet lawn, but not to let it nibble the flowering shrubs. But then there was Saint Euphemia, who had brought a bear, and knowing how bears love to catch fish, I was worried about what Roger would think; we finally made a deal that if the bear would chase those squirrels that eat all our crocus bulbs, it could stay. But the problem presented by these animals is that their powers of invisibility are not under such control as those of their saintly owners, and I don't want that bear to turn up unexpectedly in—well, for instance, in a quorum of university presidents. You may imagine I was glad to face such easy decisions as that of Saint Dorothy with her basket of fruit and flowers—very handy in the private dining-room. And when Saint Petronilla turned up with her dolphin, I simply gestured her toward the pool.

Dragons were a perfect nuisance. An otherwise decent fellow named Saint Germanus of Auxerre wanted to bring in a dragon with seven heads. I asked him to wait. But then along came that detestable Saint Catherine of Alexandria, with a very nasty dragon which she insisted was not a dragon at all.

'Is a pet, a symbol of all that is evil in my nature, which I have utterly subdued,' she said. But the dragon did not look as subdued as I should have liked, and we had high words. She wanted to have the Round Room all to herself and she wanted a priest always with her; she had some extraordinary plans for examinations: but I insisted that she scramble up the tower, and accommodate herself in our Saint Catherine bell, with her great spiky wheel, and her gigantic Sword of Truth, and her disgusting dragon.

'But I am patroness of all scholars,' she protested.

'You'll see them to great advantage from up there,' I replied, and refused to budge. She went off in a sulk.

It was with Saint George I had the worst trouble. Not only did he insist on bringing in his horse, but he also had a perfectly frightful dragon with him. I had to put my foot down.

'But it isn't a dragon,' he shouted; 'it's a dog. Watch, now. Sit, Rover!' he cried. But the dragon did not sit. It leapt up at me and snuffled me intimately and licked me, and tore the leg of my pyjamas, and uttered the most horrifying howls. Mind you, this was not wholly surprising. I have known scores of Englishmen who owned nasty, rough, smelly drag-ons that they insisted were really dogs. But this was too much.

'That's no dog,' said I, and gave the dragon a kick in the cloaca. 'It's blowing fire out of its nose. See—it's scorched a great hole in my dressing-gown.'

'Of course,' he said, haughtily; 'it's a fire-dog.'

This was the last straw. 'All dragons to the furnace-room immediately,' I shouted. 'In the morning Professor Swinton will examine them, and if they are really prehistoric animals, he will take them to the Museum.' They saw I meant it, and the dragons slithered and puffed off down the stairs.

At last the whole tribe of refugee saints was disposed of about the College somehow, and I was able, in a very slight degree, to recover my composure. But then I saw that Cleodolinda had been left behind. Saint George, a real Englishman, had been so concerned about his dog he had forgotten his girl.

'Well, young woman, what are we going to do with you?' I said.

'Oh, I suppose it's Limbo for me,' she replied in a resigned but not a complaining tone. 'I'm only an attribute, you see, not a saint, and as you've put Georgie on to help the Porter he won't have time for me. After all, I can't hang about the lodge undressed like this.'

I looked at her. She repaid looking at, but I felt our Massey College men were not quite ready for so much feminine beauty, all at one gaze, so to speak.

'I don't like to think of you in Limbo,' said I, 'but the College is crammed with your friends and their luggage and pets. So—for a while, anyhow—you may use my guest-room.'

Never trust a woman. 'Oh, you *are* kind,' she said, and hopped up and down with delight, producing a very agreeable effect. 'And you won't mind if I bring a friend, will you?'

'It depends,' said I, 'a beheaded virgin or something of that kind would be all right, but no young men. I'm expected to set an example.'

'Well, it's a man, but not a bit young,' said she. 'It's Saint Patrick, you see. The poor old sweet never thought he would be desanctified, and just when the Pope pronounced his sentence he was in one of the steam baths in Rome, and he hadn't a minute to pick up a few things, so he hasn't even an attribute to bless himself with, and—'

You know how it is. Women always overdo explanations. As Cleodolinda spoke a forlorn figure hobbled forward out of the darkness beyond our gate; a shrivelled little old fellow, covered only by his flowing beard and a very small towel on which was embroidered, in red, *Sauna Grande di Roma*. He was talking long before Cleodolinda had finished.

'Yez'll have pity on me, I know,' he said, 'seeing as how I'm a fella-Celt. Sure, amn't I a Welshman meself? Isn't it well-known I sailed from Wales to Ireland on a millstone, to convert them heathen? And wouldn't I have brought the millstone itself if that dirthy ould double-crosser in Rome had give me a minute? But awww, no! It was "Out with Saint Path-rick", and no two ways about it. You'll notice that Saint Andrew is safe and snug, right where he was. Leave it to the Scotch to get it all their own way. And that roaring ould tough, Saint David is still in his place—aw but I forgot, he's a Welshman like yourself—I mean like ourselves. Things haven't been so bad with me since the last Englishman sat

101

on the throne of Peter, and that's damned near six centuries. You've got to let me in. I'm just a poor roont old fella like yourself—'

Here I noticed Cleodolinda kick him on the shin, and he hastily changed his tactics.

'I mean to say, a fine young lad, just in the flower of his splendour, like yourself, isn't going to turn me away, and Limbo gaping before me. You wouldn't have it on your soul. And you've a giant of a soul. I can tell by the kindly light in your eyes.'

And so on. Much, much more. And the upshot was that I sent him off with Cleodolinda to my guest-room, with strict orders not to manifest themselves in the flesh except when they were safely locked in the bathroom.

But you know how people are. Especially people who have been used to having their own way (not to speak of adoration and prayers addressed to them) for over a thousand years. It worked for a few days, and then those two were prancing around in there, quite naked, waving to Saint Catherine up in the tower, whistling at the stag, and stirring up the bear by shooting pins at it with an elastic. And the Fellows, as they sit at their breakfast, have been ogling.

If it is Patrick they see, I presume they take him for a rather more than ordinarily demented visiting professor. But from the light in my young friend's eye, I have a feeling it is Cleodolinda.

And now they are in, how shall I ever get them out? Beware of compassion!

DICKENS DIGESTED

In this, the centenary of his death, I should like to speak well of Charles Dickens; the literary world has united to do him honour as one of the half-dozen foremost geniuses of our great heritage of poetry, drama and the novel. That I should have to stand before you tonight and direct at that Immortal Memory a charge of—the word sticks in my throat, but it must be given voice—a charge of Vampirism, repels and disgusts me, but when Dickens has cast this hateful shadow across the quadrangle of Massey College, I have no other course.

This is what happened.

It was the best of times, it was the worst of times, it was the age of wisdom, it was the age of foolishness, it was the epoch of belief, it was the epoch of incredulity—in short, it was the beginning of the autumn term, and the year was 1969. I met the incoming group of Junior Fellows, and among the thirty-five or so new men were some who immediately attracted my attention—but the subject of my story was not one of these. No, Tubfast Weatherwax III had nothing about him to draw or hold one's

interest; he was a bland young man, quite unremarkable in appearance. Of course, I was familiar with
his dossier, which had been thoroughly examined by
the Selections Committee of the College. He came
to us from Harvard, and he was a young American
of distinguished background—as the dynastic number attached to his name at once made clear. His
mother, I know, had been a Boston Winesap. But
young Weatherwax bore what one politely assumed
to be—in republican terms—a noble heritage
lightly, and indeed unobtrusively.

He was a student of English Literature, and he
sought a Ph.D. When I asked him casually what he
was working at, he said that he thought perhaps
he might do something with Dickens, if he could
get hold of anything new. I considered his attitude
rather languid, but this is by no means uncommon
among students in the English graduate school;
hoping to encourage him I said that I was certain
that if once Dickens thoroughly took hold of him,
he would become absorbed in his subject.

Ah, fatal prophetic words! Would that I
might recall them! But no—I, like poor Tubfast
Weatherwax, was a pawn in one of those grim
games, not of chance but of destiny, which Fate plays
with us in order that we may not grow proud in our
pretension to free will.

I saw no more of him for a few weeks, until one
day he came to see me, to enquire about Dickens as a
dramatist. I am one of the few men in the University
who has troubled to read the plays of Charles

Dickens, and relate them to the rest of his work, so this was normal enough. He knew nothing about the nineteenth-century theatre, and I told him I thought Dickens' drama unlikely to yield a satisfactory thesis to anyone but an enthusiastic specialist. 'And you, Mr. Weatherwax,' I said, 'did not seem very much caught up in Dickens when last we spoke.'

His face changed, lightening unmistakably with enthusiasm. 'Oh, that's all in the past,' he said; 'it's just as you said it would be—I feel that Dickens is really taking hold of me!'

I looked at him more attentively. He had altered since first I saw him. His dress, formerly that elegant disarray that marks the Harvard man—the carefully shabby corduroy trousers, the rumpled but not absolutely dirty shirt, the necktie worn very low and tight around the loins, in lieu of a belt—had been changed to extremely tight striped trousers, a tight-waisted jacket with flaring skirts, and around the throat what used to be called, a hundred and fifty years ago, a Belcher neckerchief. And—was I mistaken, or was that shadow upon his cheeks merely the unshavenness which is now so much the fashion, or might it be the first, faint dawning of a pair of sidewhiskers? But I made no comment, and after he had gone I thought no more about the matter.

Not, that is, until the Christmas Dance.

There are many here who remember our Christmas Dance in 1969. It was a delightful affair, and, as always the dress worn by the College men and their guests ran through the spectrum of modern university elegance. I myself always wear formal evening clothes on these occasions; it is expected of me; of what use is an Establishment figure if he does not look like an Establishment figure? But somewhat to my chagrin I found myself outdone in formality, and by none other than Tubfast Weatherwax III. And yet—was this the ultimate in modern fashion, or was it a kind of fancy dress? His bottle green tail coat, so tight-waisted, so spiky-tailed, so very high in the velvet collar and so sloping in the shoulders; his waistcoat of garnet velvet, hung all over with watch-chains and seals depending from fobs; his wondrously frilled shirt, and the very high starched neck-cloth that came up almost to his mouth; his skin-tight trousers, and—could it be? yes, it certainly was— his varnished evening shoes, were in the perfection of the mode of 1836, a date which—it just flashed through my mind—marked the first appearance of *Pickwick Papers*. And his hair—so richly curled, so heaped upon his head! And his side-whiskers, now exquisite parentheses enclosing the subordinate clause which was his innocent face. It was—yes, it was certainly clear that Tubfast Weatherwax III had got himself up to look like the famous portrait of the young Dickens by Daniel Maclise.

But his companion! No Neo-Victorian she. I thought at first that she was completely topless, but this was not quite true. Braless she certainly was, and her movement was like the waves of ocean. As for her mini, it was a *minissima,* nay, a *parvula.* She was a girl of altogether striking appearance.

'Allow me to present Miss Angelica Crumhorn,' said Weatherwax, making a flourishing bow to my wife and myself; 'assuredly she is the brightest ornament of our local stage. But tonight I have tempted her from the footlights and the plaudits of her ravished admirers to grace our academic festivities with beauty and wit. Come, my angel, shall we take the floor?'

'Aw, crap!' said Miss Crumhorn, 'where's the gin at?'

I knew her. She was very widely known. Indeed, she was notorious, but not as Angelica Crumhorn, which I assume was her real name, but as Gates Ajar Honeypot, star of the Victory Burlesque. She was the leader of an accomplished female group called the Topless Tossers.

If there is one point that has been made amply clear by the university revolt of the past few years, it is this: students will no longer tolerate an educational institution which professes to stand *in loco parentis;* good advice is absolutely *out.* Therefore I did not call young Weatherwax to me the following morning and tell him that he stood on the brink of an abyss, though I knew that this was the case. It was not that, at the dance, he had eyes for no one but Gates Ajar Honeypot; in that he was simply like all the rest of us, for as she danced, Miss Crumhorn gave a stunning exhibition of the accordion-like opening and closing of her bosom by means of which she had won the professional name of Gates Ajar. No, what was wrong was that when he looked at her he seemed to be seeing someone else—some charming girl of the Regency period, all floating tendrils of hair, pretty ribbons, modest but witty speech, and flirtatious but essentially chaste demeanour. I saw trouble ahead for Tubfast Weatherwax III, but I held my peace.

I thought, you see, that he was trying to be like Charles Dickens. This happens very often in the graduate school; a young man chooses a notable literary figure to work on, and his subject is so much more vital, so infinitely more charged with life than he himself, that he begins to model himself on the topic of his thesis, and until he has gained his Ph.D.—and sometimes even after—he acts the role of that great literary man. You notice it everywhere. If you were to throw an orange in any English graduate seminar you would hit a foetal Henry James, or an embryo James Joyce; road-company Northrop Fryes and Hallowe'en versions of Marshal McLuhan are to be found everywhere. This has nothing to do with these eminent men; it is part of the theopathetic nature of graduate studies; the aspirant to academic perfection so immerses himself in the works of his god that he inevitably takes on something of his quality, at least in externals. It is not the fault of the god. Not at all.

Very well, I thought. Let Tubfast Weatherwax III take his fair hour; he has heard of Dickens' early infatuation with Maria Beadnell; let him try on Dickens' trousers and see how they fit.

This meant no small sacrifice on my part. Whenever I met him, I said, as I should, 'Good-day, Mr. Weatherwax;' and then I had to listen to him shout, 'Oh, capital, capital! The very best of days, Master! Whoop! Halloo! God bless us every one!' Or if perhaps I said, 'Not a very fine day, Mr. Weatherwax,' he would reply: 'What is the odds so long as the fire of soul is kindled at the taper of conviviality, and the wing of friendship never moults a feather!' I began to avoid encounters with Weatherwax. The only Dickensian reply to this sort of thing that I could think of was, 'Bah! Hambug!' but I shrink from giving pain.

But I saw him. Oh, indeed, I saw him crossing the quad, his step as light as a fairy's, with that notable strumpet Gates Ajar Honeypot upon his arm. 'Angelica' he insisted on calling her, poor unhappy purblind youth. I longed to speak, but my Wiser Self—who is, I regret to tell you, a cynical, slangy spirit whom I call the Ghost of Experience Past, would intervene, snarling, 'Nix on the *loco parentis*,' and I would refrain.

Even when he came, last Spring, to ask permission to marry Angelica Crumhorn in the Chapel, late in August, I merely gave formal assent. 'I shall fill the little Chapel with flowers,' he rhapsodized; 'flowers for her whose every thought is pure and fragrant as earth's fairest blossom.' I repressed a comment that a bridal bouquet of Venus' fly-trap would be pretty and original.

I prepared the required page in the College Register, but August came and went, and as nothing had happened I made a notation—Cancelled—on that page, and waited the event.

Poor Weatherwax pined, and I ceased to avoid him and began to pity him. I enquired how his Dickens studies went on? He asked me to his rooms in the College and when I visited him I was astonished to find how Victorian, how like chambers in some early nineteenth century Inn of Court he had contrived to make them. He even had a bird in a cage: inevitably it was a linnet. The most prominent objects of ornament were a large white plaster bust of Dickens—very large, positively dominant—and a handsome full set of Dickens' Works in twenty-five volumes. I recognized it at once as the Nonesuch Dickens, a very costly set of books for a student, but I knew that Weatherwax had money. He languished in an armchair in a long velvet dressing-gown, his hair hanging over his face, the picture of romantic misery. I decided that—prudent or not—the time had come for me to speak.

'Rally yourself, Mr. Weatherwax,' cried I; 'marshal your powers, recruit your energies, sir!' I started to hear myself give utterance to these unaccustomed phrases, but with that bust of Dickens looking at me from a high shelf, I could not speak in any other way. So I told him, in good round Victorian prose that he was making an ass of himself, that he was well quit of Gates Ajar Honeypot, and that he must positively stop trying to be Charles Dickens. 'Eating your god,'

I cried, raising my hand in admonition, 'cannot make you into your god. Stop aping Dickens, and read him like a scholar.'

To my dismay, he broke down and wept. 'Oh, good old man,' he sobbed, 'you come too late. For I am not eating my god; I fear that my god is eating me! But bless you, bless your snowy locks! You have sought to succour me, but alas, I know that I am doomed!'

I rose to leave him, and as I did so—I tell you this knowing how incredible it must seem—the bust of Dickens seemed to smile, baring sharp, cruel teeth. I shrieked. It was a mental shriek, which is the only kind of shriek permitted to a professor in the modern university, but I gave a mental shriek, and fled the room.

Of course I returned. I know my duty. I know what I owe to the men of Massey College, to the spirit of university education, to that sense of decency which is one of the holiest possessions of our changing world. And as autumn wore on—it was this autumn just past, but as I look back upon it, it seems far, far away—the conviction grew upon me that Weatherwax's trouble was greater than I had supposed; it was not that he thought he was Dickens, but that he thought he was one of Dickens' characters, and by that abandonment of personality he had set his foot upon a shadowed and sinister path. One of Dickens' characters? Yes, but which? One of the doomed ones, clearly. But which? Which? For me this past autumn was a season of painful obligation, for not only had I to care for Weatherwax—oh yes, it reached a point where I took him his meals, and fed him such scant mouthfuls as he could ingest, with my own hands—but I had to adapt myself to the only kind of language he seemed now to understand.

One day—it was in early November—I took him his usual bowl of gruel, and found him lying on his little bed, asleep.

'Mr. Weatherwax,' I whispered, 'nay, let me call you Tubfast; arouse yourself; you must eat something.'

'Is it you, Grandfather?' he asked, as he opened his eyes, and across his lips stole a smile so sweet, so innocent, so wholly feminine, that in an instant I had the answer to my question. Tubfast Weatherwax III thought he was Little Nell.

His decline from that moment was swift. I spent all the time with him I could. Sometimes his mind wandered, and seemed to dwell upon Gates Ajar Honeypot. 'I never nursed a dear Gazelle, to glad me with its soft black eye, but when it came to know me well and love me, it was sure to prefer the advances of a fat wholesale furrier on Spadina Avenue,' he would murmur. But more often he talked of gradu-ate studies, and of that great Convocation on High where the Chancellor of the Universe confers Ph.D.s, *magna cum* angelic *laude,* on all who kneel before his throne.

When I could no longer conceal from myself that the end was near, I dressed his couch here and there with some winter berries and green leaves, gathered in a secluded portion of the parking-lot. He knew why. 'When I die, put me near to something that has loved the light, and had sky above it always,' he murmured. I knew he meant our College quadrangle, for though the new Graduate Library will shortly throw upon our little garden its eternal pall of shadow, it had been while he knew it a place of sunshine and of the laughter of the careless youths who play croquet there.

Then, one drear November night, just at the stroke of midnight, the end came. He was dead. Dear, patient, noble Tubfast Weatherwax III was dead. His little bird—a poor slight thing the pressure of a finger would have crushed—was stirring nimbly in its cage; and the strong heart of its child-owner was mute and motionless for ever.

Where were the traces of his early cares, the pangs of despised love, of scholarly tasks too heavy for his feeble mind? All gone. Sorrow was dead indeed in him, but peace and perfect happiness were born; imaged in his tranquil beauty and profound repose. So shall we know the angels in their majesty, after death.

I wept for a solitary hour, but there was much to be done. I hastened to the quad, lifted one of the paving stones at the north-east end, where— until the Graduate Library is completed—the sun strikes warmest and stays longest. For such a man as I, burdened with years and sorrow, the digging of a six-foot grave was heavy work, and it took me all of ten minutes.

With the little chisel in my handy pocket-knife it was the work of an instant to incribe the stone—

Hic jacet
STABILIS WEATHERWAX TERTIUS

and then, as my Latin is not inexhaustible, I continued—

He bit off more than he could chew

It was my intention to place the stone over the grave, with the inscription downward, so that no unhallowed eye might read it. Now all that remained was to wrap the poor frail body in the velvet dressing-gown and lay it to rest. Or rather, I should be compelled to stand it to rest, for the grave had to be dug straight down.

It was only then I raised my eyes toward the windows of Weatherwax's room, which lay on the other side of the quad. What light was that, which flickered with an eerie effulgence from the casement? Had I, stunned by my grief, forgotten to turn off the electricity? But no; this light was not the bleak glare of a desk-lamp. It was a bluish light, and it seemed to ebb and flow. Fire? I sped up the stairs, and threw open the door.

Oh, what a sight was there revealed to my starting eyes? My hair lifted upward upon my head, as if it were fanned by a cold breath. The bust of Charles Dickens, before so white, so plaster-like, was now grossly flushed with the colours of life. The Nonesuch Dickens, which had hitherto worn its original binding of many-coloured buckram was— Oh, horror, horror!—bound freshly in leather, and that leather—would that I had no need to reveal it—was human skin! And that smell—why did it so horribly remind me of a dining-room in which some great feast had just been completed? I knew. I knew at once. For the body—the body was gone!

As I swooned the scarlet lips of the Dickens bust parted in a terrible smile, and its beard stirred in a hiccup of repletion.

It was a few days later—last Friday, indeed— when a young colleague in the Department of English—a very promising Joyce man—said to me, 'It is astounding how Dickens studies are picking up; quite a few theses have been registered in the past three months.' I knew he despised Dickens and all the Victorians, so I was not surprised when he added, 'Wonderful how the old wizard keeps life in him! Upon what meat doth this our Charlie feed, that he is grown so great?'

He smiled, pleased at his little literary joke. But I did not smile, because I knew.

Yes, I knew.

THE KISS OF KRUSHCHEV

Any invasion of this College by uncanny and irra-
tional elements is a source of distress to me. We
have here an institution devoted to scholarship; we
toil in Massey College to raise what I like to think
of as a Temple of Reason. But, alas, from time to
time I am forced to recognize that nowhere, not
even here, is Apollo the sole shaper of human existence. Dionysian forces are also at work. But there
is one element in our college community which, I
consoled myself until recently, had never suffered
painful invasions from the realm of unreason; that
was our College Choir.

They have been with us from the beginning.
A merry, high-hearted group, they have for eight
years welcomed our summers with their song, lent
a sombre splendour to our Chapel services, and, on
such occasions as this, they have marked the season
with the widest variety of Christmas music. Nor have
they stood apart from the ideal of scholarship which
is the chief purpose of the College. They recover,
from manuscripts or rare publications, choral music
which has been unjustly neglected; they dust it off,

and bring it into the world again. And that is just how this whole grotesque incident began.

Many of you, I know, find delight in the music of Henry Purcell, who is still regarded as the greatest of English composers. He wrote superbly for the human voice, because he was himself a singer, and in his time, as Organist of the Chapel Royal, he drew great singers around him. One of these was a remarkable bass called John Gostling; not only was his voice of dark beauty, but it was of extraordinary compass. His lowest note was an F—not the F below the bass clef, which any bass can sing, but the F an octave below that—which only a very few exceptional basses can sing. Now, our organist, Giles Bryant, discovered an anthem of Purcell's in MS in the British Museum; it had quite passed out of the choral repertory because of its exceptional difficulty. It is a setting of the passage from the *Book of Job* which contains the words, "He maketh the deep to boil like a pot: He maketh the sea like a pot of ointment." Obviously Purcell had written this for his favourite John Gostling, because when the sea boils like a pot the bass soloist is called upon to perform an exceedingly long trill on that low F, and when the sea becomes like a pot of ointment an excruciatingly difficult legato passage in the deepest registers of the bass voice is called for, to produce an effect of heaving greasiness which would, properly performed, arouse nausea in every musically sensitive hearer.

Giles Bryant found it last summer, and he and Gordon Wry longed with all their musical souls to revive it in our Chapel. But where were they to find the necessary bass?

We have some good basses, but there have been few Gostlings. Our choir directors were in an anguish of frustrated desire, and the refrain of their conversation was: 'If only Igor were here now!'

I should explain that although the male members of our Choir are never wholly drawn from the members of the College, several Junior Fellows have, at one time and another, sung with them. Unquestionably the finest of these was one of our Russian exchange students, Igor Lvov. But Lvov disappeared from the College several years ago, on the 15th of December, and we never heard of him again. Russian exchange students are sometimes summoned home on short notice, for political reasons into which it would be tedious to penetrate now. So, when Igor vanished, we sighed, but accepted the situation with philosophy.

It was on a Sunday night two weeks ago that I was walking with Gordon and Giles along one of the corridors on the lowest floor of this College, listening to their plaints for the lost Igor.

'Igor could have boiled like a pot,' sighed Gordon.

'And how he would have handled that pot of ointment,' said Giles, almost sobbing.

'I can hear him now,' said Gordon, his face beautified by the light of happy recollection.

It was merely a figure of speech, but it filled me with terror. No, not terror; what overwhelmed me was that sense of doom, of realization that once again the forces of unreason had invaded Massey College. Here we go again, I thought to myself; O, ye powers that protect colleges from all that threatens them, let it not be! This year, just for this year alone, let no uncanny thing drag its trail of loathesome slime across our chronicle! But even as I prayed, I knew that it was hopeless. For although Gordon thought he heard Igor's voice only in memory, I was horribly aware that I had heard it in reality! It was just as we were passing a locked door marked Service 6.

As quickly as I could, I hurried Gordon and Giles to the gate, and bade them good-night. They walked away, happily talking about music, as I had seen them do a hundred times, and I, with heavy, doomed steps, dragged myself back to the cellarage, to the door marked Service 6. With my master-key I unlocked it, and went in, shuddering but with the courage of resignation.

'Igor, where are you?' I whispered. 'Igor, speak to me.'

'I am here, little father,' said a deep, velvety voice that seemed to come from the farthest depths of the room. For Service 6, because of the purpose for which it is used, extends far under the quadrangle. Guided by the sound of the voice, I felt my way into its cave-like recesses.

I don't know what I expected to find, but I knew Igor was there, for I never forget a voice. Names I forget, as a thousand humiliations every year makes clear, but never voices. If I had heard Igor, Igor it must be.

'Where?' I whispered, as I crept deeper and deeper into the cave.

'Here,' said Igor's voice, seemingly at the level of my knees.

What had happened? What was Igor's fate? Had he refused to return to Russia at command, and was he dragging out a fugitive's life in this darkest, most neglected, almost forgotten portion of the College? Dreading whatever it was I might see, I lit a match.

Oh, horror, horror, horror! There, in a dank tank, squatted a gigantic frog!

'Igor!' I hissed.

'I,' croaked the frog.

'Lvov!' I gasped.

'None other,' he gurgled.

'What has brought you to this?' I quavered.

'Pride!' said Frog-Igor (for from now on I shall call him that). 'Pride in our great Soviet State. Pride in the glory of modern Russia! Pride in the sound of my own voice, which is the worst possible kind of pride for a citizen of a Communist state! Sit down, little father, and I shall tell you all.'

I sat.

'Since childhood I have loved to sing,' said Frog-Igor. 'As a child on the collective, mine was the loudest voice, heard far above the sound of the machinery. As a youth in the university I was tempted to drop my studies in the crystallization of liquid manure in order to take up a career in opera. But Russia needs crystallized manure, and I stuck to it. But always I sang. Always I was in some choir. And when I came to Canada as a Soviet exchange student, I lost no time in finding a choir which badly needed me. It was a Toronto choir, named after the bourgeois-recidivist-Jew-beast Mendelssohn, and its leader was the mighty Gospodin Iseler.'

'The Mendelssohn Choir,' said I; 'a happy choice.'

'Not so happy,' said Frog-Igor. 'Very degenerate; very tainted music. Trained as I had been in the state-approved people's music of Soviet Russia I found strong traces of ideological retrogression in this music. But—I must sing, or die, so I sang what the Mendelssohn Choir sang, all the time keeping my own reservations about the material.

'At last came this time of year, the winter festival called Christmas, and the Mendelssohn Choir announced that it would offer a large composition unknown to me, called *Messiah*. You will understand, little father, that I was not pleased when I discovered, by going through the libretto with a dictionary, that this *Messiah* was a piece of overtly Christian propaganda. Yes! Shameless. But, I said to myself, these backward countries must take what music they can get. This music is degenerately modern to the Soviet ear, but there are a few good tunes and the whole score goes with a swing that is extraordinary when the source of its inspiration is considered. So—I shall consent to sing in it.

'You see, the great Iseler was very kind to me. He created an entirely new group within the choir, for me alone. Third Bass, it was called. I admired Gospodin Iseler devotedly. A man of rich spirit and Byzantine beauty, little father, and even in Russia we meet few like him.

'But still there was my problem. What was I to do about the nakedly religious nature of the text? And then I hit on a great idea. I would sing *Messiah* with mental reservations. Whenever the name of the false Hebrew God or his discredited Son occurred, I uttered an indeterminate sound, which, in the Mendlssohn Choir, nobody would notice. But in my mind I substituted the name of our mighty leader, Nikita Krushchev. And thus, you see, I preserved my integrity.

'Oh, little father, it worked at rehearsal, but when the first performance came, musical enthusiasm betrayed me. It was a great night. Massey Hall was filled to capacity with wealthy bourgeois. The smells of face-powder and mink recalled the worst days of the Czarist regime. I supposed it was because this was a new work we were launching, and I looked everywhere in the audience for the composer, but though many men had long hair, none looked like the picture of Handel on my music book.

'All went well, and my system of mental reservation worked like a—what is it you say it works like—?'

I have a fine academic command of cliché. 'Like a charm?' I prompted.

'Ah, good, good!' said Frog-Igor. 'Like a charm. But then we approached one of my favourite passages. It is in a big chorus, where everybody sings, 'For unto us a child is born,' but mentally I was singing, 'For unto us a people's republic is born,' and as we approached the climax, with the words—

And the government shall be upon his shoulder—I was thinking so powerfully of Comrade Krushchev that his beautiful, benign face seemed to rise right in front of me and—

'Yes,' I said, 'and—'

'And I made a wrong entrance,' said Frog-Igor, hanging his huge, warty head in shame. 'Before everybody else I sang, thunderously and triumphantly—

And the government shall be upon his shoulder—meaning Krushchev, you see, and all at once I felt a most terrible blow, as if I had been struck with a bullet. I raised my eyes from my music, and found that the mighty Iseler was looking at me with such hatred, such loathing, such unutterable detestation, that I dropped my score, struggled past all the other basses who sat between me and the door, and ran into the street. Oh, the shame, the bitter shame.'

'All that audience knows *Messiah* by heart,' said I. 'Elmer wouldn't care for a wrong entrance.'

'Well you may say it,' said Frog-Igor. 'As I hurried back to the College I felt worse and worse. You remember me as I was; a splendid figure of a Russian—two metres tall, two metres wide, two metres from front to back—but as I hurried through the streets I felt myself shrinking, and my free stride was becoming more and more difficult. And hot! I was perishing with shame. At last, when I reached the College I pressed myself under the gate—I could not bear to come under the glance of the Cossack McCracken—and flung myself into the cooling pool. And there, sitting on a stone, with the chill water of December washing over me, I considered my fate.

'It became clear at last. All my life, little father, and all my education, has been a rejection of super-stition. Reason is all! So says the Soviet: so also says Massey College. But in Russia, there are still those among our old people who talk of very bad, almost forgotten things. And one of them is the Evil Eye. And I knew the worst: I had done wrong, in the sight of everybody; I had spoiled the first performance of this new work, this *Messiah,* and the great Iseler had cast the Evil Eye upon me. And—there I sat in the pool and I had to face it—I had been turned into a frog.'

'Since then, I have lived in the pool all sum-mer, and when the coldest weather comes, the good Comrade Roger puts me in here, in this nice wet tank, and I sleep the winter away. But 0, little father, how I long to sing again.'

I put out my hand and patted Frog-Igor on the head. It was not a pleasurable sensation, but I have never allowed personal considerations to stand in the way of a noble action.

'You shall sing, again, Igor,' I said; 'but first of all we must do something about your personal appear-ance. Did the old people who spoke of the Evil Eye say anything about how to get rid of it?'

'Yes,' said Frog-Igor; 'it is very difficult. But you, little father, you are a good, simple man, a real member of the proletariat, and everybody pities you. Perhaps you could persuade him.'

'Persuade who?' I asked.

'The great Iseler,' said Frog-Igor. 'I can only be restored to human form again by—his kiss.'

In old-fashioned books one often reads about somebody being 'nonplussed'. I had never before paid much attention to the word, but in that instant I understood its meaning fully. I was nonplussed. Frog-Igor was going on.

'Go to him, little father. Fall at his feet; caress his knees. Let him see the tears running down your withered cheeks. Entreat for me. He will not be able to refuse you.'

It was now clear to me that, as so often happens in these invasions of the College by the forces of unreason, I was cast for an ignominious, absurdly demanding role. I spoke crisply.

'Useless,' I said. 'I know Elmer Iseler quite well. If I crept up on him and pawed his knees I don't know what he might think. You don't understand life in the democracies. All that crawling and cringing and weeping is much too Dostoevskian for twentieth century Canada.'

'Isn't there anybody else who could kiss you with the same effect?'

'There is Comrade Krushchev,' said Frog-Igor hopefully. 'He has what we call in Russia the

Proletarian Touch; it is the sovietized version of what used to be called the Royal Touch.'

I knew something that Frog-Igor, during the past seven years, had not heard. I suppose a very limited version of the world's news gets into our pool. So I temporized.

'Too far away,' I said. 'But what about a beautiful girl? In these situations on this side of the Iron Curtain it is always a princess who kisses the frog and turns him back into a prince.'

'I refuse to be turned into a prince,' said Frog-Igor. 'It is against all my principles. A bass, *da:* a prince, *nyet.*'

'Perhaps a soprano?' I suggested.

Frog-Igor looked as doubtful as a frog can.

'Or a very beautiful contralto,' I wheedled. 'The most beautiful girl in our choir?'

To make a long story short, I talked him into trying it. I put the situation squarely up to Gordon and Giles, and at the next choir rehearsal Gordon made a very graceful little speech, not harping on the Frog aspect of the problem. Only the most beautiful of the women's section, he said, was expected to volunteer.

I had feared this might create a difficult problem of discrimination, but the girls volunteered in a body. So I took Frog-Igor out of the little box in which I had brought him to the Choir Room, and put him in the middle of the table.

The girls seemed to lose their zeal. Frog-Igor leered and did his best to make himself attractive, but I thought he looked worse than before. One of the sopranos suggested that perhaps a counter-tenor might kiss him, as the Frog wouldn't know the difference. Frog-Igor spat up some unpleasant-looking black slime at that moment, and the choir realized that he understood English very well.

There was one noble contralto, a doctor by profession, who said she had had to meet worse problems in the Emergency Admissions, and she would make a start. After all, she said, it was just like mouth-to-mouth resuscitation. So she kissed him, and Frog-Igor perked up a little. The other girls were ashamed to back out after such an example of self-sacrifice, and, with a certain amount of gagging and wiping their mouths on bits of Kleenex, they all kissed Igor, and as they did so he swelled and swelled until at last he squatted before us, in the evening clothes he had worn when he was last a man, looking very much like a bass from the Mendelssohn Choir.

Oh, the joy of Gordon and Giles! It was beautiful to behold. They told the girls that every ounce of their sacrifice had been justified, and set to work at once to rehearse the great, rediscovered Purcell anthem. I have never heard anything like it. Igor boiled like a pot, and he slithered richly like grease, and one might have thought that the great John Gostling had been restored to life.

All too soon we realized that Igor's cure was not permanent. Even during rehearsal he showed signs of shrinking again into a frog, but an occasional quick peck from any female singer who had a rest at the time would put him right again. But after rehearsal I had to take him back to Service 6, to the tank.

'These girls, they are not strong,' he said; 'not strong like our Russian girls. But even a Russian girl could not help me for long.'

'Well, you can just put any ideas about a kiss from Elmer Iseler out of your head,' I said firmly.

'Ah, no; but there is still Comrade Krushchev,' he said, rolling his great eyes at me.

I knew that Comrade Krushchev had long since died in disgrace and obscurity, but I thought it better not to tell Igor.

The Sunday came—well, it was last Sunday, not to make a mystery of it—when the great Purcell anthem was to be performed at the afternoon Chapel service. Gordon had made it clear that no excuses of illness or having a cold would be accepted from any of the women in the choir, and they all turned up, looking a little discomfited, but showing a good spirit on the whole. I brought Igor in from his tank, and after half an hour's hard work they had him in condition to sing.

For the first part of the anthem I experienced a delight I have never felt before in our Chapel. This, I thought, is the perfection of religious music. And in my dark heart I began to plot to keep Igor in the tank for many years, and let him out only for services and recording-sessions which would bring the College the ample funds it so badly needs.

Igor's voice was superb. As he sang the deep did truly boil like a pot, and the sea was like a pot of ointment. But then came the later section of the anthem, very solemn, very noble, where the bass and tenor soloists together declare:

Upon earth there is not his like,
Who is made without fear.
He beholdeth all high things:
He is a king over all the children of pride.

It is tricky work, that duet, and Robert Hurd as tenor, and Igor as bass, had to watch their step carefully. I became aware that while Robert was firm, Igor was rocky. There was an excitement in his voice that alarmed me. And then, suddenly, he made an obvious, a gross mis-timing; he came in too early, and an instant later there was a horrible croak, a sound as if gas were escaping from a large balloon, and the anthem sagged to a chaotic end.

Luckily this happened near the end of the service, and as soon as the benediction had been pronounced, I sped to the Choir Room.

Poor Igor! He sat damply in the middle of the table, a frog again. A contralto—that good sport the doctor—was puckering her lips, but I knew that would do no good now. Gordon was standing in a corner, with his face to the wall, muttering incoherently. Giles, to my horror, was kicking the organ savagely. The members of the choir looked shocked and shaken, except for Malcolm Russell, who was chuckling.

I knew what had to be done. There are times, happily few in number, when I have to exert authority in this College.

'Mr. Wry, Mr. Bryant,' I rapped out. 'I will have no exhibitions of the Evil Eye in this College. Kiss Igor at once, both of you!'

'Won't,' said Gordon.

Giles is an Englishman. 'Shan't,' said he.

I knew I was beaten. There is no arguing with musicians when somebody has foozled an entry. It was Robert Hurd who explained the situation to me.

'During our last passage, about the power of God, it was pretty obvious Igor got to thinking about Nikita Krushchev,' he said, 'and when he came in wrong both Gordon and Giles rounded on him at once, and he was caught between their glares. Poor old Igor.'

Poor Igor indeed. When I picked him up he was sobbing piteously for the Kiss of Krushchev. So I put him in a little box, with some fresh lettuce leaves upon which I sprinkled a few grains of caviar, and I addressed it to Comrade Nikita Krushchev, care of the Russian Embassy at Ottawa, and dropped it in the mail-box on the corner of Hoskin Avenue.

A dirty trick? Perhaps. But you see, Igor would never have been of any further use to the College.

THE CAT THAT WENT
TO TRINITY

Every autumn when I meet my new classes, I look them over to see if there are any pretty girls in them. This is not a custom peculiar to me: all professors do it: I also count the number of young men who are wearing Chairman Mao coats, or horseshoe moustaches. A pretty girl is something on which I can rest my eyes with pleasure while another student is reading a carefully-researched but uninspiring paper.

This year, in my seminar on the Gothic Novel, there was an exceptionally pretty girl, whose name was Elizabeth Lavenza. I thought it a coincidence that this should also be the name of the heroine of one of the novels we were about to study—no less a work than Mary Shelley's celebrated romance *Frankenstein*. When I mentioned it to her she brushed it aside as of no significance.

'I was born in Geneva,' said she, 'where lots of people are called Lavenza.'

Nevertheless, it lingered in my mind, and I mentioned it to one of my colleagues, who is a celebrated literary critic.

'You have coincidence on the brain,' he said. 'Ever since you wrote that book—*Fourth Dimension* or whatever it was called—you've talked about nothing else. Forget it.'

I tried, but I couldn't forget it. It troubled me even more after I had met the new group of Junior Fellows in this College, for one of them was young Einstein, who was studying Medical Biophysics. He was a brilliant young man, who came to us with glowing recommendations; some mention was made of a great-uncle of his, an Albert Einstein, whose name meant nothing to me, though it appeared to have special significance in the scientific world. It was young Mr. Einstein's given names that roused an echo in my consciousness, for he was called Victor Frank.

For those among you who have not been reading Gothic Novels lately, I may explain that in Mrs. Shelley's book *Frankenstein, or The Modern Prometheus,* the hero's name is also Victor, and the girl he loved was Elizabeth Lavenza. This richness of coincidence might trouble a mind less disposed to such reflection than mine. I held my peace, for I had been cowed by what my friend the literary critic had said. But I was dogged by apprehension, for I know the disposition of the atmosphere of Massey College to constellate extraordinary elements. Thus, cowed and dogged, I kept my eyes open for what might happen.

It was no more than a matter of days when Fate added another figure to this coincidental pattern, and Fate's instrument was none other than my wife. It is our custom to entertain the men of the College to dinner, in small groups, and my wife invites a few girls to each of these occasions to lighten what might otherwise be a too exclusively academic atmosphere. The night that Frank Einstein appeared in our drawing-room he maintained his usual reserved—not to say morose—demeanour until Elizabeth Lavenza entered the room. Their meeting was, in one sense, a melodramatic cliché. But we must remember that things become clichés because they are of frequent occurrence, and powerful impact. Everything fell out as a thoroughly bad writer might describe it. Their eyes met across the room. His glance was electric; hers ecstatic. The rest of the company seemed to part before them as he moved to her side. He never left it all evening. She had eyes for no other. From time to time his eyes rose in ardour, while hers fell in modest transport. This rising and falling of eyes was so portentously and swooningly apparent that one or two of our senior guests felt positively unwell, as though aboard ship. My heart sank. My wife's on the contrary, was uplifted. As I passed her during the serving of the meal I hissed, 'This is Fate.' 'There is no armour against Fate,' she hissed in return. It is a combination of words not easily hissed, but she hissed it.

We had an unusually fine Autumn, as you will recall, and there was hardly a day that I did not see

ROBERTSON DAVIES

Frank and Elizabeth sitting on one of the benches
in the quad, sometimes talking, but usually looking
deep into each other's eyes, their foreheads touching. They did it so much that they both became
slightly cross-eyed, and my dismay mounted. I determined if humanly possible to avert some disastrous
outcome (for I assure you that my intuition and
my knowledge of the curious atmosphere of this
College both oppressed me with boding) and I did
all that lay in my power. I heaped work on Elizabeth
Lavenza; I demanded the ultimate from her in reading of the Gothic novel, both as a means of keeping
her from Frank, and straightening her vision.

Alas, how puny are our best efforts to avert
a foreordained event! One day I saw Frank in the
quad, sitting on the bench alone, reading a book.
Pretending nonchalance, I sat beside him. 'And
what are you reading, Mr. Einstein?' I said in hon-
eyed tones.

Taciturn as always, he held out the book for me
to see. It was *Frankenstein*. 'Liz said I ought to read
it,' he said.

'And what do you make of it?' said I, for I am
always interested in the puny efforts of art to penetrate the thoroughly scientific mind. His answer
astonished me.

'Not bad at all,' said he. 'The Medical Biophysics
aspect of the plot is very old-fashioned, of course. I
mean when the hero makes that synthetic human
being out of scraps from slaughter-houses. We could
do better than that now. A lot better,' he added, and

I thought he seemed to be brooding on nameless possibilities. I decided to change the line of our conversation. I began to talk about the College, and some of the successes and failures we had met with in the past.

Among the failures I mentioned our inability to keep a College Cat. In the ten years of our existence we have had several cats here, but not one of them has remained with us. They all run away, and there is strong evidence that they all go to Trinity. I thought at one time that they must be Anglican cats, and they objected to our oecumenical chapel. I went to the length of getting a Persian cat, raised in the Zoroastrian faith, but it only lasted two days. There is a fine Persian rug in Trinity Chapel. Our most recent cat had been christened Episcopuss, in the hope that this thoroughly Anglican title would content it; furthermore, the Lionel Massey Fund provided money to treat the cat to a surgical operation which is generally thought to lift a cat's mind above purely sectarian considerations. But it, too, left us for Trinity. Rationalists in the College suggested that Trinity has more, and richer, garbage than we have, but I still believe our cats acted on religious impulse.

As I spoke of these things Frank Einstein became more animated than I had ever known him. 'I get it,' he said; 'you want a cat that has been specifically programmed for Massey. An oecumenical cat, highly intelligent so that it prefers graduates to undergraduates, and incapable of making messes in the Round Room. With a few hours of computer time it oughtn't to be too difficult.'

I looked into his eyes—though from a greater distance than was usual to Elizabeth Lavenza—and what I saw there caused a familiar shudder to convulse my entire being. It is the shudder I feel when I know, for a certainty, that Massey College is about to be the scene of yet another macabre event.

Nevertheless, in the pressure of examinations and lectures, I forgot my uneasiness, and might perhaps have dismissed the matter from my mind if two further inter-related circumstances—I dare not use the word coincidence in this case—had not aroused my fears again. One autumn morning, reading *The Globe and Mail,* my eye was caught by an item, almost lost at the bottom of a column, which bore the heading 'Outrage at Pound'; it appeared that two masked bandits, a man and a woman, had held up the keeper of the pound at gunpoint, while seizing no less than twelve stray cats. Later that same day I saw Frank and Elizabeth coming through the College gate, carrying a large and heavy sack. From the sack dripped a substance which I recognized, with horror, as blood. I picked up a little of it on the tip of my finger; a hasty corpuscle count confirmed my suspicion that the blood was not human.

Night after night in the weeks that followed, I crept down to my study to look across the quad and see if a light was burning in Frank Einstein's room. Invariably it was so. And one morning, when I had wakened early and was standing on my balcony, apostrophizing the dawn, Elizabeth Lavenza stole past me from the College's main gate, her face marked, not by those lineaments of slaked desire so common among our visitors at such an hour, but by the pallor and fatigue of one well-nigh exhausted by intellectual work of the most demanding sort.

The following night I awoke from sleep at around two o'clock with a terrifying apprehension that something was happening in the College which I should investigate. Shouts, the sound of loud music, the riot of late revellers—these things do not particularly disturb me, but there is a quality of deep silence which I know to be the accompaniment of evil. Wearily and reluctantly I rose, wrapped myself in a heavy dressing-gown and made my way into the quadrangle and there—yes, it was as I had feared— the eerie gleam from Frank Einstein's room was the only light to guide me. For there was a thick fog hanging over the University, and even the cruel light through the arrow-slits of the Robarts Library, and the faery radiance from OISE were hidden.

Up to his room I climbed, and tapped on the door. It had not been locked, and my light knock caused it to swing open and there—never can I forget my shock and revulsion at what I saw!—there were Frank and Elizabeth crouched over a table upon which lay an ensanguined form. I burst upon them.

'What bloody feast is this?' I shouted. 'Monsters, fiends, cannibals, what do I behold?'

'Shhh,' said Elizabeth; 'Frank's busy.'

'I'm making your cat,' said Frank.

'Cat,' I shrieked, almost beside myself; 'that is no cat. It's as big as a donkey. What cat are you talking about?'

'The Massey College cat,' said Frank. 'And it is going to be the greatest cat you have ever seen.'

I shall not trouble you with a detailed report of the conversation that followed. What emerged was this: Frank, beneath the uncommunicative exterior of a scientist, had a kindly heart, and he had been touched by the unlucky history of Massey College and its cats. 'What you said was,' said he to me, 'that the College never seemed to get the right cat. To you, with your simple, emotional, literary approach to the problem, this was an insuperable difficulty: to my finely-organized biophysical sensibility, it was simply a matter of discovering what kind of cat was wanted, and producing it. Not by the outmoded method of selective breeding, but by the direct creation of the Ideal College Cat, or ICC as I came to think of it. Do you remember that when you talked to me about it I was reading that crazy book Liz was studying with you, about the fellow who made a man? Do you remember what he said? "Whence did the principle of life proceed? It was a bold question, and one which has ever been considered as a mystery; yet with how many things are we upon the brink of becoming acquainted, if cowardice or carelessness did not restrain our enquiries". That was written in 1818. Since then the principle of life has become quite well known, but most scientists are afraid to work on the knowledge they have. You remember that the fellow in the book decided to make a man, but he found the work too fiddly if he made a man of ordinary size, so he decided to make a giant. Me too. A cat of ordinary size is a nuisance, so I decided to multiply the dimensions by twelve. And like the fellow in the book I got my materials and went to work. Here is your cat, about three-quarters finished.'

The fatal weakness, the tragic flaw in my character is foolish good-nature, and that, combined with an uninformed but lively scientific curiosity led me into what was, I now perceive, a terrible mistake. I was so interested in what Frank was doing that I allowed him to go ahead, and instead of sleeping at nights I crept up to his room, where Frank and Elizabeth allowed me, after I had given my promise not to interfere or touch anything, to sit in a corner and watch them. Those weeks were perhaps the most intensely lived that I have ever known. Beneath my eyes the ICC grew and took form. By day the carcass was kept in the freezer at Rochdale, where Elizabeth had a room; each night Frank warmed it up and set to work.

The ICC had many novel features which distinguished it from the ordinary domestic cat. Not only was it as big as twelve ordinary cats; it had twelve times the musculature. Frank said proudly that when it was finished it would be able to jump right over the College buildings. Another of its beauties was that it possessed a novel means of elimination. The trouble with all cats is that they seem to be housebroken, but in moments of stress or laziness they relapse into an intolerable bohemianism which creates problems for the cleaning staff. In a twelve-power cat this could be a serious defect. But Frank's cat was made with a small shovel on the end of its tail with which it could, once a week, remove its own ashes and deposit them behind the College in the parking-space occupied by *The Varsity,* where, it was assumed, they would never be noticed. I must hasten to add that the cat was made to sustain itself on a diet of waste-paper, of which we have plenty, and that what it produced in the manner I have described was not unlike confetti.

But the special beauty of the ICC was that it could talk. This, in the minds of Frank and Elizabeth, was its great feature as a College pet. Instead of mewing monotonously when stroked, it would be able to enter into conversation with the College men, and as we pride ourselves on being a community of scholars, it was to be provided with a class of conversation, and a vocabulary, infinitely superior to that of, for instance, a parrot.

This was Elizabeth's special care, and because she was by this time deep in my course on the Gothic Novel she decided, as a compliment to me, to so program the cat that it would speak in the language appropriate to that *genre* of literature. I was not so confident about this refinement as were Frank and Elizabeth, for I knew more about Gothic Novels than they, and have sometimes admitted to myself that they can be wordy. But as I have told you, I was a party to this great adventure only in the character of a spectator, and I was not to interfere. So I held my peace, hoping that the cat would, in the fulness of time, do the same.

At last the great night came, when the cat was to be invested with life. I sat in my corner, my eyes fixed upon the form which Frank was gradually melting out with Elizabeth's electric hair-dryer. It was a sight to strike awe into the boldest heart.

I never dared to make my doubts about the great experiment known to Frank and Elizabeth, but I may tell you that my misgivings were many and acute. I am a creature of my time in that I fully understand that persons of merely aesthetic bias and training, like myself, should be silent in the presence of men of science, who know best about everything. But it was plain to me that the ICC was hideous. Not only was it the size of twelve cats, but the skins of twelve cats had been made to serve as its outer envelope. Four of these cats had been black, four were white, and four were of a marmalade colour. Frank, who liked things to be orderly, had arranged them so that the cat was piebald in mathematically exact squares. Because no ordinary cat's eyes would fit into the huge skull the eyes of a goat had been obtained—I dared not ask how—and as everyone knows, a goat's eyes are flat and have an uncanny oblong pupil. The teeth had been secured at a bargain rate from a denturist, and as I looked at them I knew why dentists say that these people must be kept in check. The tail, with the shovel at the end of it, was disagreeably naked. Its whiskers were like knitting needles. Indeed, the whole appearance of the cat was monstrous and diabolical. In the most exact sense of the words, it was the damnedest thing you ever saw. But Frank had a mind above appearances and to Elizabeth, so beautiful herself, whatever Frank did was right.

The moment had arrived when this marvel of science was to be set going. I know that Frank was entirely scientific, but to my old-fashioned eye he looked like an alchemist as, with his dressing-gown floating around him, he began to read formulae out of a notebook, and Elizabeth worked switches and levers at his command. Suddenly there was a flash, of lightning it seemed to me, and I knew that we had launched the ICC upon its great adventure.

'Come here and look,' said Frank. I crept forward, half-afraid yet half-elated that I should be witness to such a triumph of medical biophysics. I leaned over the frightful creature, restraining my revulsion. Slowly, dreamily, the goat's eyes opened and focussed upon me.

'My Creator!' screamed the cat in a very loud voice, that agreed perfectly with the hideousness of its outward person. 'A thousand, thousand blessings be upon Thee. Hallowed be Thy name! Thy kingdom come! O rapture, rapture thus to behold the golden dawn!' With which words the cat leapt upon an electric lamp and ate the bulb.

To say that I recoiled is to trifle with words. I leapt backward into a chair and cringed against the wall. The cat pursued me, shrieking Gothic praise and endearment. It put out its monstrous tongue and licked my hand. Imagine, if you can, the tongue of a cat which is twelve cats rolled into one. It was weeks before the skin-graft made necessary by this single caress was completed. But I am ahead of my story.

'No, no,' I cried; 'my dear animal, listen to reason. I am not your Creator. Not in the least. You owe the precious gift of life to my young friend here.'

I waved my bleeding hand toward Frank. In their rapture he and Elizabeth were locked in a close embrace. That did it. Horrid, fiendish jealousy swept through the cat's whole being. All its twelve coats stood on end, the goat's eyes glared with fury, and its shovel tail lashed like that of a tiger. It sprang at Elizabeth, and with a single stroke of its powerful forepaws flung her to the gound.

I am proud to think that in that terrible moment I remembered what to do. I have always loved circuses, and I know that no trainer of tigers ever approaches his beasts without a chair in his hand. I seized up a chair and, in the approved manner drove the monstrous creature into a corner. But what I said was not in tune with my action, or the high drama of the moment. I admit it frankly; my words were inadequate.

'You mustn't harm Miss Lavenza,' I said, primly; 'she is Mr. Einstein's fiancée.'

But Frank's words—or rather his single word—were even more inadequate than my own. 'Scat!' he

shouted, kneeling by the bleeding form of his faint-
ing beloved.

Elizabeth was to blame for programming that
cat with a vocabulary culled from the Gothic Novel.
'Oh, Frankenstein,' it yowled, in that tremendous
voice; 'be not equitable to every other and trample
upon me alone, to whom thy justice and even thy
clemency and affection is most due. Remember that
I am thy creature; I ought to be thy Adam; dub me
not rather the fallen angel, whom thou drivest hence
only because I love—nay reverence thee. Jealousy of
thy love makes me a fiend. Make me happy, and I
shall once more be virtuous.'

There is something about that kind of talk that
influences everybody that hears it. I was astonished
to hear Frank—who was generally contented with
the utilitarian vocabulary of the scientific man—
say—'Begone! I will not hear you. There can be no
community between thee and me; we are enemies.
Cursed be the day, abhorred devil, in which you first
saw the light! You have left me no power to consider
whether I am just to you or not. Begone! Relieve me
of the sight of your detested form!'

Elizabeth was not the most gifted of my students,
and the cat's next words lacked something of the
true Gothic rhetoric. 'You mean you don't love your
own dear little Pussikins best,' it whined. But Frank
was true to the Gothic vein. 'This lady is the mistress
of my affections, and I acknowledge no Pussikins
before her,' he cried.

The cat was suddenly a picture of desolation, of rejection, of love denied. Its vocabulary moved back into high gear. 'Thus I relieve thee, my creator. Thus I take from thee a sight which you abhor. Farewell!' And with one gigantic bound it leapt through the window into the quadrangle, and I heard the thundrous sound as the College gate was torn from its hinges.

I know where it went, and I felt deeply sorry for Trinity.

THE UGLY SPECTRE
OF SEXISM

At the college dance last week a young man, a former member of this College, approached me and screamed—in order to be heard above the music—'Are you going to have a Ghost Story for us this year?' I screamed back, 'I really don't know.' 'Oh yes you do,' he shrieked; 'I'll bet you've got it tucked away in a drawer right this minute.' Then he went to the bar to take something for his throat. Because, as those of you who attend modern dances understand, a conversation of that length, conducted while the band is giving its all, is a considerable strain on the vocal cords.

He had put his finger on a sore spot in my mind. I had no Ghost Story, and my dilemma was an ugly one: on the one hand I didn't want to disappoint you, and on the other I shrank from meeting any more College ghosts, because it is always an exhausting, and sometimes a humiliating experience.

After all, this College is well advanced in its eleventh year, and we have had a ghost story every

Christmas. Ten ghosts, surely, is enough for any college? In a modern building, such a superfluity of ghosts is almost a reflection on the contractors. Or could it, on the other hand, be some metaphysical emanation from the spirit of the Founders who were, to a man, connoisseurs of *bizarrerie*? Or—and this, I assure you, is where the canker gnaws—is there something about me that attracts such manifestations? There are men who attract dogs. There are men of a very different kind who attract women. Can it be that I attract ghosts?

Pondering thus, I wandered out into the quad, where the music was somewhat less oppressive. Yet, even in the chill air I felt myself a prey to melancholy apprehension. What was it about that music that made it so disturbing? It seemed as if it were the spirit of our time, made manifest in sound. Loud, compelling, insistent yet turbulent; rhythmic, but always threatening to break the bounds of rhythm and rage into some new and fiercely evocative mode. This was music that seemed to be imploring the gods to answer in all the primal, untrammelled majesty of a storm.

The noise mounted to a climax and I heard cheers from within. The moment had come for which modern dancers wait in worshipping expectation; the percussion man was going to perform a solo. The banging, crashing and rattling he produced was sheer sound, unhampered by any suggestion of a tune or a tone. It was heaven-storming music, and I felt myself yielding to it. My nerves were fiercely alert.

As I walked toward the College gate my glance rose, and at once I knew that something was amiss. Or, rather, was missing. Where was the great bull's head which normally presides over the exit from the Quad? Not in its place? Impossible. It must be a delusion caused by the excellent supper at the dance. But—where was the Bull? 'Bah! Humbug!' I said to myself as I stood looking out into Devonshire Place. The December wind that had been sweeping through it grew, in a matter of seconds, into a whirlwind. Dust, twigs, debris of all sorts was whirling in this tempest; some of it swept toward me and I became aware that a mass of newspaper was dashing itself against the gate, and might well blow through it. I like the quad to be tidy, and I pushed it away with my foot. To my amazement, it resisted, with a power that wind alone could not explain. I kicked at it and—how am I to tell you?— it seemed to give a cry, in an almost human voice. The sound of the percussion solo from the Hall became more demanding in its intensity, and I lost my self-possession. I kicked and pushed at the mass of newspaper with hands and feet, and the more I fought the fiercer it became, until at last it forced itself through the bars of the gate, and stood—yes, stood!—before me.

'Thing of evil,' I cried—and even as I spoke I knew that I had once again slipped into the rhetorical manner of speech which these spectres always impose upon me—'Thing of evil, what would you here? Whence, and what are you?'

The mass of newspaper appeared to be winded by our struggle, and its reply, though audible, was incomprehensible to me. But the tone was unmistakably that of a woman's voice.

'Speak up!' I demanded.

The mass of newspaper raised one of its outlying rags of newsprint and pointed toward what would have been, in a human figure, its head.

I leaned down for a closer look, because the figure was considerably shorter than I. At its top, which was twirled up into a sort of point, I was able to make out *Toronto Star, February 1, 1972.*

'You are the *Toronto Star?*' said I, half in fear, half in derision, as academics usually speak when they are dealing with newspapers.

The figure nodded its head, then pointed with what seemed to be its Homemakers' Section toward a headline which was at the place where, if it had indeed been a woman, its bosom would have been found. I put on my reading spectacles and peeped delicately at its bosom. The words there were familiar and made me recoil. They read: *The Ugly Spectre of Sexism Lurks at Massey College.*

I remembered that headline. It was on February 1, 1972, that the *Toronto Star* had printed a letter from a young woman who was aggrieved by what she considered the indefensible discrimination of this College against her sex. Not only was this place manifestly elitist, she said, but it was sexist as well, and in the modern world, this was not to be endured. I looked at the bundle of newspaper again;

there was something feminine about its general out-line, certainly, but what was it, and what did it mean?

'Frankly, you don't look like *The Star*—' I began. But the creature had found its voice and burst out in an excited squeak.

'None of that!' it said. 'I know you sexists. Next thing you'll be telling me I'm too pretty to be a great national daily. I've come to do a colour story on the Ugly Spectre of Sexism that lurks at Massey College. Where do your spectres usually lurk? Point the way and then leave me alone, you old sexist.'

'I resent being called a sexist,' I said, with dignity. 'But you are a guest here, and I shall treat you with courtesy regardless of your rudeness to me. We have no spectres but I shall gladly offer you some spirits. I could do with a double Scotch, myself.'

'That'll be fine,' said the strange visitor, in a somewhat mollified tone. I was about to go to the bar for drinks, but something happened that made it clear that however ragged and rubbishy its appearance, I was in the presence of a supernatural being, and that the atmosphere was strangely fraught. Suddenly, from nowhere, two double Scotches were hovering in the air before us, and I gestured to my companion to accept one. She immediately proved that, ghost or not, she belonged to the newspaper world by taking that which my practised eye told me was slightly the bigger. After a hearty swig had disappeared into the folds of newspaper my strange companion spoke again, in a tone that betrayed a little self-doubt.

'This *is* Massey College?' it squeaked.

'You mean you're not sure?' said I.

'The editor wouldn't give me money for a taxi,' it said, 'so I came on the wind and I've had a rough journey. That's why I'm late.'

'Late for what?' I said.

'For striking terror and dismay into your black heart,' said the creature. 'Because you discriminate against women. Because you are a barnacle on the Ship of Progress. Because you are a miserable Neo-Piscean who is trying to halt the approach of the Age of Aquarius. Because you are a fascist-recidivist-elitist-chauvinist-pig. I am here to expose you. Then your nerve will break and the Junior Fellows will throw open the gates to women and hail a new dawn.'

'You are even later than you think,' said I. 'The new dawn of which you speak was hailed on May 11 of this year when it was decided by our senior fascist-recidivist-elitist-chauvinist-pigs, meeting in solemn council, and with the full concurrence of those of our Founders who are still living, that women should be admitted to this College under the same conditions as men, beginning next September.'

'Aha! So we drove you to it,' said the figure.

'Not in the least,' said I. 'This college follows a star, but not the Toronto *Star*. You are too late.'

The figure seemed to lose height. 'You mean there's no Ugly Spectre of Sexism,' it said, in a wistful, papery voice. I felt sorry for the frail little creature.

'Why don't you just take a quick look around, and then go back and say you didn't find anything and it isn't worth bothering about?' I said.

Once again the figure became shrill. 'None of your helpful suggestions,' it squeaked; 'none of your masculine gallantry toward the defeated female. I'm onto your game; you want to disarm me with kindness, but you won't do it!'

'I must say you're very hard to please,' said I. 'And I can't go on arguing with you unless I can call you something. What's your name?'

'You'd better call me Ms.' said the figure.

'To me Ms. has always meant Manuscript,' I said, 'and you're not Manuscript, or even Typescript. You're that most dismal form of letterpress, an out-of-date newspaper. I think I'll call you Scrap, because you're scrap paper and because you're so scrappy.'

To my surprise Scrap giggled. 'Now you're talking like a fellow-creature,' she said. 'How about another Scotch?'

Hardly had I formed the thought than two glasses were in the air between us, and again Scrap grabbed the larger. I thought I saw a rude twinkle where her eye should have been. 'Here's my hand up your gown, Master,' Scrap said.

I am not to be outdone in colloquialism. 'Here's thumbing through your Index,' said I. We drank. It was very good whisky, which is not perhaps surprising, as it obviously came from the spirit world. After her second drink Scrap was quite friendly.

'I think I'll take you up on that offer of a look around,' said she. I shall refer to her henceforward as 'she' because the more Scrap drank the more feminine she became. 'Want to come?'

I nodded. But I was concerned. Where was our Bull?

'Mind you, it has to be understood that you're following,' said Scrap. 'There's to be none of this chauvinist-pig nonsense of showing the little lady over the place. I don't need a guide.'

So off we went. We started with the carrel area, and Scrap was in a perfect ecstasy, dodging in and out among the partitions, disguising herself as the contents of a waste-paper basket, and popping out at me from what she hoped were unexpected places, with cheerful squeaks of 'Boo!' It was rather like going for a walk with a mischievous dog. But as she dashed ahead of me I noticed that for all her Women's Lib principles she was uncommonly feminine, and now and then, when she was out of sight, I heard that sound which had such a stimulating effect on our Victorian forefathers—the delicate rustle of skirts. It was clear that Scrap was not wanting in feminine arts, and if I had been younger, and not a philosopher, I suppose I would have ended up chasing her.

She was delighted with the Chapel, and twitched aside the curtains behind the altar, as a likely place for the Ugly Spectre of Sexism to be lurking. She took a long look at our altarpiece, and said: 'Who's this woman, painted inside a star?' 'That is a depiction of Divine Wisdom, always represented as a woman,' said I.

'Right on!' said Scrap, approvingly.

Then we climbed the stairs, and came to the door of the Round Room. This will stop her, I thought; a spectre might lurk in a place that is full of corners, but to lurk within a circle is an impossibility. And that shows how much I knew about it. Pride came before my fall.

As we entered the Round Room the sense of being haunted descended upon me like a mist. The room was lit by an eerie, flickering blue light, which moved and stirred so restlessly that for a few seconds I could see nothing clearly. Therefore I was startled when a deep, authoritative voice, which was certainly not that of Scrap, said: 'You're late. Just like a woman. I've been expecting you. Sit down.'

The speaker was a figure so astonishing and alarming that for a moment I thought that I might swoon. He—certainly it was a he—was tall of figure, huge of chest, slim of flank, and wore elegant evening dress. Not a dinner jacket, which is often seen here; a white tie, and a tail coat of the most distinguished tailoring. But it was his head that struck awe and terror into my heart. It was huge, and it was the head of a bull. And no common bull either, but the Bull from over our gate, and from its left ear hung a massive ornament of jet, within which a fleur-de-lis was outlined in diamonds.

'The Massey Bull,' I shrieked.

'Obviously,' said the creature.

Scrap was dancing so wildly that she seemed to blow about the room on a breeze. 'You said I wouldn't find him, and I have! It's the Ugly Spectre of Sexism that lurks at Massey College!'

An expression passed over the face of the creature which I shall not attempt to describe, but it was enough to cause Scrap to crumple away in alarm. 'I am the heraldic bull of Massey College,' it said, with great dignity. 'I am, in a special and exalted sense, the totem-animal of this academic, all-male community. I stand, very properly, at the top of its coat-of-arms, and over its entrance. I am, as you may see, unmistakably masculine. I scorn to lurk. I pervade. And I demand to know what you, Master, and presumably this bundle of waste-paper here, mean by proposing to admit women under what I regard, with unchallenged right, as my roof?'

What was I to say? Fortunately I didn't have to say anything, because Scrap began to whirl in the air around the creature, squeaking: 'Admit women, did you say? Just you try to keep them out! You'll have me to reckon with. I'm Ms. let me tell you, and here I stay till this place is full of women. I'm going to make you all miserable till you acknowledge that the day of masculine supremacy is over, and you'd better get that through your big hairy head. Masculine indeed! You earring-wearer! The day of barnyard rule and barnyard ethics is done, and the glorious pennon of Unisex is being unfurled over every bastion of masculine privilege in the civilized world!'

The bull lowered his great head and fixed Ms. with red eyes. He blew a snorting breath from his nostrils that could only mean trouble. I felt that I should say something, and as I didn't know what to say of course I said something foolish.

'Surely you young people can find some grounds of compromise,' said I. They both turned on me with such anger that I feared they would attack me. To be manhandled is unpleasant, but it is a far more dreadful thing to be ghost-handled; one's metabolism is never the same afterward.

'You sit down,' said the Bull; 'we are going to debate this matter, Ms. and I, of the admission of women to Massey College. You shall be referee,' he said, and with a sharp sidewise hook of his dexter horn he tossed me into the red chair in which it is humorously supposed I preside in that room. There was nothing for it but to obey.

'Ladies first,' said I, nodding toward Scrap.

She was furious. 'There you go,' she squeaked, 'hoping to disarm me with old-world courtesy. I won't go first. You won't get a word out of me.' But then she rushed onward with an extraordinary torrent of speech in which I could only catch a few phrases like 'minority group antagonism,' 'insensitive to cultural mood,' 'oppression as an institutionalized social function,' 'dynamics of victimization,' and the like. Coming from one who was supposed not to be speaking at all it took rather a long time, and the Bull grew impatient, pawed the ground and tossed his great head. At last he was so angry that flame—yes, flame—burst from his nostrils. Scrap, so highly inflammable, was in serious danger.

Seemingly, she knew no fear. If I had not seen it with my own eyes I would not have believed what happened next. Scrap, with a furious gesture, tore from the area of her bosom a strip of newsprint, and held it in the flame, in which it was immediately consumed. But not before I saw what was printed on it. It was a lingerie advertisement, and it bore a nicely drawn depiction of a brassiere.

'Defiance!' she shrieked. 'That is the ultimate act of feminine defiance! Match it, if you can!'

The Bull laughed a deep taurine laugh. 'Typical feminine argument,' said he; 'you refuse to be considered as a sexual object, and yet you underline your refusal with a flagrantly sexual gesture. Is that your muddle-headed way of saying that you place no value on your sex?'

'I'll tell you what the value of my sex is,' snarled Scrap. 'Its value has been established by Xaviera Hollander, the Happy Hooker herself, and it's five hundred dollars a shot.'

I was dismayed by this indelicacy, and the ease with which she had fallen into the trap. The Bull sneered. He drew a paper from his breast pocket and laid it on the desk in front of me. 'I offer this as evidence in contradiction,' said he; 'this is the present male rate.' I looked at the card and blenched. It contained some intimate information about the erotic tariff of the celebrated racehorse Secretariat. I must say it made Xaviera Hollander look like cheap goods. But my sense of propriety was outraged.

'I refuse to listen to argument on this coarse level,' said I. 'Whatever arrangements you two wish to make in privacy, as Consenting Spectres, is nobody's business but your own, but I will have no part in it. This argument must continue, if at all, on a level of decency.'

'Very well,' said the Bull. 'Allow me to remind everyone present that only a month ago a Princess of the Realm, surely an example to all young women, took a public vow to OBEY the man who became her husband. And several young men in this College got up at five o'clock in the morning to hear her do it.'

This time it was Scrap who laughed, and it was immediately clear that laughter was something the Bull had not expected. He glared angrily, but he was confused, and Scrap took shrewd advantage of his confusion.

'Are you so besotted with male vanity you don't know what the Princess had in mind?' said she. 'Must I show you what feminine obedience means?'

From the mass of paper of which she was composed, Scrap produced a sheet printed entirely in red, and she began to trail it, slowly and provocatively in front of the Bull. I could hardly believe what followed. As if hypnotised, its great head began to roll to left and right, as it followed this transfixing red cloak, which gave out the characteristic feminine rustle that I had noticed before.

'Let's see who does the obeying now,' whispered Scrap.

O for the pen of an Ernest Hemingway, that I might adequately describe for you the spectacle of art and brutality that followed! Scrap was all femininity as she glided, not rapidly but with splendid grace, around the ring of our Round Room. As she moved she murmured in a low, compelling, unbearably taunting voice, 'Ah, toro, toro! Here—here to me, toro! Aha! Toro! Toro!' And the Bull, unable to help himself, responded to every word and gesture.

Do you know our Round Room? There are twenty-two tall black chairs in it, and on the back of every chair is stamped, in gold, the head of a bull. As Scrap led her victim in his fated dance, I saw that the forty-four eyes of those bulls followed every move: their forty-four nostrils stirred with growing apprehension, and I thought I saw the frothy spittle of fear dripping from their twenty-two tongues.

What was I to do? Where did my sympathies lie? I was, if you will pardon the bluntness of my speech, a quivering ganglion of irreconcilable emotions. I ought to stop the fight. I ought to help the Bull, who was as surely doomed as any bull I have ever seen in a ring. But the skill shown by Scrap thrilled me. Without knowing how it happened, I found myself standing on my desk cheering. I even snatched the rose from my buttonhole and threw it into the ring.

The fight did not last long, but it was splendid while it lasted. More and more furiously the Bull responded to the taunts of Scrap, whose elegance as a matador was beautiful to behold. Her *veronicas*, her *amontillados*, her *tournedos bonne femme* were as fine as anything I have ever seen, in the great *corridas* of Madrid. But all the time I wondered: How is she going to finish him off? She has no weapon, except that which she had pretended to hold in contempt—her feminine fascination, her charm.

As I have said, the light was ghost-light, and I have but mortal eyes. Suddenly there was a crash and the Bull was down; he had stepped on the rose I had thrown, slipped, and cracked his great head on the corner of one of our curved tables. I was cheering wildly.

But to my astonishment, Scrap was weeping. She stumbled blindly about the Round Room, looking for a corner in which to hide her head; on the floor lay the Bull, apparently dead. I thought he looked rather noble in death—until he winked at me. I had no time for reflection, because Scrap was pulling at my sleeve.

'Call me a trash-bin,' she sobbed, 'and let me get away from here.'

'But you've won,' said I. 'I presume you mean to take over the College. Isn't that what all this was about?'

'I didn't mean to kill him,' sobbed Scrap. 'I only meant to teach him a lesson. What shall I do without him?'

There are certain advantages in being no longer young. One sees a little more clearly, even without one's glasses. 'Leave everything to me,' said I. 'And you really mustn't go away. I think you'll like it here. And I think we're going to like you. Now let me put you in a nice restful place to think it all over until next September.'

And, with gallantry which Scrap did not now refuse, I gave her my arm and led her through the labyrinths of the lower part of the College, and there I put her in a very comfortable part of the Library to rest. I took care that she did not see what was printed on the door behind which I locked her, but I don't mind telling you. It said *Printed Ephemera.*

Then I hastened back to the Round Room to render first aid to the Bull. I knew that he had simply knocked his head against a reality but I thought his self-esteem might need some delicate attention.

He had gone. The Ugly Spectre of Sexism was lurking at Massey College no longer. And as I walked out into the quad I saw that he was back in his accustomed place over the gate, and I noticed, as you may notice if you choose, that, noble as he looks, and invincible as he looks, he has an undoubted black eye. But with his right eye he winked again. And I observed that he was wearing his huge single ear-ring with a new jauntiness as though he had discovered, in his brief encounter with Scrap, the truth that in the most redoubtably masculine creature there lurks some strain of the feminine.

All seemed peace in the College as I walked again in the quad. Even the music from the dance was peaceful, for the band was playing a Golden Oldie, *You're the Cream in my Coffee*

> You will always be
> My necessity
> Can't get along without you—

I hummed, and winked back at the Bull.

The great clock of Hart House struck a single resonant note. Everybody in the University knows what that sound means. 'Great Heaven,' I cried, 'it must be two o'clock.' And I hurried back to the dance.

THE PIT WHENCE YE
ARE DIGGED

O n alternate fridays during the university term, the Senior Fellows of this College entertain guests at dinner; some of our guests are Junior Fellows of the College, some are people who do interesting things in the world outside, some are visiting academics to whom we offer the hospitality of the College during their stay in the university. At our last dinner for the present year—that is to say, about a fortnight ago—we had two visitors of this latter class. One, an eminent Arabic scholar, was Dr. Abu Ben Adhem, from the University of Alexandria; the other was a Swiss, a Dr. Theophrastus von Hohenheim from, I think he said, the University of Basel. He seemed rather a queer customer; there is always a good deal of laughter at our High Table, but he never laughed; instead he smiled in a disquieting way, as if he saw a joke hidden from the rest of us. Also, he kept looking at his watch, and it was a watch that caught the eye.

'That's a handsome watch you have,' I said to him, because one must make conversation and his special subject, which I believe was some sort of physics, was unknown country to me.

'Handsome indeed,' said he. 'Very old; very precious.' He held it up for me to see. It was much larger than a modern pocket-watch, and beautifully cased in engraved gold; on the enamelled face were many dials; the figures on some of the dials were Greek letters, and others were signs which I knew—because I dabble a little in such things—to be cabbalistic. As he held it toward me he touched a spring, and the watch chimed prettily. Chiming watches are great rarities, and I have never heard one finer than his; I put out my hand to examine it, but he drew it back to himself. 'Not to play with,' he said, smiling disagreeably. I felt a little snubbed, and turned to talk to another guest.

After we have dined in Hall, the High Table group goes to the Upper Library, where we sit around a big table and divert ourselves with port and Madeira and general conversation. Abu Ben Adhem and von Hohenheim sat across the table from me, on either side of our Visitor; he is used to queer customers—they are his stock-in-trade—and I knew he would give them a good time.

Sitting on my right was one of the young women who are now included among our Junior Fellows. I know it is considered inexcusably sexist in our time to say that any girl is charming, but it is hard to break the habit of a lifetime: she was charming. She was a lively talker, and I like a girl who has lots to say for herself; quiet girls, whom some men admire so much, always make me think of clocks that have run down. She was well wound up; she seemed to regard the College port as a pleasing light thirst-quencher, instead of the mover of mountains that it is, and after a glass or two she was almost over-wound.

The talk on these occasions is often general. We fling remarks and sometimes whole paragraphs up and down the board in good, well-rounded voices. The people who say we shout don't understand academic courtesy; we are simply considerate of those who may be a little hard of hearing.

The loudest outcry on this particular night came from Professor Swinton and Professor Wilson. 'What are you two roaring about?' cried our Visitor, who has himself a voice that dominates courtrooms and makes the boldest felons tremble. 'About Scotland and the year 1974,' shouted Professor Wilson; '1974, the year that has seen the Scottish Nationalists on the march. And what better year for that? Is it not seven hundred years precisely since the birth of Scotland's mighty king and liberator, Robert the Bruce?' 'Ye're daft,' cried Professor Swinton; 'Robert the Bruce was well enough in his small way, but this year is a far greater anniversary in the history of Scots culture and imperialism, for was it not in 1774 that the great Henry Duncan was born.'

'And who might Henry Duncan be?' asked our Visitor.

Professor Swinton looked aghast. 'Man, I despair of ye,' said he; 'was not Henry Duncan the founder and deviser of the savings bank? And has not

Scotland ever since dominated the earth through the gentle, ameliorating, civilizing influence of the savings bank?'

'Hoot, awa!' shouted our Librarian, from down the table. 'Scotland's poets are her glory, and let me remind you that Gavin Douglas was born five centuries ago, to the year.'

When Scotsmen are in full cry, they must be resisted. Professor LePan threw himself into the breach. 'I'm not ashamed to say I've never heard of Gavin Douglas,' said he, 'but I remind you that a very respectable, if not positively a great, poet was born in 1774, and that was Robert Southey.'

'Southey!' shouted the Librarian, with Caledonian—nay, Nova Scotian—contempt; 'Southey! Can ye not do better than Southey?'

'Yes,' said Professor LePan; 'Oliver Goldsmith died in 1774; he popped out just as Southey popped in. And Robert Herrick died in 1674. So there!'

The Librarian uttered a wordless jeer; it was a Scottish sound rather like a power-saw striking a knot. 'You've had to take refuge in deaths,' he triumphed; 'deaths will avail you nothing.'

The rest of us rallied as well as we could to LePan's defence. Our expert on Canadian literature is Dr. Claude Bissell. 'What about Robert William Service, the bard of the Canadian north, born in 1874,' he cried, and launched at once into—

'A bunch of the boys were whooping it up
In the Malemute Saloon;

The kid who tickles the ivories
Was hitting a jagtime tune—'

But he was overcrowed by a roar from Professor Stacey. 'If you talk of Canada, tie this, if you can; who was born on the 17th of December, 1874? You don't know? Of course you don't know. But I know. It was William Lyon Mackenzie King; that's who was born on December 17, 1874.'

'Mackenzie King didn't write any poetry,' said Dr. Bissell, who wanted to get on with *The Shooting of Dan McGrew*.

'Oh, yes he did,' shouted Professor Stacey. 'It's not widely known, but I know it. And I'm bringing out a fully annotated edition of the Collected Poems of William Lyon Mackenzie King—including his five act blank verse drama *The Happy Conscript*—within the next twenty years, so all the rest of you keep your paws off it.'

'You're welcome to your Mackenzie King,' shouted Professor Careless, who was late to get into the scrap, but the more valiant because of it. 'King wasn't the only Canadian poet to be born in 1874. In twenty years I'm bringing out the Collected Poems of Arthur Meighen, including his mighty *Ode to Coalition Government;* then we'll see who was the better man.'

It was a moment for the voice of reason, of taste, of moderation and civilization, and of course it came from Professor Finch. 'Allow me to remind you,' said he, 'that apart from the lesser figures you mention, this year marks the fourth centenary of the birth of Prosper Jolyot de Crébillon, an ornament of a great civilization.'

The Librarian began a mocking chant: 'Dirty books, dirty books, Finch only thinks about dirty books!'

'Pardon me,' said Professor Finch, with that perfection of high-bred scorn and unruffled temper which is peculiarly his own; 'I presume you, Mr. Librarian, are thinking of the son, Claude Prosper Jolyot de Crébillon, whose witty novel *Le Sopha,* might seem risqué to a Calvinist mind, coarsened by the lewd rhymes of the exciseman Burns. But that was Crébillon *fils;* I was speaking of the dramatist, Crébillon *pere.*'

It seemed to me that the conversation was growing rather too warm. I sought to cool it. Now, one of my disabilities as Master of this College is that I really don't know much about anything. But I am paid part of my salary because of a pretence that I know a little about the theatre. I fished in the dank tarn of my memory for a cooling fact, and came up with a beauty. 'If you don't mind another pair of deaths,' I said, 'the world of popular entertainment lost two of its brightest luminaries just a hundred years ago.'

But I was not to have things all my own way. I never am. 'Of course one of them was William Henry Betty, the Young Roscius, who died on August 24, 1874,' said Professor Jacques Berger, with an unconvincing affectation of carelessness. I was directing a look of scholarly rigour toward him when Professor

Hume struck in: 'I don't know why you worry about theatrical deaths when 1874 was the birth-year of both Harry Houdini and Lilian Baylis,' said he. I was furious, but I smiled as sweetly as any Finch. 'I only wished to draw attention to the death, in 1874, of the original Siamese Twins, Eng and Chang. I supposed its biological interest might appeal to you.' But irony is lost on scientists who have just speared a humanist and beaten him at his own game.

While this was going on my young companion on my right had been getting rather heavily into the port, and the academic world was undulating before her in its brightest colours.

'It's all so romantic,' she cried; 'I just love Olden Times. Oh, how I wish I could make a journey backward in time; I know I'd be somebody fascinating. I've sometimes thought that I'm a reincarnation of one of those marvellous women of an earlier day— one of those mistresses, they called them then.'

We all turned to her with looks in which pity and dismay were mingled. She was a clever girl; I won't tell you what she was studying, but it was one of the really clever subjects. She had a blazing array of marks and prizes, but it is precisely these clever people who reveal a very soft core when the port engulfs them.

It was Dr. von Hohenheim who pounced. 'You really wish to journey back into Time?' said he.

'Oh, yes I do. You see I have this very, very, very strong conviction that I'm a reincarnation,' said our young guest.

Dr. Abu Ben Adhem struck in. 'Do be very careful, I entreat you,' said he. 'We are all reincarnations, but of course we are simply reincarnations of our own forbears. Travel backward in time and you will only find yourself your own great-great-great-grandmother, or somebody of that order.'

'Oh, but I'm sure she must have been somebody wonderful,' shouted the girl; 'Marie Antoinette or somebody like that. I've always understood there was French blood in the family.'

'That might very well be,' said Dr. Swinton, unexpectedly. 'Though as our friend here says, it's a wise child that knows its own father. How wise does a child have to be to know its own great-great-grandfather?'

'I'd love to know,' cried the girl, who was now in a high state of excitement. 'I'd love to go back—back to 1774, for instance—and see who I was.' She saw the doubt on my face, and shook me by the arm. 'Think how it would be—all that graciousness and politesse and lovely clothes and lots of servants and things.'

I was about to suggest that one of the other ladies present take her out for a brisk walk around the quad in the cold air. But to my dismay Dr. Theophrastus von Hohenheim rose to his feet, dominating the table.

'It can be managed,' said he calmly, and took out his beautiful watch, which he held aloft. 'Be as thou wast wont to be; See as thou wast wont to see,' he intoned, solemnly. Then he pressed the spring and the watch chimed so sweetly, so melodiously that I—I have always been sensitive to music—thought

I lost consciouseness for a moment, and when I opened my eyes, what a scene confronted me!

Oh for the pen of my great master, Ernst Theodor Amadeus Hoffman, to describe what I saw! It was our Upper Library still, and our table was the same. Our company was the same too, but we were all in the dress of 1774, and we were all—I knew it with sickening conviction—our great-great-great-great-great-great grandfathers or grandmothers of that time, though which of the one hundred and twenty-eight possibilities I could not, of course, tell. 'That is where chance comes in,' I thought to myself. And what a crew we were!

It was pleasant enough for some. There, at one end of the table, Professors Swinton and Wilson were still disputing, but now they were the great Swinton of Swinton, arrayed in the height of Edinburgh elegance, and, in the splendid panoply of a Highland chieftan, Wilson of Gunn. (I had occasionally heard Jock Wilson spoken of by his envious colleagues as a son-of-a-gun, but I never felt the truth of it till that moment). They were still deep in a haggle about Scottish Nationalism, for time had made little difference to them. They looked like portraits by Raeburn, and gave a lustre to the room far warmer even than the candle-light. The Librarian, too, was still obviously a librarian, though he had no beard, and wore a wig that had seen better days; on his left arm was a black band, and I heard him explaining to his neighbour that it was mourning for the Scots poet Robert Fergusson, who had died a few weeks ago, on the 16th of October, 1774. 'The name of Fergusson will never die,' he declared, and Dr. von Hohenheim, who was in an ominous suit of unrelieved black, murmured, 'No, never so long as it is linked with the name of Massey.'

My eyes roamed round the table. A stunning figure was Professor Baines; always the most fashionably dressed of our Senior Fellows, he was now, obviously, Beau Baines, the darling of Bath society. But our Bursar, what was he? Bearded to his waist, and swathed from head to foot in heavy, uncouth garments, with huge felt boots upon his feet, a Russian moujik in every detail, he was gazing across the table with extreme bitterness at George Ignatieff, the Provost of Trinity, who was our guest that evening; Ignatieff, like Friesen, was heavily dressed, but with what a difference! The sables and velvets of a Russian Boyar enwrapped him, and upon his head was a fur hat so immense that it might have broken the neck of a lesser man; he was drinking port straight from the decanter, and when it was empty he flung it with aristocratic nonchalance against the wall. But he was not silent; I gathered that he was attempting to secure a vast loan from a figure at his side whom I recognized as a forbear of Professor Abraham Rotstein, who was looking at his superb neighbour with the subtlety and amusement of an economist who knows financial innocence when he meets it.

Who were those unhappy creatures at the other end of the table? That Scotsman—for he could be nothing else—almost naked except for a much-worn plaid, and bearing every mark of crushing poverty—could it be Walter Gordon? Yes, it was, and he was discussing the. prospect of emigration to the New World with a figure who was so swathed in bandages that for some time I did not recognize him as Dean Safarian; he was explaining the intricacies of a recent difference of religious opinion his people had been having with the Turks; he said that as soon as he was fit to travel he, too, was going to America. These two were agreeing that to live in subjection to a master-race was hell indeed.

Nor were they the only ones who were talking of oppression. There was Robert Finch, even more elegant in the eighteenth century than in this—you never saw such a wig!—assuring Professors Stacey and Careless that any talk they had heard about imminent revolution in France was utterly without foundation. It was propaganda, he said, put about by people who did not understand the rock-like unshakeability of the French throne. But Stacey and Careless were not wholly convinced. Stacey, obviously a Tory of the darkest blue, was becoming very angry with Careless, whose less formal dress suggested some revolutionary sympathies. He insisted that revolution in the American colonies was no more than a few months away, but Professor Stacey would have none of it. 'Sir,' he roared—and I could tell by his form of speech that during some recent visit to London he had fallen much under the influence of Dr. Samuel Johnson—'Sir, I perceive that you are a vile Whig! The terms in which you speak of the man Jefferson must stand among the rankest effusions of encomiastic adulation.' 'Sir,' countered Professor Careless, 'your praise of King George is hyperbolical cant, but as it springs from ignorance rather than malignance I forgive you, and I'll trouble you for the port, if that Russian hasn't drunk it all.' 'Liberté, Egalité, Fraternité—quel blague!' said Professor Finch—perhaps I had better say the Abbé Finch—and laughed musically while getting the port first. Professor LePan, I saw, was chasing a squirrel out of the plate of nuts—a squirrel that Jacques Berger, a zoologist even in the eighteenth century, carried about in his pocket.

The noise of conversation was high. Two notable divines, The Reverend John Evans and the Reverend Northrop Frye, were hard at it; Dr. Evans defending the doctrine of salvation through works—the works one could grind out of others—while Dr. Frye was urging salvation through the refiner's fire of an exacting criticism of Holy Writ. A conversation on the fine points of agriculture was in progress between two obviously successful farmers across the table. Farmer Wells, who looked and dressed so much like John Bull that he might have stepped out of a drawing by Rowlandson, was arguing intently with Farmer Bissell—Capability Bissell he was called, because of his proven power of making two blades of grass grow where only one had grown before. Farmer Hume was fast asleep, his napkin covering his face. From beneath the table appeared a pair of glittering top boots, the property of Beau Baines who seemed to be resting there.

Everybody was talking, except von Hohenheim, who glanced in every direction in an ecstasy of malicious pleasure, and Abu Ben Adhem, who was wrapped in his Mussulman's robes and, being debarred by the Koran from drinking any port, was doing his best to eat all the dates on the table.

Everybody was talking, and everybody was behaving in a manner which I felt certain was characteristic of the eighteenth century. It wasn't bad, except that several people scratched themselves more often than is usual in modern society, and those who wore wigs were apt to remove them from time to time in order to mop the perspiration from their close-cropped heads. There were quite a few gouty feet, and one or two wore spectacles of the Ben Franklin sort. Finch, needless to say, had a quizzing-glass. And of course there was the spitting.

Everybody spat, more or less, and now and then some of them—those from the Eastern parts of Europe—blew their noses in a fashion rarely seen nowadays except in lumber-camps. They had handkerchiefs, but their purpose appeared to be ornamental. It was the spitting which took my eye, figuratively and once or twice in actuality. The two American gentlemen, Stacey and Careless, were the great proficients in this art, and they spat, as was the polite custom of the day, over their left shoulders, rapidly and with a truly American force and efficiency.

It is hard to see someone spit without wishing to spit oneself. So I spat. And that was when my own great revelation struck me.

The Americans, as I said, spat briskly, with a positively musical *brio*. But when I spat I let my head fall forward, spread my feet, opened my mouth and allowed gravity to take its course. Then I ground the result into the carpet, slowly and, as it were, compassionately. And as I did this I knew what I was; what the eighteenth century meant to me; what 1774 revealed of me.

I had been aware, as I gazed about the table, of a heaviness in the atmosphere. The air seemed infected with a wooly greasiness; I had assumed that it was Dr. Abu Ben Adhem who, like so many Arabs, was said to rejoice in oil; but I now perceived it to be the smell of lanolin. Not lanolin as you buy it for medical use, but as it exists on the unwashed wool of sheep. Now I knew that this smell came from myself. I was clothed from neck to knee in a homespun smockfrock, and about my shoulders was a sheepskin of venerable age, presumably as a defence against rain, and mist, and the damp of the Welsh hills. Because, you see, I was a simple Welsh shepherd, marked and ingrained with the consequences of his calling. Upon my head was a hat of incalculable antiquity—such a hat as Adam may have worn after the Fall—and my feet were warmly but untidily cased in more wool and gigantic greased boots. My hands were covered in tar—the tar shepherds use against that ovine disease, the foot-rot. And I had just spat as Welsh shepherds always do spit, with minimal effort, but with a primordial splendour that had something religious about it. It was thus, doubtless, that the shepherds spat on that notable occasion which we celebrate here, when they abode in the fields, keeping watch over their flocks by night.

I was roused from these reflections by a voice I knew, in the very marrow of my bones, to be a voice of authority—the voice of my betters. It was Dr. John Evans, and to any Welshman of the rank in which I found myself, the voice of an Evans of Usbutty Ustwit is like the music of the harp.

'Pass the wine,' said he. But the words fell upon an uncomprehending ear, and he saw what the trouble was, pointed at the bottle, and spoke again. 'Brénnin y pen Bilyaid,' said he, and the cruel words of abuse had an age-old familiarity. I passed the drink at once, bowing, cringing and rubbing the mouth of the bottle with my greasy sleeve as I served the gentry.

But inwardly I was stricken. Though I seemed to comprehend through my vision what others were saying, or were likely to be saying, in English, not one English word could I utter. 'Arunwaith, iëchyd da, mae Rhaglaw' said I to Dr. Evans, bowing obsequiously. But he waved me aside, as he had every right to do—him a great man of education, and me the humble shepherd of the flocks. But I glared across the table at that villain von Hohenheim, and muttered a curse in Welsh that made him wriggle in his chair, mighty magician though he was.

But mine was not the worst case. What of the poor girl who had held such high hopes of the eighteenth century; who had talked so innocently of its 'graciousness'; who had been certain that in that bygone time she would have been a mistress—and a scented, pampered mistress of royalty, no less.

She was padding about the table in her bare feet, a single ragged garment tied around her waist with a dirty string, her hair in filthy disarray and in her hand a bunch of what I took to be weeds. But it wasn't weeds. 'Won't you buy my pretty lavender: two bunches a penny?' she sang in a voice coarsened with gin. But there was a glance in her eye that made it clear that lavender was not everything she sold. Some of the men waved her away; others gave her extremely small coins which they found in the depths of their pockets. Swinton of Swinton pinched her behind, but perfunctorily, as if it were a social duty rather than a pleasure. Nobody seemed to want to buy anything at all. My heart wept for her. But yet, I thought, even from Gin Lane in the eighteenth century the modern Ph.D. may arise. I took a deep breath of hope, and immediately wished I hadn't, for the warmth of the room was working powerfully on my sheepskin.

At no time did the girl approach me, but as she passed my heart yearned toward her in pity; I hooked her to me with my crook and blessed her. 'Bendith yr Arglwdd, putain-ferch' I cried, as tears started from my eyes. But she utterly mistook my words and my intention. 'Not for twenty golden guineas,' she said, drawing her poor garment about her with pathetic pride.

I had little time to grieve over this misunderstanding, for I heard a familiar voice at my elbow. It was the College steward, putting his usual question at this time of the evening. 'May I blow out the candles?' he asked, and I nodded assent. I knew that it would do nothing to untangle the complexities of the evening to address Miroslav Stojanovich in Welsh.

Slowly, ceremoniously he extinguished each candle; in that brief moment when all the candles are out, and the electric lights have not yet been put on I heard von Hohenheim's chiming watch and, you must believe me, it was playing the same tune as before, but playing it backward, as Bach sometimes reversed a subject in counterpoint. And as it played I recovered myself, and the English tongue, completely. In the clean new light I turned to the girl beside me and said: 'Will you have some coffee? Or perhaps a little cognac?' She too was quite herself— her 1974 self,—now. 'Cognac every time,' said she.

As I went to fetch it for her, I found myself next to the unspeakable Dr. Theophrastus von Hohenheim. He smiled darkly at me, and flung me a quotation from Scripture: 'Hearken to me, ye that follow after righteousness, ye that seek the Lord: look unto the rock whence ye are hewn, and to the hole of the pit whence ye are digged.'

I am unfailingly polite to College guests. 'Isaiah 51, reading from the first verse,' said I, smiling serenely.

But he won't be asked again.

THE PERILS OF THE
DOUBLE SIGN

More than once, over the past years, Professor Douglas Baines has asked me why I never write a story about a scientific ghost. 'You should write something about haunted machinery,' he says. 'All the machinery in this College is haunted,' I reply; 'Roger has spent countless hours attempting to exorcise our heating system.' 'Of course,' he says; 'so why don't you write about that?'

The answer is that I do not *write* ghost stories. That is to say, I do not invent them. I simply confide to you the uncanny things that have happened to me since I associated myself with this College. If I were to come before you with a merely invented tale, I should feel myself to be an impostor. No: I tell you only what is true. 'Literally true?' Professor Baines might ask. No, for literal truth is not the truth of uncanny things. They belong to the realm of psychic, of subjective truth. It would be quite outside my powers to invent a scientific ghost story. My typewriter—which is a scientific marvel, and consequently always in a very delicate state of health--would refuse its task. Nevertheless I am not, I assure you, a stranger to science. I am steeped in it, but it is not of the kind that is in vogue in this university at the moment. It is the science of past ages.

This was brought forcibly to my attention last Christmas, which is to say, during the academic year of 1974–75. It is a period that will go down in the history of Massey College as The Year of the Two Hall Dons. A Hall Don, I should explain for those of you who are not familiar with the term, is the elected head of the Junior Fellows of the College, and a very important person. Last year we had two of them. One resigned at Christmas for reasons of—well, I'm going to tell you why, though at the time we agreed to say that it was because his work on behalf of the NDP became too demanding to permit him to give adequate attention to his College obligations. He was succeeded—for such is politics—by a man who was in almost every way his direct opposite. The second Hall Don was a man of balanced mind and calm and reflective temperament—a natural Conservative. The first Hall Don was a student of law, and it was a matter for wonder that he was able to keep up with his demanding legal study, while apparently giving so much of his time to the NDP. Obviously he possessed, in the highest degree, those qualities which lead to success at the bar. I need not tell you in disgusting detail what those are.

Superficially, both men seemed to be devoted to truth, as it may be determined by argument—hours and hours of complicated argument—and a close consideration of objective evidence. But the Conservative Don was a student of history, and thus a slave of Romance. The Legal Don, as a lawyer, was supposedly wedded to fact, but ah—beneath the surface he was involved in a study which does not accord with truth and evidence as we now know them—though I will not go so far as to say it was a study without its application in legal practice. He was an astrologer.

He made no secret of it. He cast horoscopes right and left. He cast one for me, and indeed published it in the College paper, *The Bull*. But it was to me alone that he confided its deeper meanings. 'You are very strongly under the influence of Jupiter,' he said, in his deep, thrilling voice. 'Oh, jolly good,' said I, uneasily. When I am uneasy I often fall into the colloquial speech of an earlier day. 'Not jolly good at all,' he boomed, and his splendid, glowing eyes darkened. 'Jupiter is the bringer of energy, right? But can we tell what he is going to do with his energy? He may put it at the service of forces that are destructive, right? Now, you have an equally strong influence from Saturn. Just suppose your Jupiter throws himself, thunderbolts and all, behind your Saturn? What then? Saturn is maleficent, so your Saturn backed up by your Jupiter produces an evil influence of incalculable force.' And there he stopped, but he gazed into my eyes hypnotically. 'What would you say that indicated?' said I, with a pitiable affectation of carelessness. 'Better you shouldn't know,' said he. 'What must be, must be, right?'

I did everything a reasonable man would do under such circumstances. I attempted to dismiss the subject from my mind. Astrology, I told myself, is a science of the past. It is utterly discredited. Its place has been taken by Sociology, Guidance Counselling and Educational Theory. Who believes in astrology now?

Ah, that was the trouble. Though I am not a whole-hearted believer in astrology as such, I was brought up a Presbyterian, and thus I am inclined to believe bad news from virtually any source. And my own observations of history have convinced me that behind what has passed as science, in whatever age and however absurd, there lurk some ill-perceived, phantasmal truths. I began to fret. When would my Jupiter throw all his unthinking, capricious force behind my malignant Saturn, and bring me to—to what? To what abyss of disgrace, to what towering folly, to—? My mind abounded in horrors: the hang-nail that turns to gangrene—the safety-belt that becomes a hangman's noose. Whenever I met the Hall Don, I thought I saw pity in his lustrous eye.

It was at about this time last year—the time when Christmas is imminent—that the presence of this strangely learned man and his grim predictions gave me an unforgettable night—a night which destroyed forever my conception of this College as an abode of peace and academic decorum. It was exactly a year ago this very night—the night of St. Lucy's Day, and also Friday 13. It is my custom, when I have been working late, to take a turn or two around the quad before I go to bed, in search of fresh air and that quieting of spirit which the darkness of night brings. As I strolled through the early winter mist, I became aware of a strange light in one of the College windows. Some windows were dark, some illumined by electric light, but this window was lit by a blue flame that undulated and quivered in a manner that could only mean one thing. Fire!

I darted into the residence where that window was, and with all the energy of my abundant Jupiter I bounded up the stair. I came to the door, and saw by the card that it was the door of our astrological Hall Don. Easily seen through the crack by the floor the curious blue light darted and flickered.

Never before had I used my master key to open the door of a private room, but this was an emergency, and I did so without hesitation. I threw open the door, ready to leap backward if there should be a rush of flame, but although the room was filled with curious light, there was no fire in the ordinary sense. A wooden box, of handsome workmanship, stood on one of the shelves, and it was from it that the blue light came.

Foolish people have called me impractical, but in an emergency I am lion-like. I rushed into the nearby bathroom, soaked a heavy towel in water, carried it back, and with deft, masterful movements I wrapped the box in it. That, I thought, will settle the hash of whatever conflagration lurks inside. But judge of my amazement when the blue light, instead of being quenched, came through the wet towel and filled the room, as before.

Nor was this the only circumstance that made my eyes start, and my hair stand on end. From beneath the towel I heard sounds—first a heavy sigh, and then a tiny, pleading voice, crying: 'If you please, sir! Oh, my preserver, my noble friend! Let me out, I beseech! Let me out in the name of Ahriman, the All Powerful!'

What would you have done? I acted without an instant of indecision. Not, I assure you, from excess of daring, but from a vastly greater positive influence—from curiosity. I was in the room of our astrologer-Hall Don, and it lay in my power to discover some of his strange secrets. I tore away the soaking towel. But of course the box was locked.

'The key,' cried the tiny voice. 'The key is under his pillow!' It was the work of an instant to find it, to unlock the box, and—what did my eyes behold?

Inside, cradled in velvet, was a globular crystal bottle, from which the blue radiance flooded the room. I lifted it, and it appeared to be filled with a mesh of deep golden threads. But as I gazed, there peeped through the golden wire, as I took it to be, a tiny face, like a piece of exquisitely carved old ivory. Its expression was imploring, and close to it two pretty little hands were clasped in anguish.

All prudence cried Watch your step! But all curiosity said Uncork him! So I did.

There was a rushing as of a mighty wind. A blue radiance shot upward to the ceiling, and there, on the desk before me appeared a little man, no bigger than a child of two, and I saw that the golden threads were a superb golden beard, that hung to his waist.

'A thousand thanks!' he cried. 'And of course, the usual reward. What's your will?'

'Great Scot,' I exclaimed. (I was, of course, invoking the spirit of Michael Scot, the medieval expert on magic and the occult, whose works are my favourite bedside reading). 'Are you a genie?'

An expression of absurd vanity overspread the mannikin's face, and he combed his fingers through the luxuriant beard. 'Indeed,' said he; 'I am the Genie With the Light Brown Hair. My name is Asmodeus.'

'The Devil on Two Sticks,' I cried, in amazement, for he was not a person I had ever expected to see in Massey College.

'As you may observe, I am slightly lame,' he said, ruefully, displaying two little ivory crutches which he had kept hidden beneath his robe. 'Now, dear friend, how may I reward you?'

My senses swam. Should I then and there deliver the College from all future care by asking for a generous addition to our endowment fund—something in the order of a few million lakhs of rupees, or perhaps a conveniently located emerald mine? But I knew my Michael Scot, and I knew what tricky fellows these genies could be. Caution, caution, I whispered to myself.

'Before we talk of that, may I not have the inestimable boon of a few minutes conversation?' I asked. 'We are quite accustomed to distinguished visitors here, but the Never-Too-Highly-To-Be-Esteemed Asmodeus, the Devil on Two Sticks himself, is a catch even for us. Now I know you won't be offended if I ask for some identification?'

'Ask what you please,' said he. 'I know you academics; you love oral examinations. Fire away.'

'Well then,' said I, 'just as a starter, tell me the precise number of angels in the Heavenly Host.'

'The figure is 301,655,722,' said he, with satisfaction.

'You mean, that was the figure in the fourteenth century,' said I.

'I am essentially a fourteenth century genie,' said he. 'Have I passed?'

'Not so fast,' I countered. 'Suppose you tell me the interpretation and origin of the word Abracadabra.'

.   'It is from the Hebrew,' said he, 'and it is a corruption of *abreq ad habra*. It means *Hurl your thunderbolt even unto death*. Have I passed?'

'Not yet,' said I. 'I am devoted to the old Three Question Formula, so familiar in folklore and magic. But you are doing well, and it is our humane custom in this university to give the examinee a short break at half time. Perhaps you would like a drink?'

I had perceived that the absent Hall Don had left an Italian wine bottle on one of his shelves, in which, through some oversight, a few drops remained. I was about to offer it to my guest, but he murmured, 'No, no; allow me,' and produced from the air a very fancy bottle of something purple, and two richly chased golden goblets. So I accepted some of that, and although it had a typically Oriental sweetness, it wasn't at all bad.

'I am wondering what your next question will be,' said Asmodeus, smiling with a corresponding Oriental sweetness as he filled our glasses for the second time.

'So am I,' I said frankly. 'It is rarely that I have a chance to ask questions of someone so well informed as I am sure you must be. You devils know everything, and I want to know everything, so where am I to begin?'

He laughed, and, presumably because of the wine, it was like the sound of little silver bells heard through some mucilaginous substance, like molasses—charming but gummy. 'Oh, I assure you we devils don't know everything,' said he. 'We have to confine ourselves very much to our own departments, which are growing all the time.'

'You mean you have departments of evil,' said I.

'I wish you wouldn't call it evil, in that narrow, ignorant way,' said he. 'You people of this world would be very badly off without what you speak of as evil. But of course Hell is heavily departmentalized, and no single devil—except, naturally, our Great

Master, Ahriman—can know everything. We have an elaborate and rapidly growing Uncivil Service, composed of departments and sub-departments, and bureaux and special committees of investigation, and all the apparatus of government. We are very busy. Now I give my attention to the Law. Indeed, all legal knowledge is summed up in me.' His eyes darted around our Hall Don's room, and they were dark with fear. 'That is how I was so foolish as to fall under the power of—him.'

'He argued you to a standstill?' I asked.

Asmodeus lowered his eyes in shame. 'You have heard of arguing the hind leg off a donkey? Something of the sort happened to me. Hence these crutches, and my pitiful imprisonment.'

I was overwhelmed by vulgar curiosity. I have always wanted to know more about Hell. 'Do you, yourself, do much tormenting?' I asked.

'Tormenting?' said he, apparently at a loss.

'Of the damned souls,' I said. 'Do you spend much time prodding them with pitchforks, or snatching glasses of ice-water from their burning lips? Do you do much in that line?'

He seemed to recover his spirits, and laughed the silvery, but gummy laugh. 'What a baby you are,' he said. 'Haven't I told you we have an Uncivil Service? The damned are kept busy, toiling away in rooms where there is only artificial light, and the only ventilation is entirely with conditioned air, doing all sorts of dismal jobs which permit them to pay the taxes that maintain the Uncivil Service.

And—this is the cream of it—they are quite unable to strike.'

'But have you no lake of burning pitch?' said I. 'And how about the Conqueror Worm That Dieth Not?'

'That is very old-fashioned thinking,' said he. 'The lake of burning pitch gave place long ago to a system of committees; every damned soul is a member of several interlocking committees, and the worst of them have what they call working lunches, where they are made to devour bad food and drink disgusting coffee while discussing projects from which all hope has been drained away. As for the Conqueror Worm That Dieth Not, we have banquets at which people make speeches that have no foreseeable end, about ideas that have no foreseeable application.'

'It sounds horribly familiar,' said I, in wonderment.

'It is,' said he. 'We in Hell are always ready to learn—'

'Stop,' I cried. 'You needn't go on—I know what you are going to say. You also have Study Groups, Symposiums, and Weekend Seminars, don't you?'

'Of course,' said he; 'where would Hell learn more than from the universities? And we are splendidly thorough. We learn all there is to be learned. For instance, I am sure I know more about this College than you do.'

'I should not be in the least surprised,' said I. 'It has never been one of my delusions that I knew much about this place. I am sure all sorts of things go on here that never reach my ears.'

'You underestimate yourself,' said he. 'They reach your ears, but you don't know how to interpret them. And that may be just as well, for if you did, sleep would become a stranger to your pillow. For instance, you know that Junior Fellow of whom you have been tempted to think well, because he appears in Chapel whenever Communion is celebrated.'

'I do,' said I.

'Would you think so well of him if you knew that he conceals the Communion wafer under his tongue, and carries it back to his room, unconsumed?' said he.

I turned pale. 'And what does he do with it then?' I asked.

'The same thing that he did with the palms he removed from the Chapel on last Palm Sunday,' said Asmodeus.

'Surely you are going to tell me what that was?' said I.

'Why surely? Because I am a devil, do you suppose I have no honour? Our code is very strict— stricter than yours—and I shan't tell you a thing.'

He was getting somewhat above himself, as devils are apt to do. But I am not wholly without experience of devils, and I know a trick or two—and a word or two that they fear. I looked meaningly toward the bottle, and wondered if I would utter a word which would make him squeeze himself back inside it. He must have read my thoughts, for he immediately became all compliance.

'You mustn't mind my little bit of fun,' he said, with a cringe. 'Of course I shall tell you anything you want to know. And this is such a very peculiar college that no one could possibly keep up with all the strange happenings here. Shall we make a little tour? You would find it of the most unusual interest.'

Should I have refused? Yes, I should never have let him leave the room where the bottle was. My control of the situation meant control of the bottle. But curiosity—ah, fatal curiosity! I nodded, and in an instant I felt myself wafted out of the window, seemingly wrapped in the little demon's robe, and we floated around the quadrangle most comfortably, looking in the windows. What we saw was pretty much what you would expect. There were Junior Fellows working, and Junior Fellows not working, and people playing cards, and people talking earnestly, and one or two scenes from which a modest man would have averted his eyes—but modesty has never been one of my foibles. There were rooms that looked like jungles, because the inhabitants were fond of potted plants: and there were rooms, usually those of mathematicians, as bare of any signs of human habitation as a Massey College room can be. In one room a young man was stirring a variety of little test tubes, which he warmed from time to time over a candle. I knew the man; he was a young immunologist.

'You see, he is making his perfume essence,' said Asmodeus, 'and he will sell it as do-it-yourself perfume kits: simply add gin and stir. Makes the wearer irresistible, especially to lovers of gin. That is how he pays his way through the university.'

From the window of another room floated a rich mingling of aromas—of soaps and langorously scented unguents. 'That is the room of your next Hall Don—the Conservative one,' said Asmodeus; 'he is devoted to the pleasure of the bath. It is the only weakness in a character of Roman austerity.'

I was surprised to hear him speak of another Hall Don, but I nodded in agreement. 'You do not suggest that there is anything unusual about any of this, do you?' I asked.

'Not this,' said he; 'but there is much more to the College than what may be seen through these windows. Look here.'

Without knowing it, I had been wafted inside the building, into a chamber unknown to me, and icy cold. Then I knew where I was; it was the large freezer, adjacent to the kitchens. On every side were trays of cold meat, and from a number of large hooks hung full sides of what I assumed to be carcasses that had not yet been cut up.

'Now this is a place of special interest,' said Asmodeus. He tapped one of the hanging slabs of meat, and it gave out a dull sound, unlike either meat or wood, unpleasant to the ear. 'Who would you suppose that was?' he asked.

'Who?' said I, with sinking heart.

His deferential smile turned to an evil leer. 'Who—or what?' said he. 'Hard to say, isn't it?'

'You cannot mean—' cried I, and whether it was horror, or the dreadful cold of the place, my voice died in my throat.

'I don't mean anything, in particular,' said he, enjoying himself immensely. 'But it is a common-place of legal knowledge that murder is more often committed by cooks than any other profession. Don't you ever wonder what became of that Junior Fellow who was here last year, and who wrote such unpleasant things about the food in the Suggestion Book?'

'He left to study elsewhere. In the States, I believe,' said I.

'Of course that is what you believe. But you don't know,' said Asmodeus.

'Give me your word that that is baby beef,' I demanded.

'Very well; I give you my word,' said he, with a subtle smile. And that was when I realized with dismay that the bottle to which I could so easily have returned him was still in the Hall Don's room, and that I had been out-generalled. Or, to be more accurate, out-devilled.

'Your teeth are chattering,' said he, 'and it is a sound I never could abide. Let us leave this place.' And in a flash we were somewhere else—somewhere very high above the quadrangle. We were, indeed, on the top of the clock-tower. Ill-natured critics of this building have said that the ornament on the top of our tower looks like a large diningroom chair, and indeed, there I was, sitting on it, with Asmodeus cuddled snugly in my lap.

How was I to get down? I knew that such a devil as Asmodeus might cast me down. I must be very careful to do nothing that might provoke my nasty little guest.

'Yes, indeed you must,' said Asmodeus, and once again I understood that my thoughts were an open book to him.

And then I thought of Douglas Baines, and his desire for a scientific ghost story. 'Can't we be scientific about this whole affair? said I; 'surely you and I can arrive at some arrangement that does not involve my being cast down from this high place?'

'We can be as scientific as you please,' said he. 'We can even use the language of science. Let's try computer science: it's very much in vogue. Let us establish the parameters of our problem. Then let's extrapolate. Here we sit—I comfortably and you uncomfortably—indulging in meaningful interface on the top of the College tower. You don't like me. I heard you think so. If we are to reach a conclusion agreeable to us both, you must immediately cease this negative input, and embrace a more positive modality. If you were to fall in the pool from here, it would not go well with you. You are a man of heavy frame and unathletic habit of life. The world would assume that, like so many academics, you had wearied of working lunches and self-perpetuating committees, and had taken flight to a quarter where you foolishly believed that they no longer existed.'

'I know,' I said; 'they would suppose that my abundant Jupiter influence had at last put itself squarely behind my malign Saturnian influence, and I had committed suicide.'

'What's all that about your Jupiter and your Saturn?' said Asmodeus, pricking up his ears.

I told him. 'The man who had you in the bottle told me that,' said I. 'And as he is an astrologer, I suppose he ought to know.'

Asmodeus laughed as I never expected to hear a devil laugh. He laughed until the tinkling of silver bells found the resonating note of the great St. Catharine bell in our tower, and it seemed to be laughing too, and the whole quadrangle resounded with Tinkle-Boom, Tinkle-Boom. The resonance of the great bell struck upward through the block of masonry on which I sat and at every Boom a disagreeable thrill ravished my person. Several of the Junior Fellows threw open their windows to see what was happening, but of course they never thought of looking so high as where I sat, in that terrible chair.

When he could speak, he said: 'He is not an astrologer, only an apprentice. If he were a fully-trained astrologer he would already be Leader of the NDP. I shall tell you a secret, though I realize it weakens my own hold over you. He has quite overlooked the fact that you are a Double Virgo.'

'I am?' said I. 'Is that good?'

'Oh, very good,' said Asmodeus. 'Jolly good, I should say. You see, he reckoned your horoscope from the instant of your birth. Good enough, so far as it goes. But the horoscopes of the Children of the Double Sign—to which special group it would be clear to a more experienced astrologer that you belong—must be reckoned from the instant of the Second Birth, which is to say, from the hour of your Baptism. And that is quite a different pair of pyjamas. By your true horoscope, you appear as a man powerfully under the protection of Mercurius, which brings you good fortune and a deliverance from all adversity. After a while, that's to say. You always have quite a spell of adversity first.'

'So what do you see in store for me?' said I.

'You will shortly be working with a new Hall Don,' said he. 'A delightful fellow, a committed Conservative, the soul of reason, and extremely clean in his personal habits.'

He smiled, as if he had given me a great gift. But I had another point to make. 'I don't imagine that the Benevolent Mercurius will allow you to throw me down from this tower,' I said, and looked him right in the eye.

He looked back, just as steadily. 'No, that is so,' he said, 'but I am not obliged to fly you down to earth, either. Good-bye!'

'Wait,' I cried; 'where are you going?'

'Oh, now that I am free once again,' said Asmodeus, 'I shall raise hell in the Law School, instead of being the exclusive slave of your Hall Don.' And he rose lightly from my lap, and with his two little crutches tucked under his robe, he flew off into the night, in the direction of the Law School.

By exertions which I still groan to think of, I got down from my stone chair, and—oh, vertigo!—reached the ladder that is fixed on the inside of our tower. It is not a descent I recommend to anyone, amid the rigours of a winter night. But at last, weary and trembling, I stood on firm ground again.

And before I went to my bed, I crept once more up to the room of the Hall Don who now, I foresaw, would be compelled to retire, and removed the bottle. For Asmodeus was a self-confident little devil and he may return. And when he does, I have the bottle, and I know the magic word; Asmodeus would be the ideal collaborator on my next book—*University Administration as a Preparation for Hell.*

Conversations with the
Little Table

Massey college is troubled with ghosts, much as lesser fabrics are troubled with mice; the most resolute determination is powerless to keep them away. Until this year, however, I have congratulated myself that they have kept clear of the part of the College that is reserved for the private quarters of myself and my family. Only once, many years ago, did a ghost tap at my bedroom door, and when I answered he quickly led me into the College proper. But of course a time had to come when I would find a ghost in the Lodgings. Anyone could have foreseen it.

It has always been my desire to keep my private life and my college life apart. If the ghost that visited me in the Master's Lodging had been a personal spectre, I would not trouble you about the matter now. But he had an undoubted relationship with the College as a whole; indeed it might be said that he was, at least in origin, a source of pride to the College. Two apparently unconnected happenings brought him here. The first was the publication, during the year past, of Colonel Stacey's book *A Very Double Life,* about some aspects of the personal character of the late William Lyon Mackenzie King; it was a significant book, deservedly successful with the public, and I recall with what pleasure we toasted it, and its author, at High Table, where we always celebrate the achievements of members of our community. The other fact was that one of my daughters moved to Hamilton, and bought a house there.

How could two such unrelated happenings work together to produce a result in Massey College? Those of you who have had experience of the occult world know that there is no chance assembly of facts that may not rouse an echo in the world of spirits. It happened like this; another of my daughters, who lives in Ottawa, wanted to send her sister a gift for her new home; she brought it to Toronto and left it with my wife and myself to be collected by the Hamilton daughter at some convenient time. It was a charming gift, a small table of the kind that antique dealers call an 'occasional table', an antique of attested Canadian craftsmanship. It was as a piece of Canadiana that its quality as a gift was raised above the commonplace; in every other respect it was just a nice little table.

'Where did it come from?' I asked my daughter.

'Oh, it has what the antique dealer called prov-enance,' she replied; 'it came from the house of an Ottawa lady named Mrs. Patteson, who was quite well known in her time as a collector of unusual things, and unusual people.'

The name meant nothing to me. We put the table in a room in our basement, to wait until it was picked up. And for a number of reasons, that was not speedily.

This was in the early autumn, and until November the table remained where it had been put. It was on the night of November the first—All Souls' Eve, as you will immediately have recognized—that I heard an unusual sound just after I had gone to bed; unusual because it was faint, but persistent. Loud sounds are not unknown in this neighbourhood during the night. Sounds attaining to the state of uproar may be heard, as students from the neighbouring colleges and residences rage through the streets, uttering cries which mount to the level of the Primal Scream. But this sound suggested a low but persistent tapping, as though someone were knocking; not the kind of knocking that one associates with academic communities—the tireless knocking of reputations and institutions—but a light hammering. I strove to ignore it, but at last I rose and put on slippers and dressing-gown, and set out in search.

It was clear as soon as I left my bedroom that the sound was inside my own house, and my ear directed me to the cellar, to the door of a room not much used, where the Ottawa table was stored. I opened the door slowly, and to my astonishment the room was suffused with a soft light—a mauve light—strongest in an open space in which stood the Little Table, and—wondrous in the telling—the Little Table seemed to be dancing a jig.

Far be it from me to pretend that I am a man of unusual courage, but in my own house I suffer no nonsense from anything, animate or inanimate. I put my hand on the Table and forced it to stand still. But when I took my hand away something happened that shattered my self-possession: the table moved toward me and began to rub itself against me in a manner that suggested a dog, but a dog with a more than doglike intelligence. The table was fondling me.

I am sure that many of you are acquainted with the book on Canadian furniture written by the great expert on that subject, Scott Symons; in it he asserts that Canadian furniture, at its finest, has a sensuous quality that can be, in certain instances, positively erotic. He says—and I have no reason to doubt his word—that on one occasion, during a meal, a dining table caressed his knee. Ghosts I can cope with, but erotic furniture destroys my self-possession; I rushed out of the room and upstairs, where my wife was still reading.

'You are pale,' said she; 'you look as if you had seen a ghost.'

'Not this time,' I replied; 'it's that table downstairs. It tried to get fresh with me. I think I need a drink.'

An ordinary woman might have laughed, or offered to get the drink, or perhaps some aspirin.

But my wife is not an ordinary woman. She rose at once, tucked the book she was reading under her arm, and led the way back to the mysterious chamber.

The mauve light flickered eerily, and as we went in the table's movement—it was like dancing—became almost frantic. My wife drew two chairs up to it, one on each side, and nodded to me to sit down. Then, to my astonishment, she placed her hands on the top of the table, with the fingers spread wide, and again nodded to me to do the same, with the ends of my fingers touching hers.

The response of the table was extraordinary. If ever a table might be said to give a sigh of relief, that was what it did. It became quiet, and almost soft under our hands; it seemed to be waiting.

'What's up?' I whispered.

My wife said nothing, but nodded to her book, which she had placed on the floor. I saw that it was Colonel Stacey's book, *A Very Double Life*.

'This must be the Little Table,' said she.

It is a commonplace to say that women have extraordinary powers of intuition. As soon as she had spoken I understood the connection. Because, as those of you know who have read it, that book describes how the late Prime Minister, and his lifelong friend and associate in spiritualism, Mrs. Patteson, used to spend long, rapt hours with a Little Table, by means of which they communicated with the spirits of the dead. Little Table; Mrs. Patteson; at last I understood.

The Little Table! The table dignified, or perhaps I should say hallowed, by all those conversations Mr. King recorded in his diary, and Professor Stacey had made known to us. I felt myself uplifted, to be thus involved with—and indeed snuggled up to by— an object so rich in association. The psychic history of Canada is scant, and here I was, so to speak, getting in on the ground floor! I felt myself unworthy. I felt that I should at once telephone to Professor Stacey, or to Maurice Careless, and ask them to come at once for—well, for what? I didn't know what the Little Table had, so to speak, on its mind.

I know the proceeding for getting answers from tables when they are in a communicative mood. I spoke.

'The usual thing, I presume?' I said. 'One rap for yes; two for no, and otherwise raps in series indicating the letters of the alphabet. Is that what you have in mind?'

Firmly, and it seemed to me joyously, the Little Table knocked once. That is to say it gave a quick tap with one tiny hoof upon the floor. It had said Yes.

'Are you there, Mrs. Patteson?' I said.

Two taps, in rather a pettish mood.

'Then who are you?' said I.

The table burst into a gunfire of tapping that startled me. 'Just a minute,' I said; 'not quite so fast.' Again the table rattled out its message. I am not at my best when confronted with problems involving figures. There seemed to be a great many taps. 'Did you say Z?' I asked. 'No, no,' my wife whispered; 'it was twenty-one taps. What is twenty-one? How many letters are there in the alphabet?' 'Twenty-eight, of course,' I hissed. 'Would you mind repeating?'

The Little Table gave two vicious little kicks, one to each side. My wife took it on the ankle, I on the shin. Then it rattled away in its telegraphic style, like one of those old-fashioned Morse instruments one heard clicking in the railway stations of an earlier day.

It was hopeless. 'Will you wait a moment,' said I. 'I want to make a helpful little chart.'

It used to be said that cobbler's children were always barefoot; by some kindred freak of Fate author's houses are always barren of pencils and paper. But at last I found what I wanted, and laboriously wrote out the alphabet, which—try as I might—proved to have only twenty-six letters, and to each letter I assigned a number. I didn't quite dare to lay this handy device on the Little Table; I feared it might scorn the simplicity of my mind. So I put it beside me on the floor. 'Now fire away,' I said; 'who is speaking, please?'

Spiteful little beast that it was, the table now tapped with tedious, insulting slowness. But at least it was possible to follow its message. Twenty-three taps.

'V,' said my wife. 'No, no; it was X,' said I.

Again those spiteful kicks. I should explain that the Little Table had what furniture experts call 'ball-and-claw feet', and it hurt. Then it tapped again, even more slowly.

This time we got it right. 'W,' we exclaimed in concert. The table tapped once.

'A,' said I.

'No, it means yes,' said my wife. 'It was W.'

Next time, twelve slow taps. L. Then thirteen taps. M. Then eleven taps. K.

'W L M K,' said I. 'Doesn't mean a thing.'

I still bear the marks of the ferocious attack of the ball-and-claw feet. But I have mentioned that women have extraordinary intuition. 'William Lyon Mackenzie King,' said my wife, in a low, reverential tone; 'it must be Mr. King himself.'

We rose and bowed to the Little Table, and it tipped its stout little person in ceremonious acknowledgement.

When I am not on duty as Master of this College I allow myself to use certain slang expressions that were current in my youth. 'Now we're cooking with gas,' I said. And the Little Table rapped once. Yes.

What should I say? Once, in my youth, I met Mr. King. He was old and near to death: I was young and impressionable, and I still remember the penetration of his glance, which seemed to be looking right through me, and weighing my possible value to the Liberal Party. He did not speak. I said—I remember the phrase perfectly, because it seemed to me to be particularly apt, under the circumstances—I said, 'How do you do, Sir?' Now I said it again, taking up the conversation from the point where it had been dropped all those many years ago.

The Little Table tapped briskly, now. Nine: pause; one, thirteen: pause; twenty-two, five, eighteen, twenty-five; pause: twenty-three, five, twelve, and twelve again. 'He said, "I am very well," I whispered to my wife. 'I know,' said she: 'I was counting.'

I shall not give you all the detail of the conversation that followed. The counting was hard work, not merely because Mr. King was a somewhat impetuous rapper, but because he was, to my surprise, an impressionistic speller. So I shall merely tell you what was said, shorn of all the psychic trappings.

'Am I to infer that you are among the Blessed?' said I.

The answer, now I reflect on it, was ambiguous. 'I am among friends,' said WLMK.

'Liberals?' I asked.

'Naturally,' came the reply.

'Ask him about Sir Wilfrid Laurier,' my wife prompted.

'Is Sir Wilfrid with you?'

One rap. 'Yes.'

'Happy, I trust?'

Here the Little Table seemed to lose control of itself. It tapped very rapidly, in a singular rhythm; eight-one, eight-one, eight-one. Which, as you have immediately grasped, is Ha, Ha, Ha! Then some very rapid tapping which, so far as I could follow it, said something about somebody's nose being out of joint. Then the laughing signal again. I was about to ask if Sir Wilfrid had suffered some posthumous damage to his nose, and how, and why, but I saw my wife frowning and shaking her head. So I dropped the subject of Sir Wilfrid.

What next? Extraordinary as it may seem, I could not think of a thing to say to the spirit of Mr. King. My wife saw that I was at a loss. 'Try him about his dog,' said she.

'Dog?' said I, not understanding.

'Pat,' said she; 'his dear doggie, his greatest friend.'

I have never cared much for dogs. But I know that dog-lovers are susceptible to flattery on the subject of their pets, and I felt that I had put my foot in it about Sir Wilfrid Laurier, and must recover lost ground. 'How's Pat?' I asked.

The table seemed to brighten up. It did some frisky tapping. Two-fifteen-twenty-three: twenty-three-fifteen-twenty-three. Bow-wow. Obviously it was Pat himself talking, so I feigned great benevolence and patted the table with the *faux bonhomie* I adopt toward other people's dogs. The table responded by rapping twenty-three, fifteen, fifteen again, and six. Woof. And, so far as I was concerned, that was enough from Pat.

I thought of people in the Other World from whom I might like to have a message. Vincent Massey, of course! Often, since his death, I have wished I could have the benefit of his advice. 'How is Mr. Massey?' I asked. The table tapped sulkily for a few seconds.

'Don't know and don't care,' was the message.

I remembered what I should have thought of earlier. Mr. King and Mr. Massey had not seen eye to eye.

'Still scrapping,' I whispered to my wife. But the Little Table overheard me, and tapped some very rapid comment which caught me off my guard, so that I was only able to transcribe the words 'opinionated,' 'insubordinate' and 'elitist'. But whether they referred to Mr. Massey or to me, I cannot say.

This was discouraging. I saw no reason why I should sit in this College and listen to Mr. King being nasty about its Founder. But what was there to say? He seemed to be so touchy. Then I had what I supposed was a happy inspiration. I noticed the copy of *A Very Double Life* that my wife had placed on the floor beside her.

'Have you read Colonel Stacey's book?' I asked.

There was a significant pause. Then a single rap. Yes.

'It's selling very well,' I said, glad to be on an ample and chatty theme at last. 'You must be pleased.'

It seemed to me that the temperature in the room dropped suddenly. 'Oh, you think that, do you?' rapped the Little Table, With unusual deliberation. I was overcome by one of my terrible failures of tact. I am generally pretty good at tact, but as it is an acquired faculty with me, and not an inherent trait, I sometimes put my foot in it, when talking to difficult people. 'I suppose you are glad to be an object of so much interest,' I said.

The Little Table rapped and rapped and rapped. 'I should have thought that my career offered enough of interest to the people of the country to which I devoted the whole of my career *comma* and my not inconsiderable talents,' it said, 'without a discussion of my youthful work among fallen women. Poor *comma* unhappy creatures *dash* 'soiled doves' was the term I always applied to them when I thought about them *dash* I went among them with but one thought in mind. I sought *comma* by talking to them seriously and sympathetically about the principles of Liberalism *comma* to win them from a life of shame to useful political activity. But so far as I could discover, not one of them ever went to the polls to cast the vote which was her democratic birth-right. I should have thought that in the present enthusiasm for Women's Liberation *dash* a cause very dear to my heart, as it was near to the heart of the noble woman who was the inspiration of all that was best in me *dash* I allude, needless to say, to my dear Mother—' And here there was a pause, which, as an old *aficionado* of political meetings I knew was meant for applause, so I applauded loudly; after I had made my hands very red, the Little Table resumed. 'I should have thought, I say, that my name would be mentioned as one of the earliest enthusiasts for the Women's Cause *semi-colon* that I should be mentioned with Henrik Ibsen *comma* with Bernard Shaw *comma* with the sainted Christabel Pankhurst and the never sufficiently to be lauded Nellie McClung. But it was not to be. No *comma* it has been suggested that my interest in women was of a carnal origin. And all because Jack Pickersgill hadn't the common gumption to destroy those damned diaries. Now you listen to me, young man—' and the Little Table rapped on and on. I was so stunned to be addressed as 'young man' that I forgot to count, and I observed that my wife was becoming drowsy under the spell of Mr. King's platform style and the tediousness of all that rapped-out punctuation. At last, after something like half an hour of telegraphed eloquence, the Little Table was still.

'Sorry about that,' said I. 'But I'm afraid there's nothing I can do about it. Shall I arrange an encounter with the author of the book? Would you like to rap with Colonel Stacey?'

Two decisive raps. No. And that was all. Worn out with our night listening to the mighty dead, my wife and I crept upstairs, to seek much needed repose.

I wanted to go back the next night, but my wife disagreed. 'He'll make another speech,' said she. 'Besides, I think it's unlucky to quarrel with spirits. Leave the wretched table alone, and I'll get it out of the house as soon as I can.' And there, for some time, the matter rested.

There is in my nature a generous portion of curiosity. I make no apology for it, and indeed I encourage and cherish it. Curiosity is part of the cement that holds society together; for many years I was a journalist, and a journalist without curiosity is useless. After Quebec's historic decision in the election of November 15 you will understand how I itched to have another talk with the Little Table. There must be something to be got out of the ghost of Mackenzie King, some scoop which I could, at the right moment, reveal to the world. So, after a few weeks of iron self-control, I broke down, and crept away by myself to the room in the depths of my house.

It was December the sixth when I went to the room where the Little Table was. My spirits rose as I saw that the glow of purple light arose from it, even more intense than it had been before. Would I be able to establish contact through it, I wondered, without the help of another person? I sat down and placed my hands, fingers spread, on its surface. I need not have worried; immediately I felt the thrill that told me the Little Table was ready to speak.

'Mr. King, are you there?' I whispered.

The retort was not in the best of humour. 'What do you think?' the table rapped. 'You've been away long enough. What brings you here now?'

'It is the sixth of December,' I said.

'What of it?' rapped the table.

'It is St. Nicholas's day,' I replied. 'He has always been kind to me.'

'Do you expect me as a Presbyterian, to pay attention to such rubbish,' said the spirit of Mackenzie King, in a series of short, brittle raps.

Off to a bad start, I thought. It is one of my weaknesses to imagine that everybody shares my enthusiasm for saints. The Little Table was clicking on.

'Superstition will be the ruin of you, Davies,' it said. 'I have seen many a man of minor talents, like yourself, go utterly to pot because of superstition. Brace up, man, *comma* brace up.'

Look who's talking, I thought. This is the man who spent so many of his private hours talking to spirits by means of this very Little Table at which I now sit. This is the man who addresses me by this tedious, farcical business of table-rapping, instead of manifesting himself and talking to me ghost to man, as a serious spirit should. But I subdued my indignation and spoke gently.

'I have come,' I said, 'because I hope that you will favour me with an exclusive interview. I should greatly value your opinion of the present state of Confederation. Taking the long view—which I assume is one of the prerogatives of your present position—what do you think is likely to happen in Quebec? Is Separatism a political gambit or a genuine threat?'

There was a pause. Then—'Don't trouble me with such nonsense,' rapped Mr. King. 'Do you suppose I have nothing to keep me busy here? My present Cabinet demands the most careful management, in spite of my success in bringing about a decisive Tory overthrow—'

I could hold in no longer. For the first time, I interrupted the Little Table. I seized it and held it firmly to the ground, thereby, so to speak, choking Mr. King off in mid-speech. This was precisely what I wanted.

'Cabinet?' I said. 'Tory overthrow? Do you mean that you are in power in—in—?' I did not know how to finish the question.

'The greatest victory of my career,' came the reply. 'I have reduced the Tories to a miserable, seedy rump, and their Leader is trying to prevent a final break.'

'What Leader?' said I, breathless with curiosity.

'Who has always been the leader of the Conservative Party, whatever puppet may have appeared to mortal eyes to hold that office?' said Mr. King.

I knew, of course. That is to say, I knew who had always appeared to Mr. King to be the Tory Leader. My mind trembled on the verge of total disorder. 'Mr. King,' I whispered, 'are you telling me that you have brought about Separatism in—' But I did not like to speak the word. To a Presbyterian it might seem offensive. I changed the form of the question. 'Mr. King,' said I; 'where are you?'

At that instant, it seemed to me that the Little Table became extremely hot. But it tapped merrily. And what it tapped amazed me greatly. Mr. King was not a slangy man, but I suppose that when he was a youth, an undergraduate in this University, he had acquired a few of the slang expressions of his contemporaries. Anyhow, what the Little Table rapped, almost giggling as it did so, was: 'None of your beeswax!'

'But Mr. King!' I persisted. 'Don't leave me just yet. You must know that your successor on earth has recently been described in an extremely influential

214

American newspaper as "perhaps the world's most gifted leader". Tell me something helpful that I may pass on to Pierre Elliot Trudeau.'

The table stopped its giggling in an instant. It became, not hot, but icy cold. 'You tell Trudeau this from me!' it banged—yes, it banged on the floor. And then it began to tap so fast that it took all my concentration to make out the letters of its clumsy, rattling language. They seemed to mean little, until I understood that the tapping was now in French. But what French! It was politician's French, which is a language in itself, understood by few. I could not make out, with clarity, what Mr. King wanted me to tell Mr. Trudeau, except that he seemed to be summoning him to join himself, wherever he was, with the utmost speed. Mr. King seemed to have a place for Mr. Trudeau in his new dominion, but I gathered that it was not in the Cabinet. I thought I caught something about 'the hot-seat.'

The Little Table was not made to withstand such vehemence. At the height of the tiráde, one of the little feet broke off, and suddenly there was silence.

I had the Little Table mended, the next day, by Norbert. He said he had a suitable piece of wood, which he had taken out of one of the fixtures of the College Chapel, that would do the job almost invisibly.

But the Little Table never spoke again. I suppose there are things, such as pieces of wood from our Chapel, that are intolerable to Presbyterian ghosts, and especially those who have achieved Separatism by what used to be called the Harrowing of Hell.

THE KING ENJOYS HIS OWN AGAIN

A hundred and fifty years is a long time, you will all agree, for a man to suffer misunderstanding and wrong. My task tonight is to attempt to put right such a misunderstanding. The length of time I have mentioned makes it clear at once that I am speaking on behalf of a ghost. Oh, if it were only one ghost! Because there are two; and I can feel them very near me as I address you now. Both are determined that I should support the version of the history of this University that they think the right one. Much hangs on which side I take.

A week ago tonight we held our College Christmas Dance. My wife and I left at about one o'clock, and went to bed, but I was unable to sleep. I had an uneasy sense that someone had been there whom I had failed to greet, because I try to speak, or at least leer hospitably, at everybody. I rose: I prowled. I went to a window and, looking down, I was surprised to see someone in the quadrangle walking alone in a posture of dejection—someone in an academic gown.

Gowns are often seen in the quad, but—at two in the morning? And was there not about the figure a singularity, a distinction greater than is common among academics? I went out into the night for a nearer look.

Whoever it was paced up and down the stone paths, and as I came nearer, I heard what was unquestionably the sound of deep sobs. The figure was weeping! Some unhappy youth who had been, as they say, given the mitt by his partner at the dance? I hid behind a tree, to hear better. The broken utterance became audible: 'O, the black ingratitude of it,' said the rich, fruity voice; 'All this fuss, and not a word—not one solitary word—about me. It's cruel, cruel!' I am not a man to withhold sympathy from any suffering soul, and I popped out from behind my tree.

'Excuse me,' said I; 'may I be of any assistance—' At that moment the figure moved into a gleam of moonlight, and you may judge of my dismay when I saw that the moonlight passed right through it! A cold greater than that of December seized upon me and my heart sank. For I knew that this much-haunted establishment was once again being visited by a ghost. But whose ghost this time?

Then I knew. It could be none other. What I had mistaken for a gown was in fact a voluminous cloak, and when the figure turned to me the elegance of the clothes beneath the ghostly yet blinding blaze of stars and orders and diamonds in the moonlight, and more than anything else that great head, that florid, fleshy face, that beaky nose, those drooping eyelids, and the splendidly curled chestnut hair could belong to but one person. It was King George the Fourth. I bowed. It is not easy to bow elegantly in pyjamas, but old theatrical training came to my aid and I think it was not a bad bow. 'Your Majesty,' said I.

'So you know me,' said the figure. 'I had concluded that I was utterly forgotten here.'

I muttered something about the University Department of History.

'Pah,' said the King. 'Deluded toadies to a totally wrong principle. I should know. I *am* History, suppressed and distorted History. O Ingratitude! How sharper than a serpent's tooth it is to have founded a thankless University.' I mumbled some disclaimer, but the King spoke on. 'It is now 1977 and this graceless institution is celebrating what it is pleased to call its Sesquicentennial. But has a word been said about the Monarch who, by a stroke of the pen, brought it into being? Don't think I'm angry. No, no. But I am hurt. Deeply, terribly hurt. So what have you to say?'

Me? It is not my job to deal with such things. Let the Public Relations people explain. Let the President explain. Let the Lieutenant-Governor, who acted as Chairman of the Sesquicentennial Committee, explain. But none of them were there. No, no; they were snug in their beds, and I was face to face with a sobbing, ignored Founder.

'I can only appeal to your magnanimity, Sire,' I said. 'You know what academics are. Simple folk whose minds rarely stray beyond the present. And really, I—what can I do?'

'I'll tell you in good time,' said the King. 'But first a matter of curiosity; something led me here; something led me to this place; some notion that in this College, at least, I might find understanding. What do you think it can have been?'

What was I to say? 'Humble as I am,' I ventured, 'I apologize on behalf of us all. I am sure no affront was intended.'

He was not mollified. A look of bitterness succeeded to grief in his countenance. 'Pshaw,' he said. 'I notice none of you forgot John Strachan. Tell me, what does this University find that is so special about John Strachan?'

I spoke without thinking. 'As our Founder—' said I, causing the King to interrupt in a temper.

'Oh Founder, Founder, Founder! Strachan was forever founding something! McGill University, your great rival—he had a finger in that pie. And Trinity, your neighbour—they toady to him there as a Founder. But in this University he wasn't a Founder, he was merely an organizer! Did he ever open his sporran and lay down a penny-piece? Because I did! This University would have been nowhere without my money.'

The word 'money' as we all know, has strong magical overtones. Silently, but impressively, we were joined by another figure, and to my experienced eye that figure was a phantom. It was John Strachan, without a doubt, in the full day-dress of an Anglican Bishop—gaiters, apron, squarecut long coat, and above all that peculiar hat like a stovepipe with a wireless aerial on either side, which gives a Bishop the appearance of one who is in perpetual receipt of messages from outer space. His square, granite face was marked with the look of intense disapproval so often seen in the Scot who has risen high in the world. John Strachan, without a doubt. The word 'money' had brought him back from the grave.

'Did I hear a suggestion,' he said in a withering tone, 'That I contributed nothing to the founding of this institution?'

'No money, at any rate,' said the King, who had no fear of this apparition. 'I laid down a sturdy thousand pounds a year, which in terms of today's money was very handsome. Indeed, I can't understand, with what must be a hundred and fifty thousand pounds of my money, why this place is in need of money now.'

'As I recall, that money was provided from public funds,' said the Bishop.

But the King did not bat an eye. 'I suppose it was,' said he; 'I could hardly be expected to fuss about where it *came* from. The important fact is that I *granted* it and you *got* it, so I suppose we may say you had it from me.'

'Your Majesty might say that,' said the Bishop, 'but other donors have given from their own pockets.'

'Meaning yourself, I suppose?' said the King.

'A Bishop does not make known his contributions to worthy causes,' said John Strachan.

'That's gammon,' said the King. 'Come along, Strachan, how much real money did you stump up?'

'I must respectfully request your Majesty not to press a question that offends against Christian principle,' said the Bishop, and I thought he seemed uncomfortable.

'Aha! Got you,' said the King; 'I'll wager fifty guineas you gave nothing at all,' and he laughed like a schoolboy.

'Sir, you are disrespectful of my cloth,' shouted Strachan, fire darting from his eyes.

'Pish for your cloth,' said the King. 'Your cloth may be well enough, but the cut and fit are abominable. If you mean I don't respect you as a Bishop, you're wrong. It is well-known that I was vastly respectful of Bishops, when I chose my own. But you were one of my niece Victoria's creations, and she had a sentimental taste for Scotchmen.'

Now it was the Bishop's turn to show hurt feelings. Tears dimmed those stony eyes. 'This is a man's reward for a life of the most stringent devotion to God, to duty and the cause of education,' said he; 'how sharper than a serpent's tooth it is to meet a thankless Monarch!'

'Fiddle-faddle,' said the King. 'What do you need of gratitude from your Monarch. Your name has been whooped and hallooed about this University for the past year, and more. You've had more gratitude than you deserve, because much of it was filched from me!'

The Bishop stopped weeping, and roared. 'You! Who slaved and contrived to set this University firmly on its feet? Who endured the reproach and ignominy of an ungrateful government and an indifferent populace? Whose hair turned gray under the strain of that shocking and discriminatory Charter you signed—without reading it, I am sure—until I was able to enlarge its scope and make a University that was truly for the people of this great land?'

'A University which you subsequently described as 'a godless imitation of Babel,' said the King; 'and after you had given it that nasty dig you skipped away and founded Trinity, which was much more to your liking. Oh, you were a mighty Founder, and such a tyrant as no King would dare to emulate. Don't lecture me as if I didn't know this University's history. Don't I remember (after my time on earth, of course) when the greedy Government took it over as an addition to their lunatic asylum, and didn't they have the ugliness to call it the University Lunatic Asylum? Not such a bad name, when you think of it. And don't twaddle about your hair going gray. No man needs to endure such things if he has a good valet.' And here King George IV touched his head with conscious pride, and indeed his splendidly curled wig was a work of art.

'Huuut!' said the Bishop. It was his version of a laugh. 'Vanity of vanities, all is vanity.'

'That's one of the truest things in the Bible,' said the King, quite affably. 'If it weren't for vanity we should still be running about in our skins, painted a horrid blue. Vanity is one of the mainsprings of human progress.'

The King seemed to be getting the better of the argument. I remembered that John Strachan's motto had been *Prudent But Fearless*. Now he showed a sudden change of mood toward what, in a character less granitic than his, might be described as soapy.

'As a Bishop,' he said, 'it would ill beseem me to show a want of charity toward any of God's creatures—even toward one whose earthly life was verra far from being a suitable pattern for a Christian King. I am truly sorry that you suppose yourself to have been overlooked by a University in whose founding you played a trifling, purely ceremonial part—

The King broke in. 'How could I have done more than I did? The University of London was being founded that same year, and of course I had a great deal to do with that. The older universities were offended, so I had to found those readerships in mineralogy and geology at Oxford to appease them. And you know how much I was involved in the Literary Fund, granting them a Charter, and as much money as I could scrape up at the time. I was always short. Generosity—it's a costly indulgence, Bishop. Literature was my real love. Byron—how I admired him; and do you know, for a time at least, he admired me. And noble, generous Walter Scott—a dear friend. I always meant to do something in the way of a Civil List recognition for Jane Austen—dear, ironical Jane, her pretty novels taught me so much about people—even though she was somewhat hard on the clergy. And in all that, I couldn't do much more than I did for little Toronto, now could I? Was it to be expected? Such a busy life, you see.'

The Bishop looked sour, like a man who has been outbid at an auction. 'Busy,' said he; 'aye, busy in the pursuit of pleasure.'

'True, true,' said the King, not in the least daunted. 'I've been called that, you know—the Prince of Pleasure.'

'And where has it brought you?' said the Bishop. 'Think, think man, upon your present unhappy state.'

'What unhappy state?' said the King, much surprised. 'I'm as happy as—well, as happy as a King. I mingle in admirable society, and I don't have to be tedious any more about rank. I can see as much as I please of the literary company I always longed for. Instead—of course it's not proper for ordinary people to kiss and tell, but I *am* a King—dear Jane Austen has been one of my mistresses for the past— oh, well over a century. No great sensation in bed, I assure you, but a wonderful talker; so I talk to Jane and sleep with other ladies whose talent lies that way.'

The Bishop was furious. 'Reprobate!' he roared, quite forgetting what is due from a Bishop to the

Defender of his Faith; 'dare you tell me that you pursue your dissolute courses unrebuked in Hell?'

'Who said anything about Hell?' said the King, much surprised. 'You don't suppose I'm in Hell, do you?'

'If not Hell, where?'

'In Elysium, of course. Where are you?'

'I am in Paradise,' said the Bishop, like a man transformed. 'In Jerusalem, the golden, with milk and honey blessed. Can you believe it, when I arrived, there was not a University, or a good private school, or an Association for the Improvement of Deserving Artisans, or an almshouse for the widows of indigent clergy, or a Society for the Relief of Decayed Gentlewomen, or a Society for distributing trusses to the ruptured poor, or a single evidence of practical benevolence in the whole of Paradise? And it has been my glorious care to found them all. And to found many, many more. And there are persons of wealth, to be cajoled and bullied and shamed into giving me the money to do it. Oh, what glorious tussles I've had with some of them! Man, it's Heaven. Work, work, work, and found, found, found, and beg, beg, beg without cease. I have turned the new Jerusalem into a splendid likeness of modern Toronto. Oh, the goodness of our bountiful Creator! He has even provided Sin—Sin in unlimited quantity and horrendous quality, for his Blessed Ones like myself to struggle with and combat and overcome. At this present moment I am busy with an area of the New Jerusalem where shameless men resort to have their bodies rubbed by unclothed women. Aye, and there is an abomination quite new since my time, a group called The Gays, and it is my resolve to assail their New Sodom. How can a poor lost soul like yourself judge of the holy ecstasy that Paradise is to a man like me?'

'I'll keep to Elysium,' said the King.

'But you ought to be in Hell,' shouted the Bishop.

'Oh it would be Hell to you, just as your Paradise would be Hell to me,' said the King. 'You'd find Elysium way over your head. The daylight hours are spent in a sort of perpetual banquet, interspersed with expeditions on the water, and there's an opera every evening. And after lights out—no, no, Bishop, not for you. Of course I build a lot of new palaces, and you should see the gardens I'm planning. And furniture! Had it never struck you that a really satisfactory hereafter would involve perpetual delicious anxieties about new furniture? And—this is God's charity at its most thoughtful—nobody ever sends in a bill!'

The Bishop's face was an arena in which Pity wrestled with Outraged Virtue. 'Man, man,' he said, 'do ye never tire of pleasure?'

'Tire—of pleasure? What an extraordinary idea. Do you ever tire of good works?'

'Never! But good works, inspired by faith—'

'What kind of faith? Do you make nothing of my lifelong faith in art and beauty? I wasn't an artist myself—except perhaps in my personal appearance—but I was a great patron, a great appreciator and inspirer, a commissioner of fine things, and a notable collector. Do you call that nothing?'

'I call it self-indulgence.'

'You, my lord, are a savage.'

'Do you call me a savage, you crowned and anointed buffoon! You jewelled and gilded puppet, good for nothing but silly folk to gape at!'

'Very well. I withdraw "savage"; it was an unworthy name for a King to apply to a Bishop of his own Church. But I shall say this; you are not a gentlephantom.'

'The rank is but the guinea stamp. I was one of the World's Workers.'

'Then we shall never agree. You were devoted to what Davies here'—the King nodded toward me—'would doubtless call the Work Ethic. Whereas I was devoted to the Pleasure Principle. I enjoyed life and I encouraged enjoyment in others. On balance I think my kind of person has done rather more for mankind than yours.'

But John Strachan was not to be talked down. 'Upon what is a University built if not upon the Work Ethic? What has the scholar to offer to his God greater than Work and Prayer?'

'What would God make of a university filled with nothing but sweaty psalm-singers?' said the King. 'God, as a gentleman and an Anglican, must certainly appreciate scholarship, intellectual dignity, connoisseurship—all the attributes of civilization, and civilization owes more to the Pleasure Principle than it does to the Work Ethic, which is moneygrubbing humbug. That was why I took pains to put a representative of the Pleasure Principle in this University at its beginning. Yes, right under your nose, my careful friend, and you never saw what I had done.'

'And what was that?' The Bishop's voice was scornful and suspicious.

'It wasn't a that; it was a who,' said the King.

'Who, then?'

'A member of my family.'

'Hut! There was no member of your family here at the founding.'

'Oh, but there was. Surely you remember him? Indeed you yourself appointed him. Have you forgotten the Reverend John McCaul, first professor of Classics, and successor to yourself as President of the University?'

'John McCaul; a man of God; a man after my own heart!'

'Perhaps. But also my nephew.'

It is impossible for a ghost to have a seizure of apoplexy, but certainly that was what the ghost of Bishop Strachan seemed to be suffering. As he fought for breath, the King continued triumphantly.

'Surely you remember, my lord, that John McCaul came to Canada under the direct patronage of the Archbishop of Canterbury? My brothers were a wild lot of fellows, and they had many sons on the wrong side of the blanket. Like any good English family, we followed the custom of the day: convicts to Australia—bastards to Canada. John McCaul was of the Blood Royal.'

With a mighty effort, the Bishop raised his hand, and, like a meteor, a volume of the *Dictionary of National Biography* emerged from one of the arrow-slits in the Robarts Library and sailed down into his outstretched hand, open at page 446 of Volume XII. The King and I read therein an entry describing the somewhat unremarkable life of one Alexander McCaul, an Irish scholar and divine, which concluded with the curt entry: 'He left several sons.'

'Aha,' said the King, 'you observe that this very Victorian compilation says nothing whatever about the good parson's wife. But she was well-known in her day. Well-known to my brother Fred, among others. Young John was his lad. You must have heard the rumours?'

The Bishop was shielding his eyes with his hand, but he shook his head.

Now it was the King's turn. He lifted his hand and at once came the response from Robarts—a volume bound in red which I had no trouble in recognizing as *University College—a Portrait,* edited by Claude T. Bissell. There, on pages 4 and 5, the Bishop and I read: "The Reverend John McCaul remained Professor of Classics, and became President of the University of Toronto. He had come to Canada in 1839 as Principal of Upper Canada College, on the special recommendation of the Archbishop of Canterbury; and this fact, as well as *certain rumours as to his royal parentage* explain perhaps his preferment in Canada, and his survival of forty years of bitter controversy over university affairs".

'There, you see,' said the King. 'It was obvious to anybody who looked at him; obvious still, if you take a good look at the portrait of young Jack in the Great Hall of Hart House. He's the spitting image of my brother Augustus Frederick, Duke of Sussex. Fred was always fond of classics, so the lad came by it honestly. Fred asked the Archbishop to find something for young Jack, and of course he did.'

It seemed to me that the King had won, hands down, and I thought it a little ungenerous of him to dance upon the body of a fallen foe.

'Come along, Dr. Strachan, we must return our books to the Library; others may want them, you know.' He tossed the history of University College into the air, and like a swallow it sped back to Robarts; the Bishop's book was slower to return than it had been in coming, and laboured in its flight, like a turkey. The King continued to rub salt into the wound.

'I think it rather shabby of the University to have grudged John McCaul some recognition of his royal parentage. I want you to take care of that, Davies. In this Sesquicentennial year, you must have—well, not the royal arms, but the arms of the Duke of Sussex affixed to the top of the frame of his picture. With a proper attaint of bastardy on it, of course. It would do a little something to make up for the University's shabby treatment of me.'

Bishop Strachan's face was still buried in his hands, but his voice, choked with tears, could be heard. 'Och, Johnnie McCaul, could ye no have con-fided your shame to your Bishop?' he sobbed.

'Oh don't be such an old Goosey Gander, Strachan,' said the King. 'McCaul's bastardy was his glory, and reflected glory on this University. Consider the Pleasure Principle and dry your eyes. You look a perfect quiz. And be realistic Strachan (His Majesty insisted on giving full, phlegmy Scottish honours to the name)—how do you expect anyone to survive as a University President who is not, in one sense or another, a bastard? Now Davies, I rely on you; have that heraldic ornament on young Jack's frame before the Sesquicentennial Year ends.'

Here was a pretty kettle of fish! But I remem-bered something Vincent Massey had told me, years ago.

'Your Majesty is by no means forgotten in this University,' said I. 'Have you visited the Senate Chamber?'

'Should I?'

'If you would be so gracious as to do so,' said I, 'you would see that above the Chancellor's great chair in that handsome room there is a splendid achievement of arms. You would immediately rec-ognize them, Sire, for they are your own. And they were placed there by the designer of that room, who was also the Founder of this College.'

'Damme, that was handsomely done of Vincent Massey,' said the King. 'I knew there was some reason why I came to weep in Massey College. An understanding spirit, that's what I discerned here.'

'Mr. Massey told me it was not managed without some dispute,' said I. 'The late Canon Cody, who was President at that time, was strongly against it; he objected that you were a bad example to Canadian youth. But in the end Mr. Massey prevailed. So you see, the Pleasure Principle is symbolized at the very heart of the University.'

'And can do it nothing but good,' said the King, beaming. Then he drew a splendid watch from his pocket. 'I must be going,' said he, 'if I am to be in time to hear *The Magic Flute;* little Mozart is conducting it himself. Farewell for the present, Davies; and you might just as well get on with that job on McCaul's portrait. Hope to see you in Elysium.'

'But not too soon,' I murmured, bowing as the King melted into the night air. I turned to take leave of Bishop Strachan, but he had gone already. Where he had stood were several little holes in the path, where his bitter tears had eaten into the stone.

THE XEROX IN THE
LOST ROOM

T hose of you who have attended several of these Christmas Parties are aware how extensively, indeed extravagantly, this College is haunted. Every year a ghost; sometimes more than one. I cannot explain how a new building in a new country—or a country that pretends it is new, although in reality it is very old—comes to be so afflicted with what our university sociologists call 'spectral density'. I suspect it has something to do with the concentration of our College community, senior and junior, on intellectual things. There is in Nature a need for balance, a compensating principle which demands in our case that where there is too much rationality there should be occasional outbreaks of irrationality. I offer my explanation tentatively, because I am no philosopher and certainly no scientist, and detractors have said that rationality is a quality by which I am seldom overwhelmed.

It could also be that there is a housing shortage in the World Beyond, just as there is here below.

Everybody is aware of the alarming rate at which the world's population is increasing. In the lifetime of some of us it has very nearly doubled. More people and thus, inevitably, more ghosts. Where are they to put themselves? Many of them are emigrating from the lands of their origin and coming to Canada, which is still comparatively open, especially in the spiritual aspect of things. That may be the explanation.

Over the years our ghosts have tended to be from the upper ranks of the spirit world; it is an odd fact that the poor and humble rarely have ghosts. Celebrated people have haunted us; now and then we have bagged a spectral crowned head, but as a general thing our ghosts are drawn from the intelligentsia. I confess with shame that this has betrayed me into a measure of vanity. I catch myself wondering, early in January, 'Who will it be this year?' And then I consult a list of anniversaries falling in the year to come. Ghosts, you know, are not always tied to the places where their earthly life was passed; now and then they are granted a freedom of movement which is called a Witches Sabbatical.

Last January I looked eagerly to see who would be on tour, so to speak, and my eye fell upon the name of Henrik Ibsen. It was the 150th anniversary of his birth, and all over the world a good deal of fuss was going to be made. Ibsen! My mouth watered. To be visited by that mighty dramatist, considered by so many people to be the greatest of his kind since Shakespeare—what a cultural *coup* that would be!

Why would he visit us? Canada reflects the social world of Ibsen as much as any country in the world today. Surely he would come to Canada, if only to sneer. And, as you know, we contain within our walls the University's Centre for the Study of Drama, and I knew that Ibsen would be in their minds, and on their tongues. Surely the great man would favour us with a few morose words. But then I reproached myself. It is stupid to count your ghosts before they are manifested. Down, vanity! Down, worldly aspiration, I cried; and they downed. But not totally. From time to time I surprised, at the back of my mind, an unworthy hankering.

When December arrived, I was nervously aware that time was getting on. Henrik Ibsen was late. It was not like him. All through his life he was known for his punctiliousness about appointments. If he said he would do a thing, he would do it, especially if it were something disagreeable. But then I came to my senses; Ibsen had promised nothing; this whole business of his visit was a foolish whimwham of my own. You should be ashamed of yourself, I said; and I was obediently ashamed of myself. Nevertheless, deep in the undisciplined abyss of my mind, that hankering continued.

The resolution of the affair came, as it so often does, on the night of our College Dance. It has long been my custom, after the supper which is a feature of our dance, to go out into the quad and take a few turns up and down. It is then that I often see ghosts. Nothing to do with the supper, I assure you, because I never take anything but a cup of coffee. Perhaps it has something to do with the excitement of seeing this quiet place turned, for one evening, into a palace of delights. So, as I paced the familiar flagstones in the chill air, I was not surprised to see a stranger stand-ing—lurking, to be more precise—in a dark corner.

My heart leapt within me. Was it he? The figure was slight for Henrik Ibsen who, as you know from his photographs, was built rather like a barrel encased in a frock coat. And the hat—where was the resplen-dent silk hat which was the great man's invariable outdoor wear? As I drew nearer it was plain that the figure was wrapped in a cloak, which, even in dark-ness, looked shabby. And the hat was quite wrong; it was a three-cornered hat. Unless Ibsen had chosen for some inexplicable reason to get himself up as a figure from the early eighteenth century, this was the wrong ghost. I was disappointed and annoyed and perhaps I spoke abruptly. What I said was 'Well?' with that upward intonation that makes it clear that it is not at all well.

'If you please,' said the ghost, 'I am looking for a modest, dry lodging in quiet surroundings.'

'This is an odd time to be looking for a room,' said I. 'You should come back in daylight and speak to the Bursar. If you are able to appear in daylight,' I added, nastily.

'Please don't be severe with me,' said the ghost in such a pitiful tone that I felt ashamed of myself. 'My need is very great, and I must find a place tonight, or terrible things will happen to me.' He was almost weeping.

'I have no wish to be severe,' said I, 'but you must understand that this college has a purpose to fulfil in the university, and that purpose makes no provision for—'

'For people in my situation?' said the ghost. 'But you are famous for your hospitality toward ghosts. Ah, but I see,' he continued, 'You are only interested in famous ghosts, and I am a sadly obscure person. That has been the pathos of my life. If I were not such a failure, I would use a stronger word than pathos; I would say tragedy.'

Poor fellow! I felt thoroughly ashamed of myself. Here I was, hankering after the ghost of a world-famous dramatist and behaving with abominable callousness to a poor phantom whose life had been a tragedy perhaps deeper than any Ibsen had conceived. Tears filled my eyes.

I should have known better. Ghosts are all rampaging egotists—forces of egotism that refuse to accept death as a fact. The ghost before me was now fixing me with a baleful glare, and I felt its hand laid with icy firmness on my sleeve.

'List, list to me,' said the ghost; 'I could a tale unfold whose lightest word, would harrow up thy soul, freeze thy young blood—'

'All right, all right,' I said impatiently. 'If you must—and believe me I know how communicative you ghosts can be—let me have it as briefly as possible, and without poetry. I'm very well up in *Hamlet*. Who are you?'

'That is my trouble,' said the ghost. 'I'm a private person, but not therefore utterly without poetry and feeling. In life I was that particular type of gentleperson called a Poor Relation.'

'Whose Poor Relation were you?' said I.

'A Rich Relation's, of course. He was a country squire in Gloucestershire. Not an ill-natured fellow. He knew I had no prospects and no luck, and he let me live in his manor house in a subordinate position, helping with the estate accounts, writing letters, teaching the children a little Latin, and sometimes drawing scale plans for his drainage projects, while he and the Vicar were out shooting. You know the kind of things Poor Relations do. I had been something of a scholar, you see, and I had hoped for a college fellowship, but I had no influential friends; I had hoped to enter the Church, but the Bishop had too many nephews, and altogether I was a failure and a dependant. I didn't complain. Not very much, that is to say. But I was a cousin of the squire, and it irked me that the servants treated me so badly.'

This was the sorriest excuse for a ghost I had ever met. Failure in the spirit world is particularly chilling, and I was beginning to shiver. But I couldn't break away. It would have been unfeeling.

'But you have apparently achieved some success after death,' said I. 'You are a ghost, and you are far from home. How have you got leave to travel?'

'That is the saddest part of my story,' said he. 'But you must hear me out. Don't bustle me.'

I groaned, but I had not the heart to leave him.

'It came to a head this very night, two hundred and fifty years ago,' said the ghost. 'It was on December the ninth, in 1728. Our good King George II had just entered the eleventh year of his long reign—'

'Yes, yes,' said I; 'I know a little history myself. Do make haste.'

'What a fidget you are,' said the ghost, rather sharply I thought for a Poor Relation. 'Then hear me. My cousin, the squire and his lady had gone to Sudeley Castle, to a ball. I was not invited. Of course not. I was a nobody and I had no fine clothes. I was left at home without even a word of apology. Nor had any dinner been ordered. My cousin's wife, who was inclined to be mean, said that doubtless I could get something in the kitchen with the servants.

'That would not have been so bad, because the servants saw to it that they ate very well, but it meant that I had to brave my greatest enemy, the butler; he took every chance to make me feel my position as a Poor Relation. And that night he was particularly tyrannous, because he was drunk. We quarrelled. He killed me.'

'Stabbed you?' I asked.

'No.'

'Shot you? The great kitchen blunderbuss, kept above the chimney, loaded in case of burglars? In

his drunken rage the butler tore it from its place
and shot you while the womenfolk screamed?'

'You have been seeing too much television,' said
the ghost. 'The eighteenth century wasn't like that
at all.'

I continued to be hopeful and romantic. 'But the
quarrel,' I said; 'he insulted you, spoke slightingly of
your birth, and your good blood was aroused. You
lunged at him with your sword, but lost your footing, and he seized the sword and stabbed you to the
heart. Please say it was like that.'

'I never owned a sword in my life,' said the ghost.
'Nasty, dangerous things. No: I'll tell you exactly
how it was. I was rather drunk myself, you see, and
we were having a dispute about how to make boot-
blacking. I had complained that the blacking he
used had too much brown sugar in it. You know,
the secret of good boot-blacking is the proportion
of brown sugar to the amount of soot and vinegar.
It's the butler's work to make it. And I said he put in
too much brown sugar. I said my boots were always
sticky. He said I lied. I said he forgot himself in the
presence of his betters. He said what betters, and I
was no more than a servant myself and begged the
Squire's old wigs. Then I absent-mindedly picked up
a table fork and stuck it into his right buttock. He
must have had very soft flesh because it went much
farther in than I had expected. Right up to the han-
dle. Then he picked up a pewter tankard and hit me
over the head, and to my surprise and indignation I
fell to the floor, dead as a nit.'

This was the lowest ghost I had ever been pestered by. A wearer of second-hand wigs! Brained in a kitchen brawl with a pewter pot! And he had the gall to haunt Massey College! Nevertheless, as a tale of low-life, this had its interest.

'What happened then?' I asked.

'That was the cream of the whole thing,' said the ghost, as near to laughter as a ghost can get. 'You see, as soon as the butler hit me with that pot, I found myself about nine inches above the ground, watching everything—myself stretched out on the floor, the cook trying to staunch the blood from my head with a towel, all the maids in hysterics, the footman saying he knew it would come to this some day, and the butler, as white as a sheet, blubbering: 'Oh zur, come back I beg 'ee. I never went fur to do it, zur. Come back and I'll go light on the brown sugar as long as I live, indeed zur, I will.' But it was hopeless. I was gone, so far as they were concerned. The butler ran off and became a highwayman, but he was too fat and stupid for the work, and he was caught and hanged within a year.

'But there was one thing about the affair that was truly impressive. The cook was a wise woman, in her fashion, and before the butler ran off she begged him to taste my blood—just a little, just to dip his finger in the blood and lick it. He refused. She took a few licks herself, to show him that there was nothing really unpleasant about it, but of course she was professionally accustomed to tasting uncooked substances. Why? Because, you see, she knew that if he did that my ghost would never be able to appear. Now you remember that, if ever you kill anybody; swallow some of his blood, or you'll be sorry. But of course in these days so many murderers are careless and ignorant that what I am telling you has almost been forgotten. I have always been glad that butler was thoroughly stupid; otherwise my fine career, my real achievement, would have been impossible.'

The ghost was markedly more cheerful, now. 'Do you know, that was the best thing that ever happened to me? From being a Poor Relation, I was suddenly promoted to Family Ghost. My cousin and his wife were proud of me, and as succeeding generations appeared in the manor I became quite a celebrity. I was once investigated by the Society for Psychical Research, and Harry Price himself gave me the coveted three star rating: Accredited Spectre, First Class.'

I continued to be patient, under difficulties. 'But what brings you here?' I asked. A ghost from Gloucestershire with a nice little local reputation—what sent him travelling?

He groaned. All ghosts groan, and it is a very disquieting sound. This ghost was a first-rate groaner.

'You read the newspapers, I suppose?' he said.

'Unfailingly,' I replied.

'Zena Cherry?' said he.

'Religiously,' said I, and made the sign of the gossip columnist—one hand cupped to the ear, the other reaching for the pencil.

'Then surely you remember her account of the old English manor house that had been bought by a Toronto entrepreneur and re-built, stone by stone, in Don Mills, near the Bridle Path?'

I did remember it.

'It was, literally, an uprooting,' said the ghost. 'But I took it philosophically. The trouble with a ghost's situation, you see, is the sameness of it. After two hundred and fifty years I was beginning to feel housebound, and I thought a new country, new people to frighten, new people to boast about me, would be an adventure. So I didn't mind the move to Toronto; the journey by airline freight wasn't bad, in spite of the delays by strikes. But when I arrived at last, all sorts of terrible things began to happen."

'Climate unfavourable, I suppose?' said I, sympathetically.

'Not that, so much as the structural changes,' said the ghost. 'Our splendid old manorhouse kitchen was thought too big for a Canadian dwelling. To begin, it was a good hundred and forty feet from the dining-room, and there was a flight of stone stairs on the way. You should have heard what the real-estate people had to say about that! And it had a flagstone floor, which was hard and cold to Canadian feet. Further, our house was a proper gentleman's residence, and without a butler and a footman and six maids and a cook and a scullion nothing more ambitious than sandwiches could be managed. So the real estate people decided that an entirely new kitchen should be built, and the old kitchen should become something called a rumpus room, where the children of the family could be at a suitable distance from their elders. I gather that 'rumpus' is the modern word for what in my day was called hullabaloo.

'To accommodate the new kitchen, the contractor bought in England and transferred to Don Mills an object that would never be seen attached to a respectable manor. It was an oast-house. You know what an oast-house is?'

I didn't.

'It's a kiln for drying hops, a great tower-like building with a pointed roof. An unseemly object. But they stuck it to the side of the manor, right by the dining-room, and put a modern kitchen in it.

'A modern kitchen is no place for a ghost. Crackling with electric current, cold things, hot things, and cramped so that one miserable servant can do the work of five. Where is the ingle-nook, where visiting grooms and coachmen can dry themselves in bad weather? Where is the cheerful fire, and the spit, the dogs, the cat and her kittens, the hens running in and out, the ducks peeping in at the door, and, in winter, the shadowy corners for haunting? But the worst thing of all was that the builders and the contractor couldn't get the name right, and they called the horrid thing an oaf-house. Who wants to haunt an oaf-house, I ask you? A Poor Relation I may have been, but an oaf—never!

'Nevertheless, I determined to make the best of it. All immigrants have a hard time in a new country, for a few hundred years. I decided to divide my time between the oaf-house, on the housekeeper's day off, and the rumpus room when the children weren't doing whatever children do in a rumpus room, which is something I never found out.

'Because, you see, the house didn't sell. Even with all the tinkering and destruction and costly misery and modern convenience it somehow failed to catch on. So the people who were trying to sell it hit on a great idea; they would let the public visit it.

'That was the end, for me. We phantoms have our feelings, and I never undertook to haunt whole-sale, so to speak. Servants I will frighten—yes, gladly. Gentlefolk of my own kindred I will provide with the thrill of a true family phantom, though I have always drawn the line at manifesting myself to more than two at a time—usually a man and his wife or better still, somebody who ought to be his wife. But haunt I must. It is part of my condition of existence, you see. Unless I make an appearance at least once a year, I am in serious trouble with—well, never you mind who. But appearing to people who have paid admission on behalf of a charity—no, no, the thing is not to be thought of.'

'I suppose a great many people visited the house?' said I. I knew what had happened, but I wanted to hear his version of it.

'They came by scores and hundreds,' said he. 'And what they did to our family manor beggars description, as Old Shakespeare says. They invited Toronto decorators to refurbish it, a room to each decorator, and the decorators themselves made my eyes start out of my head. They were men of an affected elegance—what in my day might have been called exquisites or beaux, except that these were not gentlemen—they worked for their living, and what they sold was Taste. As if anyone of any consequence ever had taste, or wanted any! They filled our comfortable old manor with spindly walnut and mahogany that might have done well enough in a fashionable bawdy-house in London, but was not to be compared with our comfortable old oak and chairs stuffed with the wool of our own sheep. They brought in pictures of people nobody had ever heard of, and declared they were by Sir Peter Lely and later masters. They stuck up curtains and threw down carpets of horrid gaudy colours, as if brown were not the only colour a lady of good family would endure in her rooms. But there was worse to come, much worse.

'They did up some of the rooms in what they called 'contemporary taste' and that was Chaos and Old Night, I assure you. They papered the floors, and stuck fur to the walls, and hung pictures by madmen, and set out furniture in which even I, as a weightless spectre, could not have sat with any comfort. And when all this was done the procession of viewers appeared. They were the friends of the Women's Committees of the charities that were to be benefited by this dreadful rape of my dear old manor, and they tramped everywhere and poked into everything.

'They seemed to have no idea of the comforts of an eighteenth-century house, and so they admired all the po-boxes in the bedrooms and said what charming little bedside tables they were, and they admired the silver chamber-pot my cousin had kept in the dining-room sideboard, for his convenience after dinner, and to my shame it was kept in full sight, filled with flowers. They loved all the modern rooms because they reminded them of their own homes. Best of all they liked the new kitchen, and said how wonderful it was that an inconvenient old manor could be so elegantly adapted for really civilized living. There were blue-haired ladies who came in aid of the Art Gallery and there were ladies with hair of improbable shades who came in aid of the Ballet, and noisy stout ladies who were patrons of Opera, and there were garden ladies who came to see the dreadful tropical plants that the decorators called 'growies' which were stuck up everywhere— as if garden rubbish didn't belong outside a respectable gentleman's house.'

'And you couldn't bear it?' said I, sympathetically.

'I could bear everything,' said he, and I swear that if ever a ghost had tears in his eyes, it was at that moment. 'Everything, that is, except the air-conditioning. Would you believe that they filled the fine old walls with metal guts that conveyed jets of air that stank of mice to every part of that dear old place—jets that squirted out where one least expected, blowing me about like a leaf in a storm and playing merry hell with my ectoplasm until I developed the worst case of phantom arthritis that has ever been seen at any of our Hallowe'en meetings. That was the finish. That settled the matter forever. I had to leave or I should have become a mere knotted bundle of malice, and would probably have dwindled into a Poltergeist of the lowest class. It was leave my home or lose countenance irreparably in the phantom world.

'So will you take me in? You are a modern foundation, I know, but your College has some of what I regard as the comforts of home. Draughts, mostly; I miss normal, healthy draughts more than you can imagine.'

I pondered, and that is always fatal, for when I ponder my resolution leaks away. He was a humble creature, as ghosts go, but his story had gone to my heart. Still—where on earth was I to put him?

'I could make myself useful,' he said, wistfully. 'I have heard that a trade flourishes on this continent—that of a Ghost Writer, and I know a lot of writing is done here. Yourself, for instance. I know you write romances, and though I despise romances perhaps, in time, I could grind out a three-volume novel about an unfortunate young man who wanted to be a College fellow, and then wanted to take holy orders, but who was slain untimely in an affair of honour with an aristocratic adversary. I promise to put in lots of theology. You could sign it, of course.'

'No,' I said firmly, 'that wouldn't do at all.'

He looked very forlorn, and he seemed to grow more transparent as grief overcame him. 'Could I copy manuscripts?' he pleaded.

I had a flash of illumination! Our Xerox machine in the College is terribly inadequate, and a copyist would be a great benefit to us—especially a copyist who was cheap.

But where was I to put him? I cudgelled my brains and then—another flash—I had the answer.

Years ago, when this College building was completed, the architect, Mr. Thom, presented me with a set of plans. I counted the rooms for occupation by Junior Fellows—and I paused. Then I went through the College with the Bursar and we counted, and counted again, and however carefully we counted there were three rooms in the plan which could not be found in the building. I made enquiry of Mr. Thom. 'Yes,' he said, in the abstracted manner which is characteristic of architects, 'when I had made all the alterations the founders called for, three rooms somehow got, mislaid. Walls were moved, and jogs and corners were eliminated, and somehow or other three rooms disappeared. They are there, in a way, and yet in another way they aren't there.'

Without a word, I led the ghost up to the top of staircase number three, until we confronted a blank wall. 'Here is your room,' said I; 'I don't pretend that I can see it myself, but perhaps you can.'

It was a risk on my part, and it worked. The ghost vanished through the wall, but I could hear his voice, and for the first time since we met, its tone was cheerful.

'Of course,' he cried; 'the very thing I've always wanted. Commodious, a charming view of the quad, several strong draughts, and no modern conveniences whatever. Bless you, sir, bless you.'

I was rid of him, for the moment. I made a chalk mark on the wall where his door seemed to be. In a day or two I would hunt him up and instruct him in his new duties as an unseen and unrequited Xerox.

As I walked back through the quad with a light heart I suddenly saw—my heart leapt into my mouth—I suddenly saw a figure, familiar to me from a score of nineteenth century photographs, standing near the gate, looking about him with an air of deep disapproval. That barrel-shaped body in the impeccable frock coat; that tall silk hat of surpassing splendour. It must be he! I was to be rewarded for my good deed! I rushed forward, my hand outstretched.

'Dr. Ibsen!' I cried; 'you have come at last. Do stay a while! Do come inside! Have a glass of acquavit! Let us have a really splendid talk about your work! And will you honour me by inscribing my copy of your great drama, *Ghosts?*'

Ibsen—for indeed it was he—bent upon me a gaze that was like being transfixed by two little knives. His thin lips parted, and a single word escaped the prison-house of his formidable countenance.

'Tvertimot,' said he, and without another word he vanished through the bars of our gate.

Tvertimot! Tvertimot—that supremely characteristic utterance had been the last word he spoke on his deathbed! I rushed into my study, dragged down my great Dictionary of the Norwegian Tongue and looked it up with trembling hands.

'Tvertimot', said the entry: 'Quite the contrary, or colloquially, Not on your Nellie'.

Well, I reflected, not a bad year for ghosts after all. We had acquired an additional Xerox, and Ibsen had dropped in for a sneer.

EINSTEIN AND THE
LITTLE LORD

I know you will understand when I say it is a great
source of satisfaction to me that this College is
regularly and extensively haunted. Every part of our
great University strives for distinction of one kind
or another, but it is everywhere admitted that in
the regularity and variety of our ghostly visitations
Massey College stands alone. Year after year our
ghosts never fail us, and they are shades of unques-
tionable intellectual distinction, the Cream of the
Ectoplasm; in this College, so often accused of elitism, our ghosts at least may truly be called the elite
of *Who Was Who*. It is hard not to fall prey to sinful
pride when I think of them.

Early in January, every year, I begin wondering:
Who will it be? Ghosts of world-wide renown think
it worth their while to drop in on us for an hour or
two, which, in the course of a busy afterlife, is uncommonly civil of them. As the custom has arisen of celebrating centenaries and anniversaries of all sorts, and
lists of these events are published at the beginning of

each year, I look down these columns with an interest that comes close to gloating, wondering who our next unearthly visitant will be. Last January there was one prize I coveted above all. This year marks the hundredth anniversary of the birth of Albert Einstein.

I see in your faces wonder, tempered with disdain. What does *he* think he would have to say to Einstein? That is the question I read in your eyes. Ah, but you see, my experience with ghosts has taught me that it is unnecessary to talk to *them;* their concern is to talk to *you.* They have no time for chit-chat. It is true I had some misgiving. If Einstein were to entrust me with post-mortem reflections on the Michelson-Morley experiments, or use me as a means of telling the world a few new things about the wavelength of light emitted by atoms, I should have to be careful not to make any mistakes in taking dictation. But on the whole I was confident. Only let Einstein come: I would find a way of coping with him.

But he didn't come. I waited; I waited. By the beginning of December I began to grow anxious. Had ridiculous pride led me into absurd expectation? Had the other world decided to humble me, to condemn the College to a ghostless year? Of course, I thought, it is not to me, but to the College, that the mighty spectres come, and the College has in no way offended. So I waited as well as I could for one long December week, and just a week ago tonight my vigil was rewarded. Einstein came.

He came unexpectedly, as they always do. It was the night of our Christmas Dance, and as some of you know, that is an affair that not merely raises the roof but rouses the dead. I had stepped out into the quadrangle, to rest my ears; nevertheless the music was still very loud, and I was not surprised to hear a quiet, slightly foreign voice say from behind me, 'Not quite my sort of thing.'

I turned and there he was, impossible to mistake. The stout, unremarkable figure, the lamentable clothes, and the large, splendid, melancholy head. He was smoking a pipe, slowly as a good pipe-smoker does, emitting tiny puffs of fragrance with audible poppings of the lips.

'You have come!' I said.

'Oh, I always meant to come,' said he, 'but I left you till near the end of my centennial year, when I knew I should be tired. Because of your rules, you know.'

What rules, I wondered? But not for long. He meant our rules about College guests. Our unbreakable rule is that no guest may be asked for a favour, and that any informal opinions expressed by a guest must be regarded as confidential. Einstein had come to us to escape the publicity that pursues an eminent ghost.

He wanted a rest, and I knew what sort of rest he had in mind. Underneath his arm was a violin. He jerked his head toward the sound of music from the dance, and in a friendly fashion he said, 'Come on; we can do better than that.'

Quite how I followed him I do not remember but in no time I was in the large room in the basement of my house, where the piano lives. I say it lives there, because I dare not say I keep it there. I am some-what in awe of it. You see, I have played the piano all my life, without ever having gained any proficiency whatever. Untold gold was spent on my musical education, but I remain a hopeless fumbler; I am perhaps the only man in musical history to play the piano with a stammer. Nevertheless, I play. Almost every day I approach the piano in my basement and endure its Teutonic sneers as I tinkle out the kind of music I like, which I confess is chiefly piano arrange-ments of music meant for other instruments, and even for the human voice.

Einstein gestured me toward the piano, and began to tune his violin. It was obvious that his pitch was perfect. I was horrified.

'Do you mean you want me to accompany you?' I said, weak with fear.

'No, no, we play together,' he said, and tucked the fiddle under his chin.

My blood ran cold. In all the vast repertoire of music in which the violin and piano can mingle there is only one piece that I would dare attempt. It is a *Humoresque* by Dvorak—the Number 7 in G flat. You know it. Popular musical taste has accorded words to it, words selected from a well-known rail-way notice:

> *Passengers will please refrain*
> *From flushing toilets when the train*
> *Is standing in the station:*
> > *I love you.*

But when Einstein speaks, who am I to disobey? So I sat at the piano, and to my astonishment I saw, on the music desk before my eyes, the score of Bach's Six Sonatas for Clavier and Violin. Einstein made a slight dip with his bow, as a signal, my hands flew to the keyboard, and there followed such a flood of exquisite music as had never come out of that piano in its existence. And it was I who was making this glorious sound! Einstein was a pretty good violinist—extremely good for a physicist—but I was a musical marvel. Little by little I took possession of this totally unaccustomed skill. Pride surged through me. I began to refine upon my playing, and to do things properly which Glenn Gould would probably have foozled. I was like a man transformed, endowed with the power to play music as I had imagined it.

Then it happened. There was a sudden discord in the bass end of the piano, and I saw that a gigantic dog had brought its great head down on the keyboard with a crash. Einstein stopped; I stopped; the dog regarded us both with eyes rimmed by nasty, wet red flesh.

'I'm sorry if Dougal has interrupted your music,' said a high, sweet, clear voice. 'But I really must speak to Professor Einstein without delay.'

The speaker was the most beautiful boy I have ever seen in my life. His graceful childish figure was dressed in a black velvet suit and close-fitting knee-breeches from which emerged legs, clothed in black silk stockings, that Marlene Dietrich might have envied. The velvet suit had a white collar of exquisite lace, and about the handsome, manly little face clustered lovelocks of long fair hair falling in a profusion of curls.

You know who it was, of course. And I, from recollections of my childhood reading of the novel of which he was the hero, was able to greet him with a cry which surely fell in familiar and welcome cadence on his ears.

'God bless your lordship! God bless your pretty face! Good luck and happiness to your lordship! Welcome to you!'

The child bowed in response to my greeting.

It was Little Lord Fauntleroy.

Modern children do not seem to know his name, or the book by Mrs. Frances Hodgson Burnett in which his story is told. But surely this is a temporary lapse of fame; his romance is undying, a superb realization of what Dr. Jung of Zürich has named the Archetype of the Miraculous Child.

Most of you are familiar with him, though there may be one or two among you, under thirty, to whom he is a stranger. But millions of readers, old and young, have thrilled to the tale of little Cedric Errol, born in New York of an American mother—whom he never addressed or referred to except as 'Dearest', because that is what his English father, who had died so young, had always called her. Cedric considered himself to be an American, and indeed he exhibited all the American characteristics, total candour, boundless self-confidence, naturally fine manners, and a democratic spirit almost too zealous to be wholly believable. But certainly in Cedric there was nothing affected about this democracy; his dearest friends were Mr. Hobbs, the groceryman, Dick the shoeshine boy, and the poor old woman who sold apples at the street-corner; he did good to many others, among the poor and needy, for whom his tender little heart was always grieved. Judge then of the reader's astonishment when he discovers that this typical little American is, because of the death of a number of relatives on his father's side, the heir of the great Earl of Dorincourt, and that his true name is Lord Fauntleroy.

How Cedric softens the hard heart of his grand-father, the Earl (a typical English nobleman, proud, domineering, with blood so blue you could use it for ink, but nonetheless a splendid creature and exceedingly rich) and how Cedric makes all his grandfather's tenants happy, and how Cedric per-suades his haughty grandfather to accept Dearest, who, though an American, is nevertheless a lady, and how Cedric gets Mr. Hobbs the groceryman and Dick the shoeshine boy to England, and settles them close to Dorincourt Castle, so that he can go on being democratic at them—all of this is familiar to you. Familiar also are the drawings done for the book by Reginald B. Birch, which made the appear-ance of all the characters, but especially the ring-leted, velvet-suited little lord, familiar to millions of infatuated readers from 1886 at least until 1925.

And there he stood, in my music room, con-fronting Professor Einstein and myself. Not only

Fauntleroy, but the huge, drooling, red-eyed mastiff Dougal, his Grandfather's pet and the little lord's inseparable companion.

I wondered what he had come for, so, with a directness which I was sure such a democratic child would appreciate, I put the question.

'What have you come for, m'lord?' said I.

He laughed. It was the characteristic laugh of an innocent child, like silver bells, and it set up an answering echo in the piano.

'I want to ask a favour of Professor Einstein,' he said.

'Certainly not,' said I; 'no guest of Massey College may be asked for favours.'

'Oh please—oh pretty-please and sugar-plums,' said Lord Fauntleroy, winsomely. 'Surely you haven't forgotten that this is the Year of the Child?'

I had forgotten. In spite of all the newspaper hullabaloo, and appeals for this, that and the other thing to increase the influence of children, I had forgotten. Certainly I had not expected the Year of the Child to have anything to do with our College Ghost.

'The Year of the Child is more important than rules,' said Fauntleroy. 'Oh, you'd probably never guess how important for the peace of the world. You know, don't you, that some dear, kind people are trying to establish a Children's Bill of Rights?'

I admitted that I had heard something of the sort. Einstein didn't bother to answer; he was regarding Little Lord Fauntleroy with big, sad eyes, the expression of which I could read. It was an expression of great weariness, mingled with a noble compassion. It was also the expression of an influential person confronted with a remorseless beggar.

'That is why I have come for advice to Professor Einstein, the author of *Why War?*' said the beautiful boy. 'The best of us want a sensible Bill of Rights. You know the sort of thing: nobody is to beat children more than is good for them, and savage people are not to eat children except in case of real necessity, and children are to be loved except when they are unlovable, and children are to be seen and not heard except for exceptional children like me, and children are to be taught sensibly by sensible people, and children are to have pocket-money but not enough to make it possible for them to get into serious trouble. And in return children undertake to be reasonable and pretend to be innocent and believe in Santa Claus and babies being brought by the doctor and all that crap—oh, what have I said!'

'You said, "and all that crap",' said I, wishing to be helpful. Little Lord Fauntleroy was hiding his face in his hands, the very picture of shame.

'I know I did,' he said. 'How could I! What would Dearest say if she heard me use such a horrid word! But He makes me do it! It's His terrible influence. Oh, if I were not the sweetest, most forgiving little soul anybody ever heard of, I could hate Him!'

To emphasize the general grief the big dog, Dougal, set up a melancholy howling, and lashed the piano keys with his great tail.

It was here that Professor Einstein intervened. 'My boy,' he said, 'if you expect us to understand you, do not begin your story in the middle and wriggle out toward both ends. I recommend the Scientific Method: state your principal thesis, develop it, and work toward a conclusion.'

Little Lord Fauntleroy took his hands from his face and looked at the great man with adoration.

'Just what I wanted,' said he; 'you are so wise, Professor Einstein, I knew you could help me. I shall do as you say. Please, may I sit on your knee?'

Einstein pondered for a moment, then said, 'No.' My respect for his wisdom rose sharply. 'Just stand where you are, and I shall sit down, and you shall tell us both, quietly and clearly, what the trouble is! Now, first of all, where do you come from?'

'From Paradise,' said the Miraculous Child. 'Oh, it's not at all the way silly people imagine. It's really a huge confederation of self-governing Paradises where everybody can enjoy Eternity with the sort of people they like best. There aren't any grown-ups in the Children's Paradise, or else it wouldn't be a Paradise for children. And of course the fact that we're all in the Children's Paradise makes the other paradises paradisal for the grown-ups.'

'Quite true,' said Einstein. 'I cannot recall ever having seen, or heard, a child since I entered the Physics Division of the Intellectuals' Paradise.'

'I was troubled by a doubt. 'One moment,' I said. 'It has always been my understanding that Paradise is for the living who have passed into rest. But you, my lord, never lived. Explain yourself.'

'Oh, you dear old silly-billy,' said Fauntleroy, putting his graceful little hand on my sleeve, as Dougal smeared my trousers with phantom drool. 'You, an author, of a sort, to say such a thing! You know jolly well that I lived more fully and gloriously than the ordinary run of children. I was loved by millions of people who had no children of their own. We children of literature are the aristocracy of the Children's Paradise. We are remembered for generations, when the real children who didn't have the luck to live to maturity are forgotten, poor little mites! We set the tone of the place. In a quiet way, we run it! There are the Dickens Group—Little Paul Dombey, and Tiny Tim, and Little Nell—and there are the Outdoors Types—Tom Sawyer and Huckleberry Finn, and Midshipman Easy, and Jackanapes, and Penrod and lots of others—and there are the littlest ones like the Bobbsie Twins and Budge and Toddy—and there are the Fairy Tale Gang—Rose Red and Snow White, and Jack the Giant Killer and all those. You wouldn't believe what a lot there are, and we are all so much more vivid than the flesh-and-blood children that we naturally take the lead. Or we did,' said the boy, his beautiful countenance darkening, 'until He came.'

'A rival?' I said.

'Not a rival,' said the boy with what in a lesser child might have been taken for a pout, 'a usurper.'

'Same thing,' said I. 'Let's hear about it.'

'Everything in the Children's Paradise was paradisal,' said Fauntleroy, 'so long as I was the boss. I took care that everybody was happy; I wouldn't tolerate an instant's discord. If any of my agents reported anything to me—'

'Agents?' said Professor Einstein; 'Spies, do you mean?'

'Don't be horrid,' said Fauntleroy, smiling his reproach. 'Just children who were either naturally very sharp, like the Artful Dodger, and Gavroche out of *Les Miserables,* or else children who were abnormally trustworthy like Casabianca—you know, the Boy Who Stood on the Burning Deck. If they saw any trouble brewing they tipped me off, and I dealt with it at once, and if the child didn't see things differently then, Dougal had a little romp with it, and that always worked.'

Dougal gave a sudden lurch that almost knocked me off my chair, and I saw what a romp might involve.

'Let's hear about the usurper,' I said.

'You know how things have been on earth for the past twenty years,' said Fauntleroy. 'Turbulence everywhere, among nations, among university students, and even among children. In fact, the modern child has simply been going straight to—'

Here he blushed deeply, and whispered something in Professor Einstein's ear.

'And the usurper came from Hell?' said Professor Einstein. 'No, from Toronto,' said Fauntleroy. 'His name is Gold-Tooth Flanagan. He is very proud of his gold tooth. He got it by ripping off Old Age

Pensioners in supermarkets until he had enough money to buy it. It was his mark of authority. It is a huge adult-size gold tooth, in the worst possible taste. But of course that sort of life can have but one end: Gold-Tooth was knocked on the head with a bottle in a police raid in Cabbage Town and to his surprise he was sent to the Children's Paradise. Of course he wanted to go to the Hooligans' Paradise, but he was too young, so he came to us instead. Nobody's fault but his own; he peaked too soon.'

'And he tried to take over the Children's Paradise?' said I.

'From the beginning,' said Fauntleroy. 'He said very offensive things. He started by picking on a literary child from the Third World, whom we have always known as Little Black Sambo; Gold Tooth called him a horrid racist name, and when I rebuked him—gently, of course, for he was new, and didn't know our ways—he asked me if I was gay. I said of course I was, and that Dearest had always loved me for being so gay, and he laughed offensively and mimicked me rudely. It wasn't until Holden Caulfield told me what 'gay' means to minds like Flanagan's that I understood that I had been insulted. Gay, indeed! Me! As if for years I hadn't been on a footing of special intimacy with Little Miss Muffet!'

'Didn't it occur to you to put Dougal on him?' said I.

'I was coming to that, just when the real trouble blew up,' said Fauntleroy. 'Of course Flanagan sat in on our meetings where we discussed the nature of the Child's Bill of Rights; they were fully democratic, so he couldn't be left out. We were trying to hammer out something along the lines I have already mentioned to you. You see, at United Nations and UNESCO all the children's business is done by adults, who have no idea of what a sensible child wants; the last thing we want is any kind of independence—make us independent and we have lost all our power. To deal as we think best with adults we must be entirely under their thumbs, which is the same thing as being on their backs: our weakness is our strength, every child knows that.'

'This child is wise beyond his years,' said Einstein.

'Indeed I am,' said Little Lord Fauntleroy. 'But Gold-Tooth Flanagan simply didn't know his business as a child. He was agitating for a Bill of Rights that would allow children to vote at the age of three, and get liquor and dope, and sue their parents for failure to bring them up properly, and ensure that when couples divorced all the assets were placed in the hands of their children—such crazy stuff as you never heard of, that would have robbed children of all their real power and loaded them down with a lot of hard work and financial responsibility. So it came to a showdown.'

'Don't tell me Gold-Tooth Flanagan won!' said I.

'For the present it is a draw,' said Fauntleroy. 'You see, the meeting became more and more unruly, and finally Gold-Tooth called Christopher Robin a Mother. At first I didn't think anything of that, because to me a mother means Dearest, but a Greek boy out of *Aesop's Fables* was sitting on the platform near me and he whispered that it was a very offensive expression, and meant somebody called Oedipus, so I asked Gold-Tooth to explain himself, and to the horror of everybody he did. Christopher Robin cried, and Alice from Wonderland hit Gold-Tooth with a croquet mallet, and when order was restored I had to speak very sharply to Gold-Tooth and he challenged me to a fight. I said I would fight him if Dougal were allowed to be the referee, but he wouldn't have that, and it looked for a moment as if things were going to be very uneven, until Huck Finn slipped something into my right hand which he said would help, and I very cleverly hit Gold-Tooth when he wasn't looking, and he fell down. But he jumped right up again and shouted Foul, and when I looked at my hand I saw that Huck had put a horseshoe in it. Then Gold-Tooth attacked me unfairly and without warning, and fought in a way that was utterly un-American, and even un-English, and when it was all over—my authority was gone.'

Here the beautiful child faltered and broke into bitter sobs.

Professor Einstein and I exchanged glances. The same thing was in both our minds. With a gentle hand the great scientist reached out towards the golden curls, and removed what was all too plainly a wig. The head beneath had been snatched bald. Little Lord Fauntleroy, at the hands of the unspeakable Gold-Tooth Flanagan, had suffered the fate of Samson.

'Have you tried rubbing it with white of egg?' the great man asked.

'Or perhaps a top-dressing of organic fertilizer?' said I.

'It will take months to grow to its full length,' said Fauntleroy, 'and we have no time. Unless the horrible plan for a Children's Bill of Rights (with which Gold-Tooth Flanagan is at this very moment interpenetrating the brain cells of the Assembly at U.N.) is thwarted, society as we have known it must collapse. Children will rule! Can you imagine what that will lead to—?'

'I am not sure that children would do worse with the world than their elders have done,' said Professor Einstein.

'That would depend on what children,' said I. 'Take the advice of a man steeped in literature and legend; this is War in Heaven, and instead of a defeat in which Gold-Tooth Flanagan is cast down into the Pit, to howl in torment with all his evil followers, he has achieved dominance.'

'Indeed he has,' said Fauntleroy. 'He's strutting around the Children's Paradise flashing his gold tooth and wearing my hair!'

'I see that you are right,' said Professor Einstein. 'Like many childless people, I tend to have an extravagantly high opinion of children.'

'You must re-read *King Lear*,' said I.

'I shall do so,' said he; 'but meanwhile, my child, do not lose heart. I shall go to the United Nations Assembly, where I still have some spiritual influence, and do what I can.'

The face of Little Lord Fauntleroy was suffused with a flush of rapture. He rushed to the great man and covered his face with kisses, while Dougal licked Einstein's violin with his huge tongue, making it disagreeably wet.

'Meanwhile, to be on the safe side, you might try this,' said I, taking a small black bottle from beneath the top of the piano.

'You dear old souls,' said the Wondrous Child, his eyes filling with tears, 'shall I really regain my hair?'

'That isn't hair tonic,' said I; 'that is a substance I use for cleaning my piano keys. It is drastic if taken internally; for instance, by anyone who was using it to clean a gold tooth.'

If I am not mistaken, the child winked at me. 'Oh what a lovely practical joke that would be,' he said. 'Of course Gold-Tooth is beyond Death, but he is certainly not beyond humiliation.' Then, seizing Dougal by the collar Lord Fauntleroy and the great dog ran toward the door. Before they reached it, they had grown dim, and vanished.

'Do you really think that children may take over the world?' I said to Professor Einstein.

'I cannot believe it,' said the great physicist. 'Have I not said that God does not play at dice with the fate of the Universe?'

Once again he raised his bow, and off we went into Bach. But because of Dougal's energetic licking his violin was sadly out of tune. The sound grew fainter, and I was aware of a decline in my own musical abilities until I found myself playing alone, and playing badly, and I knew that the seventeenth ghostly visitation to Massey College had reached its end.

OFFER OF IMMORTALITY

Many of you who are here tonight have heard several of the Massey College Ghost stories, and there are some who have heard them all. Seventeen stories up to the present, and all of them true. Yet I have never felt justified in taking the ghosts for granted; I have never dared to think— Oh, one pops up every year, and it's sure to appear on time. Ghosts do not like to be taken for granted, just as they do not like to be given orders. You will understand why I was uneasy; this is my last year as Master of Massey College, and I should have liked to round out my time here by telling you of yet another ghost. However, ' 'Tis not in mortals to command success'. I have no ghost for you.

However, there was something—circumstances of which I ought to inform you, though when you have heard them you will understand my reluctance in making them known. Not a ghost—no—but something not quite in the common run of affairs. Oh, that I had the resolution to stop now, to say no more! But—here it is.

It happened at the end of November, when we held our last High Table for this year. We don't have High Tables in December because the College Dance and this affair are our offerings of hospitality during the Christmas season. Hospitality! It is one of the guiding lights of this College. Every honour, every consideration for our guests—that is our somewhat old-fashioned principle. A guest here, is sacred.

On the Friday afternoon, when we were getting ready for High Table, Miss Whalon received a telephone call from Dr. Walter Zingg, the distinguished medical scientist and a Senior Fellow. 'I hope it won't upset the arrangement of the table too much,' said he, 'but I should greatly like to bring a visitor who has arrived unexpectedly from South America—a scientist of international renown, from Bogotá, a Professor J. M. Murphy.' That was easily arranged, and when the list of guests was being prepared Miss Whalon discovered that the University from which Professor Murphy came was founded in 1572 (which makes it substantially our senior) and that it must also be one of the most exalted universities in the world, for it stands 9,000 feet above sea level. But when she finally ran the professor down in an academic directory it said only that he was a world leader in Cryonics, and that his full name was Jesus Maria Murphy.

This did not trouble me. South America is full of the descendants of Irish immigrants who retain their

Irish names, although they are now almost wholly of Spanish and Indian blood. Jesus Maria Murphy would cause no more raised eyebrows in Colombia than such a name as Mackenzie King Stacey might in Canada. I didn't know what Cryonics was, but I didn't need to know; Professor Zingg would take care of all that.

I was not prepared, however, for the figure who appeared in the Senior Common Room under the wing of Dr. Zingg. I say 'under the wing' advisedly, for Professor Murphy came no higher than the doctor's waist. He was the tiniest human being that I have ever seen, but that was not the only thing that gave him an air of unreality; his complexion was so rich in colour, and his hair was so glossily black that he looked like a beautifully-made doll. Hair dye and an almost operatic amount of makeup; strange in an academic, but these are permissive times. When I took his hand, it was like a tiny claw, and extraordinarily cold—so cold I almost dropped it in surprise.

When I am disconcerted I take refuge in extreme heartiness and good-fellowship, which, as most of you know, is no indication of my true nature. That is what I did when I felt that cold, cold hand.

'Welcome, Professor Murphy!' I roared; 'What good fortune for us that you are able to dine here to-night! Ho, ho, ho!'

He responded with what I suppose he meant for a reciprocal exuberance. In a thin, high voice, very much like Punch in the puppet-shows I used to see in London, he replied: 'Dat what you tink, eh? Locky for you? Yes, lockier dan you know! He, he, he!'

I introduced Professor Murphy to some of the others who had assembled for dinner. Quite without self-consciousness he skipped up on top of the table, and stood there, so as to be able to address them face to face.

When an opportunity came, I looked enquiringly at Professor Zingg; he was blushing. 'Never saw him before,' he said, 'but I have to take care of him over the weekend—keeping off big dogs and mean children and that sort of thing.'

'The Professor looks to me as if he knew how to look after himself,' said I.

Certainly he had no trouble at dinner. With that exquisite courtesy for which Massey College is famous, our Librarian had seen that three volumes of the Oxford English Dictionary were on his chair, so that he would be at no disadvantage, and there he sat, perched on N-Poy, chattering away happily to Dr. Swinton, a man with an insatiable appetite for scientific curiosities; on Murphy's other side sat Professor Hume, the Master-Designate, and I knew that those two experienced hands at college hospitality would take good care of our strange guest. But I noticed that although he chased our good dinner round his plate with his knife and fork, he ate nothing, and drank no wine.

Our steward, Mr. Stojanovich, appeared beside my chair.

'That little gentleman, that Professor Murphy, asks if he might have some of his favourite drink.'

'Certainly, if we have it,' I said.

'We have it,' said Mircha; 'it is vinegar.'

'Give him the best we have,' said I.

An odd request, I thought. Vinegar is, of course, a solution of acetic acid made, as the dictionary explains, from inferior wines; Canada, which yields place to no country in the world in the production of inferior wines, has first-rate vinegar. Mircha returned, bearing a demijohn which he showed me in the distinguished manner that adds so much to College functions. I took a little in a glass, and rolled it thoughtfully over my palate; it was a rich, full Loblaw 1980. I nodded approvingly, our guest was served, and I was interested to observe that he smacked his lips and, after two quick glasses, showed an increase of his former lively spirits.

Nor was that the end of it. When we went downstairs for more conversation and wine, Professor Murphy insisted that the vinegar jug go with him, and he nipped away all evening, consuming more in liquid volume than any four of the rest of us.

This was eccentric, certainly, but nothing more. However, when we were parting for the night, the strange guest seized me by the hand, and hissed: 'I must talk to you.'

'If you wish,' I said; 'I'll ask Professor Zingg to bring you into my Lodgings.'

'No, no,' said little Murphy; 'get rid of Zingg. Tell Zingg to go hang.'

As Professor Zingg was standing right beside him, this was rude. But Professor Zingg is not a man to lose his dignity; he smiled courteously at Jesus Maria Murphy, bowed very slightly, and left the room. But I thought there was an air of relief in his manner.

In no time at all I found myself sitting in my study, facing Professor Murphy, who was curled up in my big chair, with his third demijohn of vinegar, freshly opened, sitting on the floor beside him.

A hospitable thought struck me. 'Would you like to use the plumbing?' I asked. After all, the law of gravity dictates that so much liquid intake must, at some point, impose this necessity.

'Use what?' he hissed. 'Oh, the excusado. No, no; never go. Foolish, foolish. You shall find out why.'

I can't say I liked the sound of that. But the Professor was hurrying on.

'You, Davies, you old man now, eh? You getting out of here? Dey kick you out, no?'

'Decidedly no,' I said, with some austerity, for I did not like his tone; 'I am retiring, and the College has shown me every courtesy, as is its custom.'

'Yah, yah, but you sorry to go. You want to know what's going to happen, eh?'

'Naturally I do. I am the first Master of this College; I hope the first of a long and splendid line. Not to be curious about the future would be impossible, though I know how ridiculous any such desire must be.'

'Why ridiculous?'

'Well—because of the brevity of human life.'

'Not brief at all. You not a scientist, eh?'

'No,' said I; 'insofar as it is possible to sum up what I am, I am a student of literature with a psychological bias.'

'Oh, Holy Mother of God!' said Professor Murphy. 'How you people spend your time! Still, I was just such an idiot when I was your age, a few hundred years ago. I was even a priest. Our university was started by priests, way back in the days of the Spanish Conquest; I was one of the founders and Sub-Rector for many years. But it is not easy to be a Spanish priest in the South American mountains, not if you have any real intelligence, not if you see what is right under your nose.'

I thought it better to humour this madman. Was he really claiming to be something like four hundred and fifty years old? 'So you became an unbeliever?' I said.

'Never! Unbelievers are fools, worse than unilluminated believers. I became an illuminated believer. I expanded my realm of belief. I became an alchemist.'

'An alchemist?' said I. 'Making gold, and that sort of thing?'

'Pah!' he said, and a good deal of saliva sprayed across the room at me. 'I spit on gold! In South America is gold everywhere, kicking along the ground. No, no, I studied *life*, and as time went on, and science began to lift its head above the rubbish of faith, the Illumination came, and by the middle of the nineteenth century I was one of the earliest biologists.'

'Is it widely known that you have had such a long and interesting life?' I said.

'No; better not,' said he. 'I change my name from time to time. Give up being priest, though I am still a good Catholic. But that is why I am now Murphy; lots of Murphys in Columbia. I can speak Irish. Begorrah, may your shadow never grow less, devil take you, damn your eyes, Mother Machree. Yes, now I am Professor Murphy, and head of a very big scientific section in our University.'

'And what brings you to Canada?' I said.

'I am scouting for candidates,' said he, looking at me with extreme cunning.

'For your faculty?' said I.

'No, no—for my Instituto Cryonico da Colombia. But we have strayed. We talked about your curiosity regarding the future of this College. There are lots of ways of finding out, you know.'

'Such as—?' said I.

'Well, Gematria, for one,' said he.

Gematria—the cabbala of numbers! How often had I not heard of it, that elaborate, ancient, but surely mad science of divination practised so long by the Jews, and part of the structure of their medieval scholasticism! I looked at Murphy with new eyes.

'But surely Gematria is known only among the Jews?' said I.

'If you live long enough and survive strongly enough the Jews begin to think you must be one of themselves, and they tell you secrets,' said Murphy. 'You want to know how Gematria works?'

Of course I did.

'Then you must understand that numbers are the most important things under heaven. All is number, and God is the God of Numbers. I suppose you know Hebrew?'

'I've allowed it to grow a little rusty,' I said; 'but I used to be able to read and write it pretty well.'

'Ah, then you know that in Hebrew there are no special signs for numbers, but each letter of the alphabet has a numerical equivalent, and that means that every word has a numerical equivalent also.'

'Yes, yes.'

'In the art of Gematria you divine secret things by reducing the appropriate words to their number equivalents, adding up those, then adding the integers of the sum again and again until you reach a number between one and eleven. That number is the Golden Number, and must be interpreted by knowledge of a very secret doctrine that embodies the rational pattern that lies beneath the seeming disorder of the universe.'

'Yes,' said I, 'but how are you going to make that work with English words? Hebrew suppresses all the vowels but A, and lacks several of our letters.'

'That is part of the tradition. You fill in the gaps with Greek letters that also have numerical equivalents. Greek alchemists, Jewish alchemists, they worked hand in glove. It really does work, you know. Want to try?'

'I think you want to demonstrate your skill,' said I. Of course I wanted to try. But obviously I was not deceiving him; he went off into a fit of laughter, almost silent, producing a small noise like someone crushing tissue paper.

'You do not trust me,' he wheezed. 'You think I am a magician. And so I am. But not a false magician. I am a scientist, which is a modern magician. Long ago, when our University first began, in 1572, they called me a black magician, and there are still some who make the sign against the Evil Eye when I pass them. But I wish you would trust me and let me be your friend, because I can help you greatly. Let us be friends in your Canadian manner. Call me Jesus.'

There is a Puritan buried within me. I secretly determined not to call him Jesus if I could possibly avoid it. I took refuge in cunning.

'I'll do better than that,' I said; 'I'll call you Josh. Jesus is the same as Joshua, and the short name for Joshua is Josh. You see?'

'Oh yes, I see,' said he, and I knew that he saw right through me and was laughing at my Protestant distaste. 'Now, what shall we interpret? This College, don't you think? What is its essence? What is at the root of it that will shape its destiny for centuries to come? Now wait—I must make myself ready.'

He sat very upright on my leather chair, his feet tucked under him, his eyes shut, and both his hands raised with the fingers extended. 'Now,' he said, 'tell me the full name of this place, not too fast, so that I can reduce it to numbers.'

'Massey College in the University of Toronto,' said I, and as I spoke his fingers began to flicker rapidly, as if he were tapping the keys of some invisible calculator. And indeed that is just what he was doing. I realized that I was looking at calculation as it had been during the Middle Ages, before the coming of cheap pencils and paper pads, and adding machines, and computers. He had turned his ten fingers into an abacus. Nor did he hesitate for an instant before he spoke.

'Seventeen and twenty-four, and twenty, and thirty-four, and fifty-one comes to one hundred and forty-six,' said he. 'Add up the integers of one, four six and it comes to—eleven! Oh! Oh! Eleven!'

'Good, or bad?' said I, far more anxious than I wanted to reveal.

'Magnifico! The number of revelation. The number of great teachers and visionaries in religion, science, politics and the arts. It is the number of those who live by the inner vision. Dangerous, mind you, for sometimes eleven loves ideas better than humanity, so that must be remembered and avoided. But what a Golden Number for a college! Oh, you need have no fears for this place.'

'Thank you, Josh,' I said. 'You give me great hope. I am only sorry that I shall not be here to see its fulfilment.'

'How long have you been here?' said Professor Murphy.

'It will be eighteen years next June,' said I, 'but I began work on this place twenty years ago, on the first of January, 1960.'

'Aha, well—that date and the year and date of your birth—add the integers and it comes to thirty—a three. That is very good, because three is your Golden Number also—'

'How do you know?'

'Because I took trouble to find out before I came to-night, and I knew you for a Three the minute I set eyes on you. So that is a happy—'

'Coincidence?' said I.

'There is no such thing as a coincidence,' said Josh; 'not in Gematria. It is all part of the numerical pattern that governs the world. Yes, you were a good man to begin this place, but not to continue it.'

'Why?' I dreaded what he might say, but I had to know.

'Too flighty,' said Josh. 'Lots of imagination, lots of invention, but there is a limit to what those things can do in a place like this—a place with the Great Eleven as its Golden Number. You are not always and in all things wholly serious. You have what we biologists call Jokey Genes. High time you went. Who is to come next?'

'Professor Hume,' said I. 'You sat beside him upstairs.'

'Yes, and I felt very strange things coming from him. That is why I had to have vinegar; he was heating me up, and I needed to reduce my body temperature. Tell me his full name.' And once again Josh took his calculating posture.

'James Nairn Patterson Hume,' said I.

Josh made his rapid, flickering calculation, then, to my horror, gave a pathetic little squeak and collapsed sideways. Had Pat Hume killed him? But I saw one of the tiny hands gesturing toward the vinegar bottle which sat on the floor at his side. In an instant I put it to his lips and he drank—drank—drank until there was not a drop left. His eyes opened slowly, but one was looking aloft while the other looked down, and from his tiny body mounted an overpowering reek of vinegar. If he had been drinking anything else I would have sworn he was drunk, but—vinegar? I must know.

'Jesus,' I whispered, shaking him gently. 'Jesus, are you pickled?'

He did not answer at once, but shook his head again and again, as if in wonderment. At last he spoke.

'This place must have a very special destiny,' he said. 'Its Golden Number is the Great Eleven, and that is splendour sufficient, but this Hume—this James Nairn Patterson Hume—his Golden Number is also—despampanante!—the Great Eleven. Work it out for yourself: fourteen, plus six, plus forty-one, plus twenty—and what have you?'

'How should I know?' I said; 'I'm just one of your frivolous Threes; I can't be expected to add in my head. *What* have you?'

'Badulaque! Analphabet! You have ninety-two and even you should see that when you add the integers—nine and two, dog of a Three—you get eleven. So this College, already shaped by Eleven, is now to have a Master who is also an Eleven, and what will happen then—Oh, rumboso, rumboso!' His eyes seemed fixed upon some rosy vision.

'What will happen? Tell me,' I said, shaking him.

'Oh, do not ask me to tell,' said Professor Murphy. 'Instead, why don't you join me in the Great Silent Chamber of the Immortals in the University at Bogota, and from time to time we shall come back here and behold with our own eyes the wonders that are sure to be brought forth.'

I was mystified. 'Great Silent Chamber of Immortals?' I said.

'You know of my work,' said he. 'Am I not the Praefectus of the Instituto Cryonico of Bogotá?'

'I suppose so,' said I, not very tactfully; 'but what's Cryonics?'

'Oh, you Threes, you have the minds of ballet-dancers! Cryonics, numbskull, is the science that will save mankind by preserving indefinitely the lives and abilities of people chosen for that purpose. It is achieved by a carefully calculated arrest of the cellular death which eventually brings ordinary mortals to the point of physical and spiritual death; that arrest is managed by draining the body of most of its blood, and substituting a formula for which ordinary vinegar may serve as a temporary substitute; then the body is placed in a very cold chamber, and all its activities, but not its cellular life are kept on ice, so to speak, until they are needed. Then, a gradual melting-out, and there's your man, practically as good as new and in my case, more than four hundred years old. Think what an accumulation of wisdom and experience that means! What we alchemists began so long ago as a search for the Philosopher's Stone was achieved in our Andean heights when we discovered—Oh, to hell with modesty!—when *I* discovered, that all that was needed was a sufficiently low temperature and plenty of vinegar. Now—here is your chance, and you must be quick, for this evening has been an exhausting one for me. Will you fly back with me to Bogota? I promise you that in a week you will be emptied of your disgusting thick blood, and you will find yourself in a flask, reduced to the temperature of liquid nitrogen. All you have to do is leave a call at the desk—just like a motel—and in a hundred years you will be shipped back here to see what this great College has achieved.'

I was tempted. I confess I was tempted. But I thought I should first talk the matter over with my wife. Later, when I had Professor Murphy's calculations checked by a Jewish scholar at one of the synagogues on Bathurst Street, I discovered that my wife is also a Three, just as I am myself, and it is unwise to neglect her opinion.

'May I have till tomorrow to make up my mind?' said I, and the Professor's nod was so feeble that I became greatly alarmed about him.

But we Threes have substantial powers of improvisation. It was clear that the Professor was so overcome by what he had found out about Massey College that he needed first aid, and of a special kind. So I did my unscientific best. Taking him in my arms, I carried him up the back stairs to the College kitchen; it was like carrying a wineskin, for the vinegar within him kept sloshing around most unaccountably. But I got him on one of the kitchen tables without having been seen during our wobbly progress through the College, and I undressed him, right down to his skin. Former priest that he was, I was not surprised to find that he was wearing a tiny hair shirt, which is still in my possession, more or less, for Miss Whalon uses it as a tea-cosy. I managed to rouse him sufficiently to drink a couple of large beakers of vinegar, then I brought jugs of ice-water, doused him thoroughly, and tucked him up for the night on a shelf in our large, walk-in refrigerator. In that embracing chill he fell instantly into a child-like sleep, and so I left him.

I went immediately to my wife, and put the great question up to her: was I to go to Bogotá and a chilly life eternal, in order that, from time to time, I might return to Massey College and spy on what my successors were doing? She thought for a while, and then said: 'I wouldn't, if I were you. Don't be a Massey College ghost; it would be most unbecoming. Don't you remember the line from our theatre days—"Superfluous lags the veteran on the stage"? When you have made your exit, take off your costume, clean the assumed character off your face, and leave the theatre.'

These were wise words, as I had expected them to be. So I went to bed; went to sleep; and forgot the whole matter.

I was sharply reminded of it only last week, when we had our annual Christmas Dance. A great feature of that affair is the buffet, which is a splendidly theatrical creation at which all the guests survey, before they eat, the miracles of cuisine that our chefs have prepared. Elegantly displayed turkeys, splendidly ornamented fish, jellies and potted meats pressed into fantastic and festive shapes, cream puffs filled with cream, so that their whiteness takes on the likeness of swans, wonderful little tartlets like jewels of topaz, and ruby and emerald. Cakes decorated in High Baroque styled that are themselves the epitome of Christmas, and happy youth and good cheer. As always, I looked at it with pride; this was just the sort of show to appeal to a man whose Golden Number is Three. And then—

I don't want to continue. I'd much rather not. But there are imperatives of historical truth which even a Three dare not brush aside. There, at the centre of the main table, was—No, no. No, I say!

Well, it was a roast suckling pig. At any rate, that was the way it was garnished. Certainly it had an apple in its mouth, and around the little eyes were outlines of white icing. Tips of pink icing extended its ears, which were not wholly pig-like. I looked hopefully between the markedly un-piglike buttocks for a curly tail, but there was none.

Turning to our Bursar, Colin Friesen, I said, controlling my voice as best I could: 'That's unusual, isn't it? Where did you get it?'

'It must have come in a big order,' said he. 'Nobody seems to know anything about it. It is a novelty. Delicious! Vinegar-cured, I should say. Try a bit of the crackling.'

But I declined. A flighty Three I may perhaps be, but I can boast, as I hope all my successors will be able to boast, that I have never, knowingly, eaten a guest of this College.

Made in the USA
Monee, IL
12 December 2023

48933507R00173